A novel by...

BEATRICE BRADSHAW

Hired
BY MY RICH
Highland
Husband

A Scottish marriage of convenience romance

Love was never part of the deal...

Whisky heir Max Drummond needs a wife – fast. If he doesn't marry by his thirtieth birthday, he'll lose his Highland inheritance.

Freelance journalist Rowan MacKay is out of options. With her grandmother's care bills piling up, she needs cash.

When she stumbles onto Max's Scottish estate for a story, she never expects him to offer her a deal that solves everything: one year of marriage in exchange for financial security.

No emotions. No entanglements. Just cold, hard practicality.

But life at Dunmarach isn't as simple as a contract. Rowan's fire clashes with Max's control. And what starts as an arrangement soon turns into heated looks, slow-burn tension, and nights that break every rule of their deal…

Content Note

This romance is written in British English ('realise' instead of 'realize'). There's also a bit of a Scottish accent here and there – the story is set in Scotland, after all.

Please be aware: this book contains several explicit / smutty open-door sex scenes and a good sprinkle of profanity.

It also touches on topics that could trigger certain audiences, such as parental neglect, an accident, cognitive decline, grief, and divorce. It's best to be prepared.

Your mental health matters. <3

To all the girls who've been told they're too much: never let anyone dim your light. The world needs it.

Chapter One

Maxwell Drummond had faced billion-pound mergers, hostile takeovers, and raging CEOs, but nothing had prepared him for this. It wasn't so much the ultimatum that bothered him. It was the fact that he hadn't seen it coming.

And knowing his late father, he should have.

Outside, a rare burst of late-July heat pressed against the ancient stone walls, but inside the castle, the study remained cool, heavy with shadows and the scent of leather and paper. Max stood with his cold hands clasped behind his back, shoulders rigid in his tailored suit, and watched the Highland landscape stretching before him. After years of absence, the backdrop of his upbringing felt like a noose around his neck.

'I trust you understand the clause?' Richard Blackwood's voice grated against Max's patience like sandpaper, setting his teeth on edge.

Max turned and fixed the solicitor with the same stare he used to intimidate boardroom opponents in his capacity as CEO of M.A.D. Capital Partners, one of London's most formidable private equity firms.

His firm.

'Perfectly. Though, I can't see what my marital status and

place of residence have to do with me inheriting Dunmarach. I can manage it from my London office.'

'Your father was clear in his wishes.' Blackwood shuffled the papers on the massive oak desk. 'Marry by your thirtieth birthday and live in Scotland, or the estate passes to the trust.'

His thirtieth birthday – in one week.

Outrageous.

Max fought the urge to loosen his tie, refusing to show any sign of discomfort. Of weakness. 'And what of the distillery?'

'The same applies. Everything – the castle, lands, and Drummond's Finest – will all come under trust ownership. We've maintained operations with the trustees' appointed team handling day-to-day matters. Your involvement hasn't been required thus far. Though it would have been welcomed.'

Max barked an empty laugh. 'Spare me.'

'We ensured the estate's stability when you were…otherwise occupied. The trust exists to safeguard the Drummond estate. Should you fail to meet the conditions, it will come under trust ownership. The trustees would have the authority to sell assets, restructure operations, and make decisions in what they deem the estate's best interests.'

Max set his mouth in a hard line.

So they'll gut the place for profit. What do I care?

He had built his own life far away from here for a reason. His jaw went rigid as memories surfaced. His father's voice, clipped and cold. The weight of silence between them.

His parents couldn't even bear to look at him.

All they wanted was their favourite son back, Dunmarach's original heir. But they had lost Martin. And it was all Max's fault.

Thirteen years after the accident, he still heard the sickening crunch of metal. Felt the darkness. Blue lights strobing through the rain. The sharp tang of blood and hospital disinfectant. Drifting in and out of consciousness, nurses murmuring. Max hadn't been able to move. Hadn't been able to attend his brother's funeral.

One month in hospital. And the day after he got out, his parents sent him away to university in England.

That old cocktail of rage, guilt, and inadequacy churned in his gut. He had spent over a decade building walls around these memories, treating emotion like a sinking venture to be shut down.

He had turned himself to stone.

Yet here he was, reduced to that seventeen-year-old boy again by wood panelling and stale air. The ruthless financial genius Maxwell Drummond, brought low by a dead man's parlour tricks from beyond the grave.

Two years after his death, no less.

Max still tasted the bitter coffee from that morning two years ago when his secretary had interrupted his 9 AM meeting with news of the boating accident. A rented yacht, a Caribbean storm. His parents had been mediocre sailors at best. The Coast Guard had searched for two weeks before declaring Murdoch and Charlotte Drummond lost at sea, leaving him to arrange a funeral for nothing but air and regret in mahogany boxes that would never rot. The fresh dirt on his parents' graves had matched the decade-old soil on Martin's.

Max had left the next day without a backward glance. That was the only time he had visited Scotland in thirteen years.

Until now.

His father had created the trust after Martin's death. As a failsafe, one more reminder that Max had never been the heir his father wanted. The message had been clear: the trust was to protect Dunmarach *from* Max, not *for* him.

So he had buried himself in his company and let the estate be managed in his absence, refusing to engage. Refusing to look back.

Now he was trapped in his father's fortress of dark wood

and disapproval again. Murdoch Drummond's presence, a blend of Highland peat and patrician judgement, had followed Max through every boarding school dormitory, Cambridge lecture hall, and London boardroom. It was still here in these walls.

'I see,' Max said. 'Is that all?'

Blackwood's mouth contorted into what might have been meant as a sympathetic smile if he had been capable of that. As the trust's managing trustee, he had mastered the art of delivering bad news with just enough regret to make it seem like he cared.

'Your parents believed marriage would provide stability,' Blackwood said. 'Help you embrace your responsibilities here.'

'Rather than living large in London?'

This wasn't about stability or structure, it was about fixing him. About replacing what they had lost. They might have thought a wife and a home could make him more like the son they had buried.

'One week to get married.' His fingers tapped against his thigh. 'You've waited until I have *one week* before my thirtieth to mention this rather crucial detail.'

'The trust's timing isn't my responsibility. The trustees believed that if you were serious about Dunmarach, you would have returned before now. Your parents...well, they hoped that time would lead you back here without the need for ultimatums. Clearly, that hasn't been the case.' Blackwood straightened his wire-rimmed glasses. 'Their will granted the trust temporary control of the estate following their passing. It stipulated that you could inherit on your thirtieth birthday, provided you fulfilled the conditions. The trust wasn't legally required to disclose those conditions until now. Although I did advise your parents and the trustees to inform you sooner.'

'Did you now?' The whisky decanter clinked against the

glass as Max poured two drams. He was sure Blackwood was lying. But he wasn't sure why. 'How conscientious of you.'

Blackwood accepted the offered drink with a curt nod. 'The trustees saw no need to rush matters. They preferred to wait until…the time was right.'

'Don't bullshit me, Richard. I'm not a boy anymore.' The crystal tumbler threw shards of light as he raised it. 'The right time? You mean the right time to make it impossible for me to fulfil the conditions. The trust is doing this on purpose. You obviously want me out.'

'We'll do what's necessary to ensure Dunmarach's future.' Blackwood sighed and set his untouched drink aside, unable to suppress his smug 'game-over' face. 'And your parents wanted you back home where you belong.'

'Is that so?' Max stalked back to the window, the floorboards creaking beneath his Italian leather shoes. His father's mounted stag head seemed to mock him from above the fireplace. 'Funny how "belonging" wasn't a priority when they shipped me off to uni the day after I got out of hospital.'

'Your brother's death affected them profoundly.'

'Don't.' The word cracked like a whip.

'They lost a child. They were grieving.'

'Were they? And what about me? Believe it or not, I was grieving, too. I lost my big brother, goddammit!'

'You chose to stay in London after Cambridge.'

'And my parents chose to pretend their surviving son didn't exist.' Max's attention fixed on the worn line of carpet where his father had so often paced.

Who was Blackwood trying to fool? This was a coup. The trust wanted to cut Max out, and his parents had handed them the knife. Maybe they had actually thought they were safeguarding the estate with this clause, maybe this was another punishment. One last reminder of everything he wasn't. Impossible to tell now.

'The stipulations are clear.' Max straightened his cuffs, a

habit he had developed in boardrooms when preparing to deliver a killing blow. 'One week to secure a bride or lose everything. No need for this performative concern.'

His reflection skewed across the dusty glass of Martin's old trophy case. Academic awards, rowing medals, rugby trophies. A shrine to the golden son. Max's own achievements were absent, though he had matched every one of his brother's accomplishments.

Not that it had ever mattered.

'They wanted—'

'What they *wanted*,' Max cut in, 'was a reliable, pliable successor. What they *got* was me. Now, if we're quite finished with this touching family retrospective, I have calls to make.'

'Maxwell…'

'Thank you for your time. I'll have my team review the documentation.'

The solicitor gathered his papers. 'Of course. Good luck.'

'Save it.'

Once alone, Max crossed to the antique globe bar, lifting the lid to reveal a collection of decanters. He poured himself another generous sip of the family's single malt. The tumbler was cool against his palm as he inhaled the notes of peat and oak.

One week to find a wife or he would lose everything.

'Fucking hell.' He tossed the drink in one burning swig. He had spent years building his private equity firm, crafting an identity separate from the suffocating weight of family legacy.

Laird.

The study walls seemed to close in, heavy with portraits of Drummond ancestors who had managed what he couldn't – maintaining the family line, protecting the legacy, being worthy of the name. But what made him furious – no, ready for war – was being played by the trustees, a bunch of backwater bureaucrats led by Blackwood. They thought they had him cornered.

And no one put Maxwell Drummond in a corner.

If he were to lose Dunmarach now, this would prove his father right. It would mean letting Martin down.

He couldn't let either of those things happen.

Max had made himself into a winner, took what life offered and gave nothing in return. He had made himself untouchable. Not by chance, but by choice. Insecurity, vulnerability – those were weaknesses he couldn't afford, chinks in the armour. In his world, survival belonged to the calculated, not the sentimental.

Watching Dunmarach fall into the trust's hands? Not on his watch. If he had to marry to keep it, then so be it. Marriage was nothing but a contract, and contracts he understood.

He traced the boundaries of the study, cataloguing potential candidates among his London acquaintances with the same precision he applied to takeovers and mergers. There must be someone who would grasp the practical nature of such an arrangement. Someone who wouldn't expect more than he could give.

Grace, the barrister? Too sharp for the inevitable divorce. Nadia from the tech company? Too much like him, married to her work. He let out a dry chuckle. Who was he kidding? They would all laugh in his face. What would such a conversation even sound like? 'Lovely weather. Fancy getting hitched, so I don't lose my ancestral pile to a scheming trust?'

Another harsh laugh echoed off the oak-panelled walls.

Over the years, more women had come and gone from his bedroom than he could count. And none of them gave a shit about him. He had well taken care of it. His thumb flicked over his phone screen. A decade of affairs left him with plenty of numbers, but not a single person he would trust with his legacy.

Not a single person he would trust, period.

He had designed it that way, hadn't he? Keep them at arm's length, never let anyone close enough to see the fractures and shadows.

Martin's old rugby scarf still hung on the coat rack, blue now faded to grey. Max's hand caught on it as he passed, and the soft wool seemed to taunt him. Perfect Martin, who had never struggled to connect, to belong. Who had filled this office with laughter instead of grim silence. Who could do no wrong. Always perfect. Flawless.

If only they knew…

The alcohol burned in his empty stomach. Seven days to find a wife. He hadn't even shared breakfast with anyone, let alone contemplated sharing a life, business or otherwise. Relationships had never been his style. Affairs, yes, countless, but he had always made sure to leave while it was still dark.

A sudden gust rattled the windows, and the old house groaned around him like a ghost. Everything in this room belonged to the dead. Martin's awards, his parents' disappointment. And now he was expected to conjure up a bride and bring her into this mausoleum of morbidity – or roll over and hand it all to the trustees, making a joke of himself in the process?

The glass clinked against his father's desk as he set it down. Piled clouds hunkered over the hills in the distance. He loosened his tie at last. Losing the estate would be a heavy financial blow, but it wouldn't break him. His investment company had made him wealthy in his own right.

But the thought of watching smug trust managers taking away the Drummond legacy sent a bracing pressure through his chest. The distillery his ancestors had built, the castle that had sheltered eight generations of his family. All that made a Drummond a Drummond – stripped away. He could already imagine the whispers in the private clubs, the knowing looks at industry events. The great Maxwell Drummond, who had conquered Britain's financial sector but couldn't keep hold of his own heritage.

The heir who lost it all.

Such a tasteless cliché.

He had spent years trying to forget this place. Martin had loved Dunmarach with a passion that Max had never understood. But standing here, watching twilight creep across the hills their family had stewarded for centuries, he felt the weight of what his brother had always known: this wasn't just property to be managed. This wasn't a random business he could rip to shreds and sell for parts. Dunmarach was more than land or legacy. It was the core of who they were.

And Max was the last of them.

He owed it to Martin's memory to preserve what his brother had cherished, what should have been his to protect if fate hadn't had other plans.

If he hadn't…

The irony wasn't lost on him. Max had spent years running from this place, only to find himself struggling to keep it. He lifted the glass in a mock toast to his reflection in the window. 'Happy early birthday, idiot.'

Outside, the Highland dusk unfurled over the estate like a shroud. A distant rumble of thunder echoed across the hills, and, for a moment, he could have sworn he heard Martin's laugh in it. That generous sound that had always filled these halls before…everything. His brother would have found this situation hilarious.

Max would find a solution. Discuss this with his legal team. Discover a loophole. But as the darkness gathered and the whisky dwindled, even Max Drummond couldn't convince himself it would be that easy.

Chapter Two

The ceiling fan wheezed above Rowan MacKay's head, stirring the stagnant July air without cooling it. She slouched over her laptop in the faux leather armchair. Highland midges battered themselves senseless against the B&B's grimy window. On the screen, her bank balance glowed like a neon sign advertising her failures.

'Fuck's sake.' She jabbed at the calculator app again, as if the numbers might rearrange themselves into something less terrifying. The extra fees for her gran's care were due next week, and her last freelance payment was still 'processing'.

The springs gave a loud screech as Rowan flopped backwards onto the bed. The tiny room's musty air carried hints of damp and decades-old cigarette smoke.

Her phone blinked to life, and her gran's face lit up the screen.

'Hello, ma wee treasure! Just checking ye're all sorted up there.'

Her grandmother's voice loosened the knot in Rowan's chest. The familiar childhood endearment felt especially precious now, knowing how her gran's world was shrinking. Moments and faces fading into shadows she could no longer reach. It wasn't the forgetting – like taking her medication or the fact that her husband had passed almost two decades ago. Although that was part of it, too. She'd only been in the care home for four months, but it already felt as though everything was slipping away too fast. For now, she could still press the right speed dial on the phone in her room and be cognisant of who she was talking to.

God only knew for how much longer.

'I'm fine, Gran. The room's...' She glanced at the suspicious brown stain on the ceiling, '...rustic.'

'And the story? That castle?' There was a pause, then, 'Did I ask ye that already? These days ma mind's like one of those puzzle boxes.'

The casual mention of those memory lapses made Rowan's throat constrict. Three years ago, the early-onset dementia diagnosis had hit like a sledgehammer. As if the small stroke hadn't already been enough.

'What are ye writing again?'

'A feature about the castle, the distillery, and the new heir. Or so I hope.'

'And any luck wi' that?'

Nope, not really. Rowan glanced at the battered folder next to her laptop, crammed with material about Dunmarach Castle. It was the perfect hook for a young journalist hustling her way into the good graces of *North By Scotland's* editor. Possibly her shot at a stable job. Real exposure. Even if it was only for a Highland lifestyle mag.

Dunmarach. A castle with a distillery on the brink of releasing its new 30-year-old single malt. Industry whispers hinted it might knock any *Glenwhatsitnot* off its pedestal. A new Highland malt with a pedigree so pristine and a back-story so secretive, it practically sold itself.

Supply and demand, two of the apocalyptic horsemen of capitalism.

And the timing couldn't have been juicier.

Not that it mattered much to her personally or the wider world, but whisky geeks were dying to know what Maxwell Drummond planned to do with the distillery when he took over. Insiders suggested that his thirtieth birthday marked the day he'd officially take control. It was all rumours, though. He hadn't made a single public statement since his parents' deaths two years ago. Or before that. Nobody knew the man. No interviews, no press releases, not even a token nod to PR.

For a journalist with half a brain, that kind of silence was catnip. Who wouldn't want the inside scoop on that?

'Still in the planning stage,' Rowan hedged. 'But I'm getting there.'

She'd tried playing nice for weeks, had gone through all the proper channels. Emails, polite calls, even the odd grovelling voicemail. But the distillery's management wasn't interested in press. The Drummond brand was thriving on exclusivity. No open days, no advertising, no comment. She'd have to dig out whatever she needed for the article on her own.

'I've got a good feeling about it, Gran. Something will come of it.'

'That's ma lass.' Her gran's voice brightened. 'Always landing on yer feet, like yer maw. Have tae have yer wits aboot ye.'

The comparison twisted something in Rowan's gut. Her mother was still pulling double shifts at the hospital. A quarter of a century spent treating wounds, dispensing medication, administering infusions, and raising a child on her own – and what did she have to show for it? A dodgy back and a daughter who'd gone to uni but still couldn't afford decent accommodation in Glasgow.

Well, Rowan would find a way to give Gran the care she deserved and her mum a nice wee vacation. Even if it meant scaling castle walls to do it.

That was the reason she was here.

'Oh, did I tell ye? Yer grandda Joe called. Said he'd be round the morn. I've been waitin' on him.'

Rowan's heart cracked. 'Och, Gran... I'm not sure if...' Then she forced cheer into her voice. 'You know what? I think you *did* tell me. That's great news! Now, have you had your tea already?'

After saying goodnight, Rowan returned to her research.

Of course, tracking down a millionaire wasn't as simple as sliding into his DMs. Officially, the estate was managed by a trust. They'd stonewalled every email, dodged her calls, and made it clear they weren't taking media inquiries, either. The trust might have been keeping everything running, but the castle – and its true secrets – belonged to Maxwell Drummond.

The castle's website was sparse, but she'd dug up a few old articles. One rare society photo from a couple of years ago showed a stern-faced young man in his mid-twenties, all angular cheekbones and brooding intensity. Dark hair, grey-blue eyes, and a face that looked like it had never cracked a smile but could probably crack marble. The tailored suit framed his broad shoulders. Even staring the camera down as if it had challenged him to a duel, the man was strikingly handsome. City-boy polish with a hint of Highland warrior lurking underneath.

The kind of man who had his trousers ironed but still carried you into his castle for a nice round of ravishing.

Jeez, girl. Hormonal much?

It was an older article that caught her professional eye. Thirteen years ago a mysterious car accident. Maxwell had survived, his older brother hadn't. The details were frustratingly vague, cloaked in that polished language posh families used to cover their secrets. And then, as if the universe hadn't kicked his balls hard enough, his parents had vanished in some freak storm near Antigua two years ago.

She chewed her lip. 'No wonder you prefer to stay down in London, looking all scowly and frowny.'

No time for sympathy for the devil, MacKay!

Her credit card balance was creeping ever closer to the limit. And her gran's weekly physiotherapy and private dementia care sessions weren't going to pay for themselves.

'Sorry about your tragic backstory,' she said to his glowering photo and tried to squash her guilt. 'But I need a story more than you need your privacy.'

Principles are for those who can afford them.

One good story was all she needed. One piece to finally prove she could hack it in journalism.

Dunmarach castle stood empty most of the year. Perfect for her plans.

'Right then, Mr Moody MacDarcy.' She straightened her shoulders and pulled up the satellite view of the estate. 'Let's see about getting past your defences.'

The late-summer sun was already surrendering to dusk when Rowan finalised her plan – one that tap danced gleefully between investigative genius and a potential criminal record. She wrestled into her most ninja-appropriate attire: well-worn Doc Martens that had survived at least six music festivals, black jeans, and a black leather jacket. Her notebook disappeared into her trusty backpack, along with an emergency Mars bar. Breaking and entering was hungry work. She threw in a day-old sausage roll to appease potential canine interference.

Best to be prepared for the wee angry dugs.

The B&B's antique hallway clock groaned out nine chimes as she crept past the front desk. Mrs Bellamy, the owner, didn't even look up from her crossword puzzle.

'Popping out for some fresh air,' Rowan chirped, while her conscience performed mental gymnastics. She'd always been up for shenanigans, but this was her first attempt at planned trespassing. For a greater good, but still.

The path to Dunmarach wound up a hill through woodland, leaves crunching and brittle twigs splintering beneath her steps. After twenty minutes, the trees thinned and revealed the first proper view of the castle. It loomed at the edge of the world, towers stark against the fading light, with nothing but the rugged Grampians and endless sky beyond. Grey stone spires rose against the craggy ridges, their proud contours mellowed by wind and rain and time. Streaks of evening light broke through the heavy clouds and caught the slate roof, making it gleam like wet silk.

'Holy shite.' She fumbled for her camera. This was what she needed. Something unique, something with soul. The kind of story that could launch her career.

Her heart raced as she approached the wall, equal parts excitement and terror coursing through her veins. The oak's lowest branch was within reach – if she jumped.

She'd tried everything above board, hadn't she?

Sometimes, the right thing was whatever got the job done. Rowan took one last look around and jumped for the branch. Her fingertips scraped the rough bark and slipped. Landing with a muffled thud, she glared up at the tree as if it had insulted her.

'Second time's the charm. Or third. Or…' She bent her knees and launched herself again. This time, she snagged the branch with both hands. A triumphant grin split her face. She swung her legs and hooked one over the branch with all the grace of a drunken sloth. 'Definitely not a career burglar.'

With a series of grunts that would have done any gym hulk proud, she hauled herself up and paused to catch her breath. Squinting at the scene below, she saw the castle's manicured grounds stretched out like a carpet. No security in sight. No cameras. And no bloodhounds.

After dropping onto the grass, she straightened and

dusted off her black jeans. She'd get a few photos, maybe peek through some windows. Just to get a vibe. Totally harmless. Professional and investigative, albeit in a morally grey way.

Okay, more like anthracite.

Probably charcoal.

Didn't matter, she was in now.

Suddenly, the air thickened, and a sharp chill crept up her spine. A twig snapped behind her. Rowan froze, and her heart stopped for a beat.

Security? A groundskeeper? Rottweilers?

Then a deep, dark voice behind her boomed, 'And what, exactly, do you think you're doing?'

Her first instinct was to run; her second was to run faster. She turned. And there he was, like a shadow against the looming castle: the most furiously beautiful man she'd ever seen.

She knew that face.

And it looked angry. Very, very angry.

Maxwell Drummond was a lot taller in person, his imposing presence filled the space between them like storm clouds. His eyes, grey as the castle walls, fixed on her with an intensity that made her skin prickle.

Well, fuck.

Chapter Three

Max had sought peace in the gathering dusk, wandering across his grounds. Now, he spotted a slight figure in dark clothes, dropping from the old oak with surprising grace. For an instant, he thought the whisky was playing tricks on his eyes.

But no, there was an intruder on his property, flicking leaves from her jeans with the casual ease of someone tidying up after a picnic.

'And what, exactly, do you think you're doing?' The words came out low and dangerous, laced with the anger he had been suppressing all day.

She spun around, and Max stared into the greenest eyes he had ever seen. Unrepentant. They bore into him with the same calculating focus he had noticed in boardroom rivals. Everything about her bristled with rebellion, from her scuffed boots to the worn black leather jacket. Yet, she held herself with the confident poise of someone who had strolled into a thousand places she didn't belong and made them her own.

'Would you believe I'm doing a survey on tree mainte-nance?' Her tone was far too cheerful for someone caught trespassing.

He narrowed his eyes as she smiled at him, wide and unwavering. Though there was a flicker of something else beneath it. A slip in the act, maybe. Bluster, definitely. Straight red hair fell over her shoulders, framing the kind of heart-shaped face that belonged on a Highland single malt label. Her chin was set with quiet stubbornness, freckles dusted across her nose like cinnamon.

'No.' Max advanced and let his height dominate the space between them.

She didn't move an inch, let alone quiver. Why didn't it work? It usually did, and this woman was at least a full head shorter than him.

A low heaviness sat in the air. The weight of an impending storm, though whether it was in the sky or standing before him was unclear.

'You are breaking and entering,' he said.

To his surprise, she laughed. *Actually* laughed. 'Breaking implies damage. I simply…creatively accessed public heritage.'

The sheer audacity radiating from this petite figure before him!

'Private property,' he corrected. 'And you are trespassing.'

'Ah, but that's debatable. Did you know Dunmarach Castle was open to the public every summer from 1952 to 2002?' She pulled out a small notebook and flipped through the pages with theatrical flair. 'The tours were popular until—'

'…until my father ended them.' Max cut her off, unnerved by her interest in his family's past.

Somewhere in the distance, the sky grumbled low and long.

'And now I'm ending whatever game you are playing. Leave, or I'll call the police.'

'Hmmm…' She cocked her head and studied him with unsettling directness. 'No, you won't.'

'I assure you, I most certainly will.'

'Nope.' She popped the 'p' with aggravating confidence. 'Because that would mean publicity. Questions. Journalists. *Kerfuffle.* And you, Mr Drummond, seem like someone who values his privacy over *kerfuffle.*'

'So you know who I am.'

'The brooding, absent owner of Dunmarach? Hard to miss.'

She gave him a measured once-over, and he was suddenly aware of his dishevelled state: tie loosened, three buttons undone, shirt half-untucked.

'Though you're more...rumpled than your rare press photos. Almost as if Hugh Grant was your stylist.'

'Get off my property.' Only one week left for him to say that.

'I will. After you answer a few questions about the distillery's history and—'

'No.' He stepped closer, close enough to catch the scent of her shampoo, something warm and bright. 'I don't give interviews, especially not to trespassers who—'

Lightning tore through the clouds, thunder booming down after it. Fat drops of rain began to fall, quickly becoming a deluge that would turn the ground into treacherous mud. It was as if the Scottish Sea had decided to move location. The woman yelped, clutching her backpack to her chest as if it held the Crown Jewels.

'Brilliant,' she muttered. 'Bloody brilliant.'

Max should have let her get soaked. Should have watched her trudge back to wherever she came from. Served her right for sneaking onto his estate and disrespecting him.

Instead, he heard himself say, 'Inside. Now.'

She blinked rainwater from her lashes. 'Sorry?'

'I expect you don't have a car.'

'No, I walked all the way from the village, like the peasant I am.' She gestured toward the valley, where sheets of rain had reduced visibility to mere metres. Lightning split the sky and briefly illuminated the large iron gate further along the wall. Beyond it, the torrent was already transforming the muddy track downhill into something resembling chocolate mousse.

'I would personally ensure you got back, but I don't drive.' The admission tasted sour. 'I gave my driver the night off, and it's too muddy to walk all the way.'

The rain made the ground dangerously slippery, and this woman breaking her neck on his land wasn't a headline he wanted to wake up to. He didn't need any more problems.

'Och, dinnae be daft.' She set her shoulders, rainwater streaming down her face. 'My boots have seen much worse at Glastonbury.'

Another thunderclap shook the ground beneath their feet. The storm had positioned itself overhead.

'Out of the question. This is different,' he said and watched as her left boot made a sucking sound when she shifted her weight. 'That track will be impassable in three minutes.'

Her eyes flickered toward the castle, then back to the threatening sky. She beamed as if a thunderstorm were her idea of a good time. 'Okay.'

Max turned around. 'Come. Before we both get pneumonia.'

He didn't wait to see if she followed. The rain plastered his shirt to his skin, reminding him of how undone and ridiculous he must look.

As if Hugh Grant was my stylist. Fuck off.

It wasn't just the worry about her breaking her neck on his land. Something about her pulled at a sense of honour he thought he had buried long ago.

The young woman – he still didn't know her name – caught up with him as he opened the door.

'For someone who was about to call the police two minutes ago, you're being surprisingly hospitable,' she said.

'Don't mistake necessity for hospitality.' He ushered her into the warmth of the kitchen and turned on the lights. Water dripped from her hair onto the flagstone floor, forming small puddles. 'Once the rain stops, you're leaving, Miss…'

'Rowan,' she said promptly.

'Pardon?'

'My name. It's Rowan MacKay.' She stuck out a hand as if this were a normal introduction and not the result of her criminal activities. 'Freelance writer and journalist, occasional trespasser, and very grateful for the shelter. Pleased to meet you.'

Max ignored her hand. 'Stay here. Don't move.'

He made his way to the linen cupboard next door in the laundry room and used the moment alone to collect himself. What the hell was he doing, letting a stranger in? The alcohol must have addled his judgement. He grabbed a clean, dry shirt from the shelf and swapped it for his wet one.

When he returned, she was examining the kitchen's Aga oven with shameless curiosity. As if Dunmarach were a museum. Which it wasn't and never would be.

She rubbed her hands together. 'This is original, isn't it? Must be at least seventy years old.'

Max frowned. How did she seem so at ease here? Most people stumbled over themselves to avoid irritating him. For good reasons.

'I don't know, and I don't care.' He tossed her a towel, trying not to notice how her wet clothes clung to her slender curves. 'And stop snooping.'

'Not snooping, observing.' She dried her hair vigorously. 'There's a difference.'

'Is there also a difference between breaking in and "creative accessing"?'

Her smile was quick. 'Oh, absolutely. One shows robust initiative.'

Despite himself, Max felt his lips twitch. He squashed the impulse. 'You're ridiculous.'

'So I've been told. Usually right before people agree to help me.'

'I'm not people.'

'No.' There was something knowing in her tone that unmoored him. 'You're most definitely not. But you *are* helping me, so…'

Max turned away. 'I'll phone Mrs MacPherson to see if there's a room ready. You can stay until the storm passes, not a minute longer.'

'Your housekeeper?'

'Yes. She lives in the village and comes in once a week.' At least that was what he thought. The trust took care of the details. And Max had no idea why he was explaining himself to this insolent brat.

Or why he had offered her a room.

'Ah. Part of me hoped her name was Mrs Danvers – you know, like in *Rebecca* by Daphne du Maurier?' She wrapped the towel around her head. 'Never mind. Former English lit student speaking. So it's just you, rattling around in this ginormous place?'

Max's jaw set as he tried to look anywhere but at her. The rain had turned her heather grey t-shirt almost translucent, clinging to her small, hard peaks and the gentle dip of her waist. He caught himself tracking a droplet down the curve of her throat and pulled his gaze back to her face.

'My living arrangements aren't your concern.'

'Wrong. Everything's my concern. Occupational hazard.' She tilted her head, sending another trickle of water down her neck. 'I'm a writer. Can't help it.'

He pulled his phone out of his pocket and stepped away. From the weight of her observant stare.

'Excuse me.' He brought up Mrs MacPherson's number. Thankfully, it connected after only two rings.

'Mrs MacPherson?' He kept his tone clipped and professional to mask his discomfort.

He hated how little he knew about the place now. The estate was a loose thread he hadn't bothered to pull at in years, leaving it to others to keep it from unravelling, while he poured himself into London's cutthroat financial world.

'Apologies for the late call. Which guest rooms are prepared?'

The east wing was being aired out and the south tower needed repairs, but the Blue Room in the family wing was always kept ready.

What a mess. He was forced back to play lord of the manor, and he didn't even know which rooms were habitable. The castle had stood empty since his parents' death, maintained by a skeleton crew. Mrs MacPherson and her team came weekly, going through their basic cleaning routine. Old Grant tended the grounds, and there was a night watchman – Thompson? Tomkins? – who patrolled the perimeter. Slater and his crew took care of the distillery down by the loch.

Max hadn't had a say in the management, so he hadn't cared.

And now he had a rain-soaked intruder watching him fumble through the basic remnants of Highland hospitality.

'Yes, the Blue Room will do,' he said. 'Thanks.' He hung up before she could respond.

Rowan was still studying him. Those green eyes seemed to miss nothing. 'Interesting place for a finance mogul to call home.'

Home.

His shoulders stiffened as he pivoted to the doorway. 'First floor, third door on the right. I trust you can find it without climbing any more trees or sticking your nose where it doesn't belong.'

'Sure. Thank you, Mr Drummond. Or do you have a proper title?' She didn't even try to conceal her sarcasm.

'Laird Maxwell Drummond of Dunmarach. Or…just Maxwell.' The correction surprised them both. He cleared his throat. 'The title is meaningless to me. And if you're staying under my roof, you might as well use my name. I'm twenty-nine, not ninety-two.'

'Maxwell,' she repeated softly, testing it out. Something in her voice made him turn back to face her.

She looked rain-dampened and ruffled, yet somehow more alive than anyone he had ever encountered. Their eyes met, and for a beat, the air seemed to hum with possibility.

Then Max turned to leave. 'Goodnight, Miss MacKay.'

'Rowan,' she replied. 'And I'm twenty-four, not…'

But he was already halfway out the door before she could finish her sentence.

As he retreated to the study, footsteps echoing through the empty corridors, his pulse kicked against his collar. He couldn't shake the image of rain-darkened auburn hair and challenging emerald eyes.

He had invited her to stay. A complete stranger. Caught trespassing, no less. Had he lost his mind? She didn't look like an arsonist or a thief, though. Blame Drummond's Finest. He usually stuck to the occasional dram, savouring it.

Not today, though. Today was chaos.

She had invaded his life like a badly timed shareholder meeting, wielding that vexing grin.

Worse. She had made him curious.

He didn't do curious.

The way she had said his name grated against his composure. Her voice had a timbre that suggested she found him both amusing and transparent, a combination that made a muscle in his jaw twitch.

What a weird woman.

No. He didn't want to wonder why she was here or what drove her.

He wanted her gone.

He needed to scour away the irritating awareness that had lodged beneath his skin like a splinter, to erase the memory of those keen eyes dissecting him.

Tomorrow morning, she would be leaving, taking her notebook, her probing questions, and that unnerving ability to scratch at his walls.

Good riddance.

Yet as he climbed the stairs later, an uncomfortable feeling clung to him like an ill-fitting coat: Rowan MacKay was more than a minor annoyance. She was dynamite in boots.

Chapter Four

R owan felt trapped inside a Wedgwood teacup. The Blue Room lived up to its name in spectacular fashion. She ran her hand over the silk damask wallpaper. 'So this is what old money looks like when it goes colour blind after centuries of inbreeding. Hmm!'

The room was three times the size of her own in the flat-share in Glasgow. A four-poster bed dominated one wall, with carved oak posts that reached toward the ceiling. The mattress, when she tested it with an experimental bounce, squeaked in protest.

What must a girl do to get a bit of memory foam once in her life?

She got up and hung her wet clothes over a carved Victorian screen, dripping onto the Persian rug.

Probably the first time in half a century that anything got wet in this bedroom.

She wandered around and found an oversized jumper in one of the drawers, faded black with 'Cambridge University' emblazoned across the chest. It smelled of mothballs and fell to mid-thigh, hanging loose and shapeless. But it was comfy and dry.

'Right.' She pulled out her notebook. 'If I'm going to

borrow without asking and continue my life of crime, I might as well take notes.'

A portrait of a long-dead Drummond hung askew, his enormous 'stache seeming to judge her. She flopped into a blue armchair. 'Och, I bet you never had to worry about care home bills or rent.'

Her thoughts drifted to Maxwell Drummond. The way he'd towered over her in the rain… She scoffed. As if that could intimidate her. She'd broken up knife fights on Sauchiehall Street. So, obviously not.

But nice try, Moody MacDarcy.

His eyes had blazed with thinly veiled fury, the colour of the sky just before lightning strikes. Rain dripped from a jaw that hadn't relaxed in at least two decades. He moved like a man who expected the world to bend around him, yet there'd been something uncertain in the way he'd fumbled through basic hospitality. And that moment in the kitchen when their eyes had met…like touching a plug socket with wet fingers. Thrilling and dangerous and stupid as hell.

Also: impossible.

'Focus, MacKay.' She jotted down a few observations in her notebook. The room's dimensions, the quality of the furnishings, details that spoke of faded grandeur. Her pen scratched across the page as she sketched out possible angles for the story.

Elusive heir returns to crumbling castle…

No, too Gothic romance. Though speaking of romance… She glanced at the bed again, imagining Maxwell sprawled across those crisp white sheets. The unwelcome thought sent an inappropriate shiver through her.

'God, no.' She buried her face into a throw pillow. 'Ew. Gross.'

No. She was *not* attracted to Mr Darcy's emotionally constipated Scottish cousin. Even if he did wear that white shirt like it had been painted on impeccable pecs when the biblical downpour had hit.

Rowan jumped up, needing to move. 'Time for some creative research.' She inspected every corner of the room. The enormous wardrobe yielded a collection of hunting tweeds that hadn't seen daylight since the days of Queen Victoria. In a chest of drawers, behind a stack of extra blankets, she found a dusty photo album.

Was this still research, or was it snooping? Before she could ask her conscience to decide, her hands were flipping through the pages. Then she stopped. An image showed a younger Maxwell, maybe fourteen or fifteen, laughing with friends on a rugby pitch. His face was open and happy. Cute. Nothing like the closed-off fortress of a man she'd met tonight. There were other pictures, too. Family gatherings, picnics, holiday snapshots with Maxwell and an older boy, arm in arm, sharing the same set of grey-blue eyes.

She recognised him from the articles.

His dead brother.

Rowan closed the keepsake gently, her fingers lingered on the soft, grained leather cover. She didn't know the full story, but the happiness in the pictures carried an undercurrent of loss.

Maybe that was why he was so…guarded.

Rain still thrashed against the windows as she finally crawled into bed, her notebook clutched to her chest. The sheets smelled expensive. Like everything else in this place, they carried the weight of history and wealth she could never grasp.

Wealthy didn't mean trustworthy, though.

She could only hope that he wasn't a serial killer. 'The Laird with a Lust for Blood. Cracking title.'

She sensed there was a story here. Not another fluff piece about Highland heritage and whisky, but something more substantial. Something about legacy and loss, about the price of privilege and the weight of inheritance. About a man who seemed to have shut himself away in a prison of his own making.

'Game on, Maxwell Drummond,' she murmured as sleep pulled at her consciousness. 'Let's see what secrets you're hiding.'

Max stared at the ceiling. He had hardly slept. No wonder. The alcohol had burned off shortly after he'd gone to bed, leaving him with nothing but circular thoughts about Dunmarach and a dull headache.

And then there was Rowan MacKay.

He would have to have a chat with Thompson – Tomkins? – about security. This stranger had waltzed right through, armed with nothing but brass nerve and a knack for making him feel like he was the one who had shown up uninvited.

Unacceptable.

The morning ritual of selecting a suit usually centred him, but today even Savile Row's finest felt like a polished veneer. He avoided his reflection as he fastened his tie, unwilling to see the evidence of a night spent strategising impossible marriage scenarios. His usual mask of boardroom confidence wasn't holding as well as it used to.

He had enough on his plate as it was.

'One week to conjure a bride.' He smoothed non-existent wrinkles from his jacket. 'And now there's a ginger menace camping in the Blue Room.'

The universe, it seemed, had a cruel sense of humour. Here he was, scrambling to find someone – anyone – willing to enter a marriage before his thirtieth birthday stripped him of his inheritance, and all he had acquired was an unauthorised, disrespectful houseguest.

He needed coffee.

As he strode down the corridor, a sound stopped him dead in his tracks.

Was this…singing?

Yes. A voice, bright and lilting, floated through the Blue Room's door like sunlight through stained glass. Some pop song he vaguely recognised. The melody curled around him and lifted the castle's oppressive weight for a fleeting moment.

Then reality crashed back.

He was standing outside a guest room like a creep, listening to a trespasser sing in his shower.

Completely unacceptable.

Max willed himself to move and descended the stairs with purposeful strides as if he could outrun the way that song had made him feel.

In the kitchen, he centred himself on the ritual of coffee-making and let the familiar motions ground him.

'Six days,' he reminded himself as the dark liquid streamed into his cup. Less than a week to secure his inheritance by marrying.

Completely and utterly unacceptable.

He heard the singing again. It grew louder, accompanied by footsteps. His grip clamped on the counter as Rowan's voice preceded her into the kitchen, still humming that tune. He shouldn't turn around. Shouldn't wonder how the morning light would make her hair gleam, or—

He turned.

She wore his old Cambridge jumper like it had always been hers, bare legs beneath the hem. Her hair was damp and dark and she looked…as if she belonged here, in this space that hadn't felt like his in thirteen years.

'Morning, *Maxwell*.' Her voice carried a hint of the song. 'Oh, yay! You made coffee! Aren't you a darling!'

And with that, she snatched his fresh brew from the machine.

The sheer gall of it rendered him speechless. For the first time in his adult life, Maxwell Drummond – who could reduce other CEOs and board members to stammering with a single raised eyebrow – found himself without words.

She had stolen his coffee.

His coffee.

And he had thought she didn't look like a thief.

The rage started in his chest and spread outward until his fingertips burned with heat. But any angry retort died on his tongue as she closed her eyes, making a sound of pleasure that shot straight through him.

'Mmm,' she purred, 'proper good stuff. Not that shitty instant muck.'

Her throat moved as she swallowed, and he tracked the motion with an intensity that had nothing to do with anger. His fingers drummed against the counter, a tell he thought he had trained himself out of years ago. He turned to the coffee machine, shoulders rigid as he started another brew.

'The rain has stopped, but it will take a while until the mud is dry. My driver will be here in thirty minutes. He can take you to the village or wherever you need to go.'

'Trying to get rid of me already? And here I thought we were having such a lovely time.'

'Breaking and entering is *not* my idea of lovely.'

'Creative accessing, Maxwell,' she corrected and moved closer.

'I see you added theft to your criminal record.' He gave her his most throat-cutting glare. It slid off her as if her skin were made of Teflon.

'Wrong. *Borrowing*,' she countered. 'I'll return the jumper. My clothes aren't dry yet. And I don't want to catch pneumonia, you know.'

'Keep it.' The words slipped out before he could stop

them. He covered his slip with a scowl. 'Consider it payment to leave and never return.'

Rowan laughed. 'Oh, Maxwell. That's adorable.' She hopped onto the counter and started to swing her bare feet with calculated casualness. 'But we both know I'm the most interesting thing that's happened here in aeons.' Her eyes sparkled as she leaned forward. 'Besides, if you really wanted me gone, you wouldn't have let me stay last night. Admit it, Maxwell. I'm fascinating.'

The coffee machine hissed as he jabbed at buttons. 'You're a nuisance and a trespasser.'

'And yet here I am, drinking your coffee.'

Max turned away, needing distance from those knowing eyes. He wrenched open a drawer and searched for bread. The large kitchen suddenly felt too small, too intimate. 'I suppose you want to be fed before you leave.'

'Careful. That almost sounds like hospitality. Or charity. Though I'd check the expiry date on that bread if I were you.'

He frowned at the green spots on the loaf. 'I'm sure there's more somewhere.'

'I'd try the bread box right over there. You know, the thing that has "BREAD" stamped right across the front?' She took another sip and grinned. 'Do you even *know* how to make breakfast?'

He slotted the slices into the toaster and muttered under his breath as he turned back to the coffee machine. Grabbing a mug from the cabinet, he placed it beneath the spout. The machine sputtered to life again and began to pour a stream of rich brew. 'Don't worry. I manage.'

'Mmhmm.' She reached past him to adjust the settings on the toaster he had forgotten to check. 'Is that why you're about to cremate perfectly good toast?'

He bristled. 'I don't usually—'

'Cook? Concede that food doesn't magically appear, carried in by the fairies or the underpaid help?' She hopped off the counter and moved with easy grace, found a knife and a plate in the cupboards, and took the butter from the fridge. 'Tell me, does your butler polish your shoes with unicorn tears, or is that for special occasions?'

'I don't have a butler.'

'No? What about a valet? Please tell me someone helps you dress. These suits can't be easy to put on with that stick up your ar—'

'Enough.' The word sliced through the air. 'You know nothing about me or my life.'

'No. I don't.' She caught the toast mid-air as it popped. 'But I know what kind of life produces someone like you. Private schools, never having to worry about choosing between heating and eating. Other people wiping your bum.'

'You think I've never struggled?'

'At least not financially.' Colour surged to her cheeks, and for a split second, her confidence faltered before resolve hardened her face. 'I think your struggles involve choosing between the Porsche and the Jag.' She spread butter with quick, efficient strokes. 'Some of us can't even fathom that sort of problem.'

'Spare me the working-class hero act. You really think performatively breaking into castles solves anything?'

'No, but writing about it might.' She shoved a slice of toast into his hand while she took a bite out of hers. 'My gran's care home bills went up again. Now it's three hundred quid a month for specialised dementia care. That's money I don't have. On top of rent that keeps climbing, while my income doesn't. I'm freelancing, and it's fucking tough.' Her voice wavered, and she masked it with a smile. 'Every month, I do the maths. Every month, it doesn't add up.'

Max wasn't used to people laying their problems bare, and it needled under his skin. He didn't know whether to admire her honesty or resent her for making him feel something he would rather ignore.

'There are other ways—'

'What, like investing? Inheriting? Bitcoin? Asking Uncle Pimsy for a loan over a dram of Macallan?' Bitterness crept into her tone as she hopped back up onto the counter. 'Do you know what it's like to lie awake wondering if you'll have to choose between your gran's care and your own roof?'

The coffee scalded his tongue. 'I'm neither responsible for you being a judgemental brat, nor for your financial situation.'

Her lips pursed, like she'd bitten into something rotten, and she gestured around the room. 'No, you're part of the system. This kitchen is larger than our flat. And by the looks of it, you probably spend more on a suit than I make in a month.'

He scoffed. 'That's not—'

'Fair? True? Both, actually.' She set her mug down hard enough to spill coffee over the rim. 'Don't get me wrong, it's nice of you to let me stay. But you have a literal castle while people are choosing between food and medicine. And you don't even know how good you have it.'

He stared at her as if he were seeing her for the first time. The scorching spark in those green eyes, the daring lift of her chin. The morning light hit the copper in her hair, matching the pots and the blazing conviction in her eyes. She was certifiably mad, breaking into his property, stealing his clothes and coffee, and lecturing him about wealth inequality while perching on his counter like she owned it.

And yet…

There was something compelling about her complete disregard for everything. Most people tiptoed around him, intimidated by his position, power, wealth. She bulldozed through all of it with the delicacy of a wrecking ball, equipped with nothing but bull-headed confidence and righteous indignation.

Her passion was irritating, but also…refreshing. When

was the last time he had met someone who cared about anything with such fierce intensity? Never. She spoke about her grandmother with so much devotion, willing to risk trespassing charges to help her. The financial difficulties she described stirred something in him. Three hundred pounds – a sum he would spend without thinking on a dinner – stood between her grandmother and proper care. While she was right about his privilege, she was wrong about him not noticing. He noticed things.

And suddenly, like a key clicking into a lock, everything aligned. An idea formed, dangerous in its simplicity.

Max had exhausted every avenue. His legal team couldn't find a loophole or contest the clause of the will. And he had made them work on it nonstop since yesterday. The trust insisted that a wife would signify he was capable of committing to something beyond a quarterly earnings report. He needed someone who had nothing to gain beyond what he offered, and nothing to lose by leaving. He glanced at Rowan, dangling her legs off the counter with crumbs on her borrowed jumper. Against all logic, she fit the bill.

He needed a wife within one week. She needed money. They were practically solving each other's problems already.

The idea was absurd. Unorthodox at best. No sane man would consider this a viable solution. His lawyers would have aneurysms drafting the contracts. But desperate times called for desperate measures. The more he thought about it, the more the pieces clicked into place.

And it wasn't as if he had better options.

He didn't believe in fate; he wasn't a fool. But even he couldn't deny the fortuitous nature of this encounter.

It still was lunacy, of course. Rowan was nothing like the socialites he casually dated now and then. She would dismantle his world piece by piece, just to see what he was made of.

Perhaps that was what this mausoleum of a castle needed.

What *he* needed?

Ridiculous notion. He needed no one.

But at least she had the fire to match his ice, the courage to challenge him, and enough genuine compassion to balance his cynicism. Plus, her clear disdain for his wealth meant she wasn't after his money. Even if money was what she lacked.

A marriage of convenience. It could work. She would get financial security for her grandmother, he would get his inheritance and triumph over the trustees. And if the opportunity offered itself…

Max cut that thought off before it could form.

But watching her gesture with her toast, rambling about healthcare, he was already turning over how to phrase the suggestion.

'I might have a solution if you would shut up and stop ranting for two minutes.' His voice sliced clean through her tirade.

She paused mid-gesture, toast hovering. 'A solution? What, are you going to start a charity for impoverished writers? Are you buying the NHS?'

'You need money. I need something else.' His tone was precise, measured. The same one he used for million-pound deals.

'Woah. If this is leading to some dodgy proposition involving your bedroom, I should warn you: I know jiu-jitsu.'

'Don't be crude. And what makes you think it would happen in the bedroom?' The mental image of her legs hooked around him here on the counter sent a tingling pressure up his spine.

A hint of pink climbed the sides of her face at his words.

Interesting.

'First, I need to know that I can trust you,' he said.

'Cross my heart!' She drew an X over his Cambridge logo with dramatic flair. 'Scout's honour. Though I was kicked out of the Brownies for questioning authority, so maybe that's not the best oath.'

Max pinched the bridge of his nose. 'I need a wife.'

'I'm sorry, what?'

'To inherit everything – the castle, the distillery, the estate – I need to be married before my thirtieth birthday in six days.'

'And that's relevant to me because…?' But her eyes sharpened with interest.

'Because I'm offering you a business arrangement. A marriage of convenience. Marry me. One year, strictly professional. You get financial security, I get my inheritance. We both win.'

She stared at him for a few seconds. Then she burst out laughing. 'Oh, that's brilliant! For a second there, I thought you were…' Her words fizzled out as she studied his face. 'Fuck. You're serious.'

'Entirely.'

'You want to marry me? Me. The woman who broke into your castle less than twelve hours ago.'

'Creatively accessed. And think of it as a business merger.' His voice remained steady despite his racing pulse. 'You need capital, I need a partner who won't try to take advantage. You have no reverence for my position or wealth, which makes you…suitable.'

'Suitable?' She repeated the word like it tasted funny. 'Have you *met* me? That's the worst proposal in the history of proposals. And I once got asked by a guy doing a handstand in Wetherspoons with his arse out.'

'This isn't a proposal, it's a proposition.'

She didn't seem interested. This wasn't going according to plan, which rarely ever happened. What would Martin have done? Martin wouldn't have ended up in this kind of mess in the first place. And Max was only standing knee-deep in disaster because Martin wasn't here.

And Martin wasn't here because of him.

Rowan's cheeks flushed crimson, her fingers toying with the hem of his jumper.

He wasn't ready to let her off the hook yet. 'Only one year. Financial security for you and your grandmother. One-third paid at contract signing, one-third in twelve monthly instalments, and the final third as a settlement after the full year, along with an amicable divorce.'

Emotions flashed across her face like pages in a flip book. Disbelief, outrage, consideration, calculation, doubt, temptation. The honesty of her expressions fascinated him. How did she survive this world being so readable?

'You're absolutely mental,' she said finally. 'Completely round the bend. Aff yer trolley.'

He held her stare and ignored the way his heart pounded. 'Is that a no?'

'It's a "you can't be fucking serious, pal".'

But she was thinking about it. He saw the gears turning.

'What's the catch, Maxwell?'

'Besides legally binding yourself to a stranger for a year?'

'Yeah, besides that minor detail.'

He straightened his tie, buying time. 'We would need to be convincing. The clause specifically prevents marriage fraud.'

'So we'd have to… What? Hold hands at events? Share a bed?'

'Live together. Appear as a normal couple.' He kept his tone impersonal. 'Nothing inappropriate.'

'Right, because there's nothing inappropriate about a fake marriage.' She slid off the counter and paced barefoot on the stone slabs. 'This is insane. You're insane.'

'I prefer the term visionary.'

'But you hardly know me!'

'I know you're brazen enough to break into a castle for a story, but so principled you had to tell me why you need the money. You're educated, articulate, and capable of handling yourself in any situation. Most importantly, you seem to dislike everything about my lifestyle, which means you won't try to maintain it after we separate.'

She stopped pacing and stared at him with huge eyes. 'That's surprisingly astute.'

'I am an astute businessman.'

'You're a madman.' But she was smiling now, that daring glint back in her eyes. 'What if I'm a rare female serial killer? A black widow?'

'Then I suppose I'll die knowing I made an interesting mistake.'

A startled laugh slipped out. 'God, you really fucking mean it.'

'I do.' He allowed himself a calculated smile. 'Though I would appreciate if you would stop stealing my coffee.'

Chapter Five

Rowan wasn't accustomed to private chauffeur-driven cars – she wasn't accustomed to cars in general – but now she was gliding through the Highland landscape in a sleek Maybach like some kind of budget Bond girl.

It was a far cry from Glasgow's buses, where the air was seasoned with candy-floss vape, weed, and McDonald's. No death glares from power-mad drivers who'd shut the doors in her face.

No, this private Benz, with its buttery leather seats, felt like riding in a spaceship through a parallel universe. It also felt like a weird flex. Was Maxwell trying to make her feel important to convince her to say yes to his grotesque proposal?

His driver – a stoic man named Oliver who looked like he'd been carved from a similar block of granite – hadn't uttered a word since leaving the castle. Rowan stared out the window, replaying the morning's events like an absurdist play.

'Marry me,' he'd said. Calmly. As if that weren't completely bonkers.

Her mind ricocheted between outrage and a strange,

unnerving flicker of intrigue. One year. A whole year living in a castle, all expenses paid. Enough money to cover her gran's care, help her mum, and get a decent laptop that didn't sound like a dying badger. It was tempting.

But marriage?

She was twenty-four; marriage hadn't been on her horizon. Not even with Ben, and he'd been near flawless husband material. In theory. Until he'd followed the international hipster call to Berlin two years ago and dumped her arse.

And she should've seen that coming.

Rowan knew how to be the fun one, the bold one, the first to say 'another round?' at the pub. But real friendships and relationships, the kind that stuck? That was a lot trickier.

Maxwell's mental. And I'm no less mental for even thinking about it.

Trusting a man like this – controlled, cold, and from another world – felt like walking into a catastrophe with open eyes. And what would it say about her if she agreed to this? Trading her independence for a cheque.

The car pulled up outside the B&B, and Oliver opened her door with the same blank efficiency he'd shown throughout the brief journey.

'Thanks, mate.' She paused. 'Do I have to tip you, is that how it's done?'

Oliver shook his head. 'No, Miss.'

'Anyhoo, thanks for driving me.'

He gave a curt nod and tapped the brim of his cap with two fingers. 'Only doing my job.'

'Still nice. See ya!'

The B&B's reception area smelled of stale biscuits and wet walls. It was still early and Mrs Bellamy wasn't around as Rowan trudged past the desk, wearing Maxwell's jumper like a trophy for getting access to a reclusive millionaire.

Mission accomplished, next level unlocked.

After the castle's vastness, her room felt even smaller. A

suspicious brown stain on the ceiling had developed overnight, forming what looked like a crude map of Scotland. She sat down on the bed and pulled out her phone. 'Time to check on the troops.'

Her mother answered on the fourth ring and sounded exhausted. Night shift again.

'Everything awright, love? It's before nine. You never call this early.'

'Can't a daughter check on her favourite mother without ulterior motives?'

'Not when that daughter's you. There's always something going on in that head of yours.' A pause. She *heard* her mum's smile fading. 'I don't want you to worry, but your gran had a wee tumble last night.'

Rowan sat bolt upright. 'What? What happened? Is she okay?'

'Aye, a little bump on the elbow when she got out of bed. She was looking for your grandda again. Thought he'd just stepped out to get her flowers. Got confused about where she was, and when.'

The familiar guilt writhed in Rowan's stomach. 'I should be there.'

It wasn't the physical fall, it was the mental slipping. Each time Gran confused the present with the past, Rowan felt her fading away further. And if the care home couldn't manage…

'Naw, love. You should be following your dreams, that's what you should be doing. Found your story yet?'

She laughed, slightly hysterical. 'Oh, you could say that. I might have half-accidentally broken into a castle and met its brooding owner.'

Her mother yawned. 'What's that now?'

'Nothing, Mum. Journalism stuff.' She picked at a loose thread in the blanket. 'Listen, about Gran's fees…'

'Don't you worry about that. I've picked up some extra shifts—'

'Mum, no. You're already working yourself to death.'

'Better than the alternative.' Her mother's voice carried that unyielding tone Rowan knew all too well. She'd inherited it, after all. 'We'll manage. We always do.'

'Aye, I guess so. Now go to bed and get that well-deserved beauty sleep. I love you!'

Hanging up, Rowan stared at her phone. Even the idea of writing that story felt absurd when she couldn't even pay her gran's bills with it. She checked her emails, hoping for good news from another travel magazine that had seemed interested in her pitch. Instead, she found a rejection for the current commission that might as well have been copied from a template:

Dear Ms MacKay,

Thank you for your work on the Drummond and Dunmarach feature. Unfortunately, due to editorial changes, we won't be moving forward with the piece at this time. We appreciate your efforts and wish you the best in your future projects.

Rowan blinked. Read it again. They'd let her pitch the story, let her sink time and money into research, let her think she had something solid – only to drop it without a reason. No kill fee, no explanation. Just a boot to the bum.

'Editorial changes, my arse,' she muttered and deleted the email. 'You don't want to pay proper rates.'

Another email informed her that, due to financial constraints and the economy, her weekly gig writing blog posts for an HR company had been terminated effective immediately, cutting off her only trickle of income. Even though their staff consultants wouldn't pick up the phone for her meagre hourly rate.

Fuck. Fuck. Fuck.

Rowan pressed the heels of her hands against her eyes until colours flared behind the lids. Purples and greens, bruises blooming in the dark. Her chest felt stuffed with broken glass, shards catching and tearing with every inhale.

Twenty-four years old and what had she achieved? A collection of rejection emails and an overdraft that grew like a malignant tumour.

She'd done everything right, hadn't she? University, internships, networking events where she'd smiled so hard her face hurt, pretending she belonged among trust fund babies who treated journalism as a hobby before daddy or mummy got them a proper job.

If she couldn't make it as a journalist soon, what was the point? How much longer could she chase dreams that didn't pay?

The memory of her final shift at The Last Drop popped up. Sticky floors, bass that thudded in her bones for hours after, fishing pound coins from puddles of spilt Tennent's, some steamin' lad trying to grab her arse while she collected glasses. She'd left that life, surviving on coffee, crisps, and Irn Bru. Day shifts at the café, nights at the club, uni in between. The thought of returning to that made her insides curdle.

The tears came hot and sudden. She buried her face in the pillow to muffle her hiccupping sobs. Her shoulders shook with the effort of containing them, an earthquake of frustration and fear that threatened to split her open.

Her gran's face swam before her eyes, confused and vulnerable under the care home's fluorescent lights. 'Did I tell you about Joe visiting?' she'd ask. Her late husband was the one place where her mind found rest and safety.

Rowan had only faint memories of her grandda – she'd been six when he'd passed – but she knew he'd adored the ground her gran walked on, and vice versa. They'd met at Glasgow's Barrowland Ballroom and never spent a day apart for thirty-four years – until he'd died suddenly from a heart attack eighteen years ago. And until that day, Joe MacKay had brought his wife coffee in bed every morning.

That was the kind of marriage Rowan wanted. Not the draining situationships her friends were involved in. And certainly not something like her mother and her biological father, who'd left her mum two years after Rowan's birth and hadn't been part of their lives since.

And most definitely not a stone-cold business deal.

The tears dried as she stared at the ceiling stain, her mind churning. What was the alternative, though? Going back to Glasgow and watching her gran lose out on the care she needed? Letting her mum work herself into an early grave? Accepting another soulless gig for pennies?

No.

It couldn't go on like that.

She opened her laptop and started writing. That always helped to clear her mind and tame the chaos.

A few hours later, Rowan had her notes sorted. Writing kept her from going mad. She exhaled past that tight knot in her chest. Her stomach growled. Yep, the old sausage roll earlier had been a mistake.

Beggars, choosers, blah blah…

Her thumb hovered over her mother's contact photo. A selfie from last Christmas, Gran mid-eye-roll in the background as Mum grinned under tinsel-draped antlers. She wanted to talk to her. But her mum would ask questions Rowan couldn't answer. If anyone knew what it meant to rush into marriage and regret it, it was her mother. The screen turned hazy, and Rowan tossed the phone onto the bed, where it sank into the duvet's faded floral valleys.

Another stomach growl.

Rowan put her boots on, cinching the laces tight around her ankles. Time for a pie and a pint at the pub down the road. Tax-relevant travel expenses, after all. Hashtag free-lancer life.

Two hours later, the chips sat heavy in her gut. Rowan turned around on the bed, springs screeching like banshees, and stared at her phone. Now it was Pat's contact photo that grinned at her. A shot from last Halloween, their faces painted like zombified Spice Girls.

'Hey Pat, fancy being my witness when I sell my soul to a posh wanker for healthcare cash?'

The words curdled in her mouth.

'Remember that castle I mentioned? Turns out the lord of the manor's got a marriage kink. Pass the vodka.'

A text message from her mother interrupted her thoughts:

> MAW (21:37) Last update for today: Gran's arm's fine, but she's too tired for a call. Give her a ring the morra. Love!

Small mercies. The ceiling stain had morphed into what looked like Australia. The former penal colony. She chucked a sock at it and missed. Maxwell's jumper still hung off her frame. She'd half-considered burning it, half-considered never taking it off. A tactile reminder of his stupid proposal.

'Business merger,' she scoffed to the empty room. 'Merging what? My overdraft with his ego?'

Her notebook lay open to yesterday's entry: *Dunmarach Castle – crumbling empire or capitalist relic?* Beneath it, fresh ink bled through the page: *Would you marry the laird for a year's rent?* Followed by: *Asking for a friend.*

Somewhere in the village, a dog howled. She imagined it was singing a lament for her dignity. A moth kamikazed into the lampshade, casting shadows that danced across the ceiling.

Rowan grunted and flung an arm over her eyes. 'All right,

MacKay. Let's get some sleep. Tomorrow, the world will look different.'

That was what her gran always said, and she was always right.

Or at least used to be.

Sunlight stabbed through the threadbare curtains, and Rowan blinked awake to the ceiling's evolving Rorschach test and a mouthful of jumper fabric.

The jumper.

The proposal.

She sat up, vertebrae realigning into something approximating human posture.

The mirror above the sink offered a harsh critique: yesterday's mascara smudged into raccoon-chic, a crease from the pillowcase on her cheek like a duelling scar.

Her phone buzzed with a message from her bank. 'Your overdraft limit has been reached.'

Okay. That's it. I've had it.

This was the opposite of a fairy tale, but if it solved the problems that kept her up at night, she could live with a few moral compromises. Temporarily.

And it was a unique opportunity.

'Let's look at this logically,' she muttered to herself. 'One year of your life. That's all. Pretend it's some weird reality show. *Big Brother* meets *Downton Abbey*.'

She counted the points on her fingers. 'You get a story. Gran gets proper specialist care. Mum can cut back on shifts.' Her voice strengthened. 'And Max gets…whatever the hell he needs this for. Everyone wins.'

She grabbed her laptop and pulled up the castle's image again. The grey stones glowed in the light, proud and ancient and full of stories waiting to be told.

Besides, how many journalists could say they married a Highland laird for research?

That's some gonzo journalism shite. Highly unethical, of course.

The lump in her chest loosened. Maybe she wasn't selling out. Maybe she was being smart for once, playing the game instead of letting the game play her.

Rowan pulled out her notebook, trying to make sense of the morning's events and the whole chaos:

Pros of fake-marrying Maxwell Drummond:
- Money for Gran's care
- Help Mum (stop being the one who lets her down)
- Sell article (probably) — advance career?
- Save enough to buy wee flat
- Live in actual castle
- Gorgeous grumpy husband (shut up, brain)
- Could write book about experience???

Cons of fake-marrying Maxwell Drummond:
- Actually marrying a stranger (snores?)
- Living with Mr Darcy's evil capitalist twin
- Probably illegal???
- Pride and principles completely destroyed
- Mum might murder me

Her pen hovered over the page. The minuscule, morally still-intact part of her brain screamed that this was like cycling through a minefield. The weight of her decision squeezed her chest. What would it mean for her pride? For her independence? Her (flexible) morals? She thought of her mum's exhausted voice, of her gran's grip on reality loosening day by day, and of the mountain of bills multiplying like rabbits on Viagra.

Once she did this, there was no turning back. No retreat. And that thought sent doubt skittering across her mind like a spider she couldn't catch. But then again...

'Fuck it!'

The phrase exploded from her like a battle cry, slicing through her hesitation. Pride wouldn't pay the bills, and independence was worthless if her family crumbled under the weight of it. She grabbed her bag and marched downstairs, pausing only to scribble a note for Mrs Bellamy, before heading back up to the castle – straight into madness.

All rise... Here comes the bride.

The walk back to Dunmarach stretched before her, a winding ribbon through heather and gorse before the forest grew denser. Pewter clouds let single rays of morning sun in, painting the hills in brushstrokes of gold. Rowan stopped and let it sink in. This place was as much a part of her heritage as Glasgow's concrete streets. Strange, how she'd grown up Scottish but had seen more of Glasgow and Ayrshire than of the Highlands. She knew her ancestors had been cleared and relocated during the Highland Potato Famine in the mid-nineteenth century like countless others. But that was all.

The breeze carried the sweetness of rain-soaked earth, so different from the familiar urban cocktail of bus diesel, piss, and chippy grease.

She breathed it in and something stirred beneath her ribs.

This was her land, too. These peaks and valleys, these prehistoric stones. Her ancestors had been forced out of these glens, driven to the Central Belt by hunger. And they survived. She didn't know their names or their faces, but she felt their strength in this land. The thought made her walk a bit taller as she picked her way to Dunmarach.

The brass door knocker was cold in her hand. She lifted it once, twice, three times. Each knock echoed like in the stillness of mid-morning.

Maxwell opened the door himself.

So really no butler. Well, well.

His eyes widened at the sight of her.

'I won't be cleaning,' she announced before he had the chance to speak. 'And I have conditions.'

'Let's discuss these conditions inside.'

'Nope, right here. First: I keep my job. My writing comes first. I want access to the castle's records. Also, and this is a no-brainer, no shagging.'

'Is that all?'

'For now.' She didn't look away, half-expecting him to object. But he merely nodded, as if her job couldn't possibly matter. Or the shagging.

'Oh, one more thing. You have to tell me your middle name. I refuse to marry someone when I don't know their full name. For all I know, you could be a Maxwell Bartholomew Percival Gandalf.'

That earned her an actual laugh. Short and surprised, like it had snuck out without his permission. 'It's…Alexander.'

'Maxwell Alexander Drummond. Rowan Drummond.' She tested the name. 'Weird, but could be worse. Do we have a deal?'

Maxwell stared at her. His eyes, a mix of slate and ice, were unreadable. He looked as if he was weighing whether she was worth the trouble.

Then he stepped aside and gestured for her to enter. 'We have a deal.'

The words left goosebumps on her skin. Crossing the threshold of the imposing front door, Rowan couldn't shake the feeling she'd signed a contract with a very well-dressed, handsome devil.

But hey, at least hell came with free central heating.

Chapter Six

Rowan whistled low as she entered the study behind him. 'Damn. Did Hogwarts have a jumble sale?'

Max suppressed a grunt, but her comparison wasn't wrong. Floor-to-ceiling bookshelves dominated one wall, their volumes bound in leather and gilt. A stone fireplace commanded another wall, topped by the Drummond family crest carved in stone. Heavy curtains framed windows that overlooked the loch, filtering the Highland morning into something gothic. Stag head, dark wood, leather, the works.

Max hated it.

He took his place behind the enormous desk and regretted it immediately. This was his father's chair. It felt like a pair of too-tight shoes.

Rowan didn't sit down in either of the chairs facing the desk. Instead, she began to rove the room like a curious cat, letting her fingertips drift across leather-bound volumes. Her black skinny jeans and grey 'Fuck the Patriarchy'-jumper clashed with the neo-Gothic grandeur as if she had wandered onto the set of the wrong film.

He fought the urge to roll his eyes.

She moved with deliberate slowness and examined each object as if cataloguing evidence.

'So this is where all the important man-decisions happen, eh?'

'If you're quite finished with the social commentary—'

She paused at a display case, studying antique duelling pistols. 'These fully loaded? In case this goes south?'

He slanted his eyes. 'Can we focus, please?'

'On your spectacularly insane marriage proposal? Sure.'

'One year,' he repeated. 'Complete financial security for you and your family.'

'And in return?'

'You play the role of devoted wife. Attend events, charm the trustees, convince everyone this is real.'

'So wife isn't enough, you request devotion? While you play the role of…?'

'Myself.'

She laughed.

'Take it or leave it, Rowan.'

'Take.'

She didn't flinch. Clearly, a woman who stuck to her guns once she made up her mind. He admired that.

'The terms need to be clear,' he said. 'No room for misinterpretation.'

'Mmm. Like the fact that you're basically buying a wife?'

'I prefer to think of it as a mutually beneficial arrangement.'

'A business merger.' She took a book from a shelf and flipped through it. 'With wedding rings instead of contracts.'

'Oh, there will be contracts.' He pulled out a portfolio. 'I had my lawyers drew up a draft as soon as I heard of the trust's requirements.'

She turned. 'Prenup, I suppose?'

'Among other things.' He spread the preliminary documents across the desk. 'Non-disclosure agreements, terms of separation, financial arrangements. It can be revised within thirty days of marriage, provided both parties are in agreement.'

'How romantic.' She replaced the book and moved to inspect antique maps. 'Do I get a say in these terms, or am I supposed to sign wherever you point?'

'That's why we're having this discussion.'

'Ah.' She drifted to another shelf, this one holding family photographs, and picked up a silver frame. 'Is this you?'

He knew which photo she meant without looking. Him at seventeen, with Martin. Their last summer. Just weeks before… 'Put that down.'

She set it back, but her eyes lingered on the image.

'The terms,' he said, 'include public appearances. We'll need to be seen together, behaving like a normal couple.'

'Define normal. Because if you expect me to simper and hang off your arm like some trophy wife—'

'I don't care how you do it, but I expect you to be convincing. The trust overseeing the inheritance will be watching for any sign of fraud.'

'So what, we share meaningful glances?' Her fingertips touched a ceremonial Sgian Dubh. 'Snog in public?'

'Some physical affection would be expected, yes.'

'Christ. But to be crystal clear: I'm not saying "to obey" in the vows.'

Her reflection in the windowpane was overlaid with the grey-green of the loch outside. She was a conundrum, an unpredictable element that clashed with the staid world he had built for himself. He had never met anyone like her, so infuriatingly opinionated and oddly authentic. She was a nuisance, yes. But she was also a practical solution to his problem. A means to an end. An opportunity.

'This isn't a romance. We're not getting married in a church. That won't even come up.'

'Great.' She turned to face him, hands on her hips. 'Because I'm not a dog. I don't obey anyone.'

'I'm beginning to notice that.'

Her lips quirked. 'Smart man. Also, write that down, I want full access to the archives.'

'Absolutely not.'

'Non-negotiable.' She stopped next to a floor lamp and ran her thumb along the fringes. 'I'm a writer, and this place is a goldmine of stories. That's part of my payment. I came here for a story, Maxwell. I'm not giving that up.'

He stood and braced his hands on the desk. 'These are private family records!'

'And I'll be family, won't I?'

'You'll be my wife in name only.'

'Give me something to work with.' She advanced on the desk. 'Stories. History. Things that matter.'

'These records are sensitive and private.'

'So supervise me.' She was at the desk now, mirroring his pose. 'Watch me like a hawk if you must. But I need something more than playing house. I'm a journalist and writer, not a gossip columnist.'

'That remains to be seen.' He was pulled into those eyes. She was tiny compared to him, yet somehow she made him feel like he was the one being cornered. She would have killed it in any boardroom, and she probably didn't even know it. Or didn't care.

'Limited access,' he conceded. 'Under supervision.'

'And I keep the rights to anything I write.'

'Within reason.' He straightened, trying to regain the upper hand in the conversation. His back was already wound up tighter than during his last high-stakes deal. 'Nothing that could damage the family's reputation.'

'Reputation? You're the one who proposed to a random trespasser. Besides, your precious family secrets are safe with me. I'm interested in the distillery's history, not your great-aunt Gertrude's scandalous affair with the gardener.'

Max let out an involuntary groan.

He was slipping. Years of manoeuvres, takeovers, and million-pound deals, yet this woman led him around by the nose like some green graduate fresh out of business school. Maxwell Drummond, losing control of a simple negotiation because a redhead in a provocative jumper knew precisely which buttons to push.

'What, worried I'll expose your historic scandals?' Her smile was cutting. 'Afraid I'll find evidence of cattle rustling and illicit stills?'

The sight of her circling his father's study made his teeth grind. Rowan MacKay seemed to thrive on challenging him. She negotiated like someone who had learned the hard way that nobody would fight her corner if she didn't do it herself. It was bracing, in an irritating way – like a splash of ice water to the face.

'Sign the NDA first. Then we'll discuss what constitutes a scandal.'

She tapped her index finger on the desk. 'Speaking of scandals and such – *how* convincing do we need to be in public?'

'Enough to fool the trust, so I keep my family's estate and distillery. That's paramount.'

'That's not an answer.' She leaned forward. 'I need specifics, Maxwell. Where are the lines?'

He forced himself to maintain eye contact, though something about her direct gaze turned the silence between them into a thread pulled too tight.

'Hand-holding,' he ground out. 'The occasional kiss. Nothing inappropriate.'

'So you've said. But define inappropriate.'

'For God's sake—'

'No, I mean it.' She didn't back down. Of course not. 'If

we're doing this – and it looks like we are – I need to know what I'm agreeing to. Where do we sleep? What happens at social events? Do we dance? Share food? Pecks or tongue-hockey? What's the script here?'

'It's not that I've done anything like that before, so we'll have to improvise.' He ran a hand through his hair, forgetting his usual composure. 'We can have separate rooms. But as I said, we'll need to act…couple-like.'

'Couple-like,' she repeated.

'What do you want, woman? A detailed manual?'

'Maybe!' She threw up her hands. 'Because right now this feels like signing a blank cheque with my body as collateral!'

'It's not the nineteenth century, you're not my property. I won't touch you if you don't want me to. Never.' The words hung between them, heavy with implications.

And if she wanted to? Would he touch her? A spark of something untamed made his pulse hitch and a slow burn worked its way up his neck. 'What else?'

'Separate bedrooms,' she said. 'I can't sleep with other people next to me. Too much…breathing and moving and snoring. Ugh.'

'But not on our wedding night. And we'll need to share when we have visitors. Although considering that most of my family is in the graveyard, that shouldn't be much of a concern.'

'Share a room or share a bed?'

He loosened his tie. 'That would depend on the circumstances.'

'Circumstances?' She gave him a dry look. 'Either we're sleeping in one bed or we're not.'

'The trust requires proof of cohabitation. But cohabitation doesn't equal consummation.'

She was closer now, examining a chess set near the desk. 'I won't fake that kind of intimacy.'

He stopped and took a breath. 'As I said, I wouldn't ask

you to. We'll need to be convincing, but we don't need to be intimate.'

For a fleeting moment, he allowed himself to imagine Rowan spread across his sheets, her keen tongue occupied with activities far removed from verbal sparring, while his own tongue… The thought hit him low in his gut – not the usual contained attraction he felt toward the women he dated, but something more primitive, powerful. Like the first cut of whisky straight from the still, burning and pure. Part of him wanted to discover if that resistant spirit carried through to intimate moments, if she would challenge him there, too.

Max pushed the thought aside. He had no patience for distractions. He had a legacy to save.

'Good.' Her face gave her away, reddening slightly. 'Because that's off the table.'

This blush would be his undoing. It made her vulnerable in ways she wasn't even aware of. Damn, it made *him* vulnerable. He had always kept his composure tight, but the way colour betrayed her…

'Agreed.'

They stared at each other across the desk, the dusty air charged between them. He noticed details he shouldn't – the subtle arch of her eyebrows, the determined set of her mouth, the bow of her lip.

'What about dates?' she asked.

He blinked. 'What?'

'Real couples go on dates. They have inside jokes, shared experiences. We need a backstory that's more than "met under a tree while committing minor felonies".'

'You're the storyteller. Think of something. I don't care.'

'We met through mutual friends.' She ticked points off on her fingers. 'You were instantly smitten with my incredible wit and charm. I found your brooding darkness irresistible. Whirlwind romance, surprise proposal, small wedding because we're private people.'

One brow ticked up. 'Smitten?'

'Would you prefer besotted? Enchanted? Bewitched? Consumed with yearning?'

'I'm beginning to regret this already.'

But he wasn't, not really. Something about her quick mind made this feel less like a business transaction and more like something else. Something it shouldn't feel like.

Fun, perhaps?

He didn't do fun.

Fun had died with Martin.

'Too late.' She flashed a smile that was half daring, half devil-may-care. 'You're stuck with me for a year now, Maxwell Alexander Drummond.'

The use of his full name struck a nerve he didn't know was exposed. 'Are we agreed on the terms, then?'

'Almost.' She planted her hands on the desk again, leaning so close that he could see the flecks of gold in her irises. 'One more thing.'

'What now?'

'If we're going to convince people we're in love, you need to stop looking at me like I'm something you scraped off your shoe.'

'I don't—'

'You do. And I get it. I'm not your type. But if this is going to work, you need to at least pretend you want me around.'

The words hit harder than they should have. He studied her face. The determination in her eyes, the rawness beneath her bravado. She wasn't his type, true. Too short, too petite, almost boyish. And far too annoying.

No, she was something altogether more fascinating.

And that thought was unsettling.

'I'll work on it,' he said.

'Amazeballs.' She loosened her stance. 'Whatever this is, whatever we're doing – we're partners. Equal partners. No pulling rank or hiding behind your title. Got it?'

Something in her tone made him pause. 'Okay.'

'Now, where do I sign?'

He pushed the preliminary documents toward her. Her brow furrowed in concentration, one finger tracing lines of legal text.

What had he done?

This woman was going to turn his ordered world upside down. She would push him, rile him up.

Too late now.

'These need work,' Rowan announced, breaking into his thoughts. She pulled a red pen from her backpack and began marking the papers. 'The language is too vague here.'

'You have experience with contracts?'

'It might surprise you, but working-class kids attend universities, too. Also, I read a lot of publishing agreements.'

He leaned forward, drawn into her rapid-fire commentary on the documents. Her suggestions were clever, practical, and silly. She had written 'LOL NO' next to one particular clause.

'I also think we'll need to practise.' She set down her pen.

'Practise what?'

'Being a couple. The little things. How we touch, how we look at each other. It needs to be natural.'

'I suppose.'

'Och, don't look so terrified.' Her eyes sparkled with amusement. 'Your body is yours. I promise not to ravish you against the bookshelves.'

'That's reassuring.'

'Though it would make an awesome story.' She gathered the marked papers into a neat stack. 'Rich laird seduced by common writer among ancient tomes.'

As she handed him the documents, her fingers met his. There was a tiny electric spark. Unwanted, yet undeniable. He pulled his hand back, determined to ignore it.

'This isn't a romance,' he reminded her.

'God, no. Ew. It's business. A deal.'

She held out her hand in all seriousness. It was adorable. He looked at her offered palm, then back to her face. No artifice, no games – just determination and perhaps a hint of the same madness that had possessed him to suggest this in the first place.

And they hadn't even known each other for twenty-four hours.

He took her small hand. Her skin was warm, her grip firm. 'A deal.'

'Excellent.' She nodded but didn't release his hand.

Neither did he. 'You'll have to move into the castle.'

'Good thing I already brought my bag,' she said with a wink.

'You're going to be nothing but trouble, aren't you?'

'Oh, my dear Maxwell.' She spoke in an exaggerated, posh accent and squeezed his hand once before letting go. 'I already am.'

'I'll have the documents revised. We can finalise everything tomorrow.'

'Perfect.' She stretched. 'That gives me time to practise my noble gestures.'

'Rowan.'

'Yes, *darling*?' She batted her eyelashes.

'Get out of the study.'

She let out a laugh. 'As you wish, *honey*.' But she paused at the door. 'This is bonkers, you know.'

'I know. I'm only doing this because you're the lesser evil.'

'Maybe that's what I *want* you to think. Well, I guess you're about to find out. But we're probably both going to regret it.'

'Probably.'

She nodded once. 'See you around, future husband.'

The door closed behind her, leaving him alone with the

ghosts and the lingering scent of her shampoo. He looked down at the papers, covered in her decisive red markings, and felt something between dread and anticipation settle in his chest.

What had he done, indeed.

Chapter Seven

Rowan surfaced from sleep like a diver. When she slanted her eyes open, the room was so blue that she actually felt underwater. She blinked at the ceiling, where ornate plasterwork swirled into Celtic knots.

Knots.

Like…tying the knot.

'Jesus fuck,' she whispered. 'That's happening.'

She swung her legs over the side of the bed and padded across the room.

The ensuite bath was a converted cupboard, all awkward angles, despite the fancy tiles. Rowan stepped under the shower head and let hot water sluice over her shoulders.

'Okay, MacKay. You're marrying a stranger for money. No biggie. Just another Tuesday.'

The soap smelled expensive, like something that had never sat on a Boots shelf. She sniffed it. 'Bet this costs more than my weekly food budget.'

Wrapped in a towel that felt like cuddling a cloud, she surveyed her reflection in the mirror. Same face, same constellation of freckles across her nose. But something felt different like she'd stepped into an alternate reality where working-class writers from Glasgow lived in Highland castles.

Her favourite Taylor tee – soft from a hundred washes – felt like a rebellion against the room's grandeur. The logo was faded almost to illegibility, the black cotton gone dark grey. She gathered her damp hair into a messy bun.

Baby steps into the landed classes.

The corridor outside stretched like something from *The Shining*, clad in wood panels. She counted doors as she walked, trying to map the layout in her head. The whole place felt like a museum after hours.

She found Max at the kitchen island, looking like he'd stepped out of a financial magazine's 'Power Breakfast' spread. His suit was pristine and his movements precise as he tapped his spoon against a hard-boiled egg. A glass of orange juice and two slices of toast completed his breakfast.

So he knows how to feed himself. That's a relief.

The morning light caught his profile, turning him into the picture of masculine refinement. Soon she'd be having such private moments regularly. His finger would wear a ring that matched hers.

Well, it was decided. So…

'Morning, fiancé!' She bounced onto a stool, consciously disrupting his calm. 'Ready for our last day of unwedded bliss? Will we have a hen and stag night? You can hang out with the *actual* stag on the study wall, and I—'

He didn't even look up from his egg. 'Good morning.'

'That's it? Just "good morning"? We're getting married tomorrow, and you're acting like we're scheduling a dentist appointment.'

'Would you prefer sonnets? Interpretive dance?'

'Save the hot stuff for the honeymoon.' She nabbed a slice of his toast, earning a cutting glare. 'Speaking of which… We should sort out some details. Like, are you allergic to anything? Because if I accidentally kill you with a peanut butter sandwich, that'll look suspicious.'

'No allergies.' He took a purposeful sip of orange juice. 'You?'

'Mainly capitalism and patriarchal oppression.'

'Evidently.'

'What about transport?' She leaned forward, elbows on the marble counter. 'Can I take one of your fancy motors for a spin? I promise only minimal scratches.'

'There are no fancy cars, and you won't need to drive. You'll have a driver at your disposal. Oliver is always on call.'

'What?' Her jaw dropped. 'Like, all the time? Is that even legal, or does it fall under modern slavery? And just to let you know: I don't have a car, but I *do* have a license.'

'The insurance wouldn't cover it.'

As if someone like him would need insurance. He could pay for a new car from the loose change he'd find in one of his suit pockets.

'For the love of Taylor, Maxwell. I can take the bus like a normal person.'

'You may call me Max, that's more suitable for our arrangement. And, in case you haven't noticed, there are no regular buses here to get around. This isn't Glasgow, it's the rural Highlands. Oliver will take you wherever you need to go.' His tone was clipped and final.

She snatched an apple from the bowl in front of him. 'What about the wedding? Please tell me we're not doing the Highland circus with bagpipes and all that.'

'Small ceremony here at Dunmarach. Only a few witnesses – Oliver, Mrs MacPherson, Blackwood, and Slater from the distillery.'

'No bridesmaids, no party, no Jägerbombs?' She smirked and bit into the apple.

'It's a business deal, Rowan, not a pub crawl. The ceremony is a formality.'

'I know. And where's that formality taking place?'

'In the study.'

'Ah, Mini-Hogwarts. Cosy. And what am I supposed to wear? My best Primark dress might not cut it.'

'Good point.' He pulled out his phone, thumbs flying across the screen. 'Mrs MacPherson will handle it.'

'You're texting her now? About my dress?' Her eyebrows shot up. 'You know, I'm starting to think you're not a real person. You're some sort of robot trained to be the most efficient man in the history of efficiency.'

'Think what you want, but you need to look the part for the official portrait. And I don't suppose you have a wedding dress in your backpack along with your "Eat the Rich" collection.'

'Portrait?' She nearly choked on her apple. 'Like, proper oil and canvas?'

'Photography.' He pushed aside his empty plate. 'We're not completely medieval.'

'Could've fooled me, what with the castle and the arranged marriage.' She took a gulp of coffee to hide her racing thoughts behind the mug. 'So, about the whole "living together" thing. What are our meal arrangements?'

He sighed. 'We'll eat together when our schedules align and the occasion warrants it. Other than that, I'll be busy with work most days or travelling for business. Mrs MacPherson will organise a cook.'

'Noted. But tell me again how we're going to convince people we're in undying, everlasting love?' She crossed her arms.

He set down his phone, finally meeting her eyes. 'We'll practice, as you said. Physical affection, getting used to each other.' His tone was curt. 'To be convincing.'

'Oh, right.' Her neck burned.

They stared at each other across the counter, the morning silence stretching between them.

'Come here,' Max said quietly.

Rowan slipped off her stool and rounded the counter. He sat still, his posture was rigid. Like he was bracing himself for something unpleasant. She frowned. Was this as awkward for him as it was for her? He didn't strike her as the touchy type. But if they were going to sell this charade, they had to start somewhere. Her pulse ticked faster as she stepped into his space.

'So.' She put on a breezy tone. 'This is about fooling the trust, right?'

Max gave the barest nod, but the stiffness in his shoulders betrayed him. He clearly didn't *want* to do this, but he seemed to think it was necessary.

'We should start with something simple,' he said.

'Yes. We need to figure out how to touch each other without looking like we're about to break out in hives.'

He stood up. An all-around impressive specimen, no doubt about that.

It's simply not fair. He must have a micro-penis or something. Well, I shall never find out.

Rowan inched nearer, enough to catch his scent – clean and woody, with a hint of something darker and more complex.

And then something happened.

He lifted his hand, and time crystallised around the gesture. His fingers caught a wayward strand of her hair with unexpected gentleness, like cradling the flame of a match. The touch whispered across her cheek as he tucked it behind her ear, but then his thumb traced the arc of her cheekbone.

The grey in his eyes warmed to a clouded blue. Something unshielded flashed in their depths, gone so quickly she must have imagined it. But his thumb lingered against her skin for one heartbeat, two, three.

Her usual arsenal of quips and comebacks evaporated. She

was caught in this impossible moment where Maxwell Drummond touched her like she was precious.

When he withdrew his hand, the morning air felt chilly against her face. Rowan searched for her misplaced composure while her pulse did its best impression of a drum solo.

This was a performance, nothing more.

So why did her skin still feel branded where his thumb had been?

'Well,' she managed, her voice slightly unsteady. 'That was…almost convincing.'

'Promising start.' His face gave nothing away, but something in his voice sounded rougher than usual.

'Okay, next move. Put your arm around me, Maxwell.'

'Max.'

'Right, yes. Your arm, Max. Around me. Like couples do.' It felt safer to hide behind her usual cocky self. 'I promise I won't bite. Unless you're into that sort of thing.'

The look he gave her could have frozen hell over twice. But he complied.

She shifted. 'Relax a bit, will you? I'm your fake fiancée, not a grenade that's about to go off. Loosen up.' She ducked under his arm, fitting herself against his side. 'Aye, like this.'

His body was warm and solid, his jacket soft against her cheek. 'Look, my shoulders fit perfectly under your armpit. Like a roll-on deodorant.'

She sensed a caged power beneath his suit that made her breath catch.

'Okay, next up: hand-holding.' She took his right hand with her left, lacing her fingers through his. Max's skin was warm, his grip firm but gentle. The contact sent sparks racing up her arm.

'We're a couple. Happy and in love.' She tried to keep her tone light. 'Are you feeling the love yet? Are you?'

Max ran his thumb over her knuckles with careful intent,

as if he was testing the edge of a blade. She felt every point of contact, the warmth of his palm against hers, the way his fingers laced through hers.

The most shocking part was how right it felt. And something molten pooled low in her core.

Oh no. Oh hell no.

'This isn't bad.' Her voice came out softer than she intended. 'Very…couply.'

'Mmm.'

That damn thumb kept moving, tracing patterns that sparked a fire under her skin. How could this human block of marble display such gentleness?

'We should try a proper hug. That might also be expected.' She turned in his hold, and suddenly they were chest to chest.

His hands found their place at her waist, warm through her thin tee. She put her palms on his chest and felt his heartbeat quicken beneath the fine wool. Rowan pulled back and looked up. His eyes were even darker than they'd been before.

Oh, she was in so much trouble.

'This is a little weird,' she said.

'A little.' But he pulled her closer.

She looped her hands around his neck. 'I think we need to stay like this for a minute. Get used to each other.'

'Probably.'

Rowan let herself lean into him and put her cheek on his chest. He let his hand glide down and rested his palm on her lower back with the right amount of pressure. And just like that, all awkwardness faded, replaced by a strange sense of… safety. He felt like an anchor while her world was spinning. A rock her tide could surge against without fear of breaking either of them.

'Max?'

'Mmh?'

'Your coffee's getting cold.'

'I know.'

'Okay.'

So they stood there in the castle's kitchen. Her own breath slowed, matching his rhythm until they were inhaling and exhaling in sync. The whole world shrunk to the sound of their breathing.

No. No. No.

'Surprisingly effective.' She looked up at him again. 'We'll make a great fake couple.'

His face was unreadable. 'It will do.'

She stepped back to put distance between them. 'I'm going to go. Practice my adoring gazes.'

'I have work to do.' His eyes stayed fixed on some point over her head. 'You won't see much of me.'

'Of course, the hamster wheel.'

'Try to refrain from setting anything on fire.'

'No promises!' She turned and left the kitchen, heart lurching in an erratic rhythm.

What the hell had that been? They'd gone from banter to intimate embraces in a matter of minutes. She hurried towards the stairs, her thoughts spinning. This was a potential disaster. A beautiful, chaotic, terrifying disaster, and she was pretty sure she was about to dive headfirst into the deep end.

So. Much. Trouble.

Rowan trudged up the grand staircase. Three hours of wandering the grounds hadn't cleared her head. If anything, Dunmarach Castle's looming presence had only thickened the haze in her mind.

'Welcome to your new life in unearned privilege,' she muttered and pushed open the Blue Room's door. 'It's fine. Everything's—'

The words died in her throat.

A dress lay across her bed. Pale champagne silk charmeuse. The straight silhouette spoke of another era – the 1920s when women first dared tell men to piss off. Short flutter sleeves and a boat neckline with delicate pearl beading along the trim.

Maybe Mrs MacPherson had some kind of sixth sense about these things, or maybe she'd read her size and style from the old clothes hanging in the Blue Room.

Mrs Mac, you magnificent fairy godmother!

And Rowan hadn't even met her in person yet. But that was how it was supposed to be, right? Never be heard or seen.

One thing Rowan was hell-bent on changing while she was at Dunmarach.

She approached the dress cautiously. A pair of pearl drop earrings rested on the pillow, gleaming with quiet elegance. Likely as antique as everything around here. She picked them up and rolled one drop between her fingers.

Her wedding.

And she was doing it on her own.

Rowan's phone felt heavy in her pocket. She should call her mum, share this moment – despite how weird it all was. But shame churned in her gut. Lying to her mother had never been her strong suit. Some daughter she was, selling herself like a plot device in a Victorian novel.

And there was no point in telling her gran. It would only confuse her.

Her thumb hovered over the call button. She had to do it, even though this call felt like defusing a bomb while blindfolded. She tracked restless circles around the room, her sock-clad feet silent on the worn Persian rug, as she spun her rehearsed tale. Mutual friends, instant connection, whirlwind romance.

Let's get it over with.

'A week?' Her mum's voice shot through the speaker. 'You've known him for a week? Have you lost your mind? What does he do for work? Does he treat you well?'

'I know how it sounds—'

'Do you? Because it sounds like my sensible daughter's gone mental. What did you go to university for?'

Rowan leaned her forehead against the cool window pane. 'When you and Dad eloped to Gretna Green—'

'Oh Christ, not that old chestnut.' A resigned sigh filtered through. 'Your gran's been filling your head with those stories again, hasn't she? All that nonsense about love at first sight and destiny.'

'You were nineteen,' Rowan pointed out. 'At least I'm twenty-four.'

'Aye, look how well it turned out for me.'

Rowan closed her eyes, her next lie tasting like copper pennies. 'It's different with Max. When you know, you know.'

A long pause followed, punctuated by the familiar sound of her mum's ceramic mug being set down on the kitchen counter. 'Stubborn as a mule.'

'Wonder where I got that from?'

Her mum's laugh was soft, almost wistful. 'You're going to do this regardless of what I say, aren't you?'

'Pretty much. But... Maybe you can come up here tomorrow?'

'Naw, love. I have work. I'd have taken the day off if I'd expected my only child to get married.'

'Okay, yeah. It's a bit spontaneous.'

'Are you sure about this, Rowan MacKay? You haven't even mentioned him to me at all before. That makes a mother suspicious.'

'Whirlwind romance, as I said. And aye, totally sure.'

Big, fat lie. Or rather, she *was* sure – but not for the reasons her mother thought.

I'm doing this for yous.

'For the record: I'm not on board. But all I will say is… Don't make me come up there in a month and clip your ear for being an eejit, love. If it all goes tits up, you better get your arse back home before I come and drag you myself. Same goes for him. If he hurts you, I'll cut his baws and make him eat them.'

She swallowed past the lump. 'Thanks, Maw.'

'Rowan?' Her mother's voice mellowed. 'You're still my wee girl, and I'm looking out for you. But I also know you're smart, so I'm choosing to trust you. Against my better judgement. Be careful, darlin'. Okay?'

'Always.'

The call ended, leaving Rowan alone with the weight of her deception. She let the tears fall. There was no holding them back, anyway.

That was the hardest part. Now let's see if I can say yes to the dress.

She stripped down to her underwear, avoiding the mirror's judgement. The silk slipped over her head like water and draped over her skin with surprising weight. A few inches too long, but otherwise perfect.

Her reflection stared back. The girl who'd shared Ben's cramped student flat for two years, who'd navigated casual hook-ups on futons and questionable sofas after their break-up seemed far away now. That Rowan belonged to a world of instant noodles, Buckfast, and late-night kebabs.

This Rowan right here wore silk and pearls, and tomorrow she'd marry a man who moved through the world like he owned it.

Nothing like her usual type.

And yet.

She remembered how his thumb had stroked her cheek. How his heartbeat had quickened when she'd touched his chest. The way his eyes had darkened when…

'Nope.' She shook her head hard and smoothed the silk over her hips. One last look in the mirror, one deep breath.

'Fuck me sideways. I'm getting married tomorrow.'

Chapter Eight

Max stood at the study window and watched puffy clouds scud across the Highland sky, like sheep herded by an invisible collie. Behind him, the small gathering of witnesses shifted and murmured. Their presence made the study feel smaller, more confined. Even the air was dense. Mrs MacPherson had attempted to soften the room's severity with white roses and sprigs of heather in crystal vases.

Max adjusted his cuffs, a habit that steadied him. But the gesture rang hollow today.

His wedding day.

It didn't feel like it.

It didn't feel like anything.

The registrar arranged her papers on his father's desk. The same desk where Max had proposed this arrangement three days ago. Where his father had spent countless hours managing the estate. Now it would witness a marriage. One his parents would have disapproved of.

And yet it was their fault.

A quiet knock preceded Oliver's discreet entrance. 'She's ready, Sir.'

Max nodded once, shoulders straightening beneath his

suit. The classical music – Pachelbel's *Canon in D*, because Mrs MacPherson insisted some traditions must be observed – seemed to pause with his breath as the door opened again.

Rowan entered like the first light of dawn after a long, dark night.

The dress flowed around her petite frame. Her hair was loosely swept up, exposing the elegant line of her neck. And she wore his grandmother's pearl drops. Their soft gleam echoed the dress's sheen.

She looked…right. As if she had stepped out of one of the portraits lining the walls. It unsettled him more than he cared to admit.

Their eyes met across the study. Her lips quirked in that half-smile that suggested she found the whole situation absurd.

'Quite the shindig,' she murmured as she took her place beside him. 'Love what you've done with the place.'

'Behave,' he whispered back.

The registrar began to speak. 'We are gathered here today…'

Max let the words wash over him and tuned into the subtle warmth of her presence at his side. She stood still, her small hand in his, but he felt the tension thrumming through her. The urge to steady her was unexpected.

'Do you, Maxwell Alexander Drummond, take Rowan MacKay as your lawful wedded wife?'

The ring was heavy in his pocket. Rose gold and cairngorm, worn smooth by generations of Drummond women. Using it for this arrangement held a hint of betrayal, but needs must.

'I do.' His voice came out calm. And why wouldn't it? There were no promises to honour, no love, nothing else inappropriate. Just paperwork and smoke and mirrors.

'And do you, Rowan MacKay, take Maxwell Alexander Drummond as your lawful wedded husband?'

'I do.' A hint of humour coloured the words as if she couldn't believe it.

The ring slid onto her finger with surprising ease. It was a touch too wide, but they could fix that later. Her breath hitched as the metal landed against her skin, but her hands were steady as she placed a plain band on his finger. It felt alien, constricting.

'I now pronounce you husband and wife. You may kiss the bride.'

Rowan squared her chin, green eyes bright with challenge and something else he couldn't name. He bent down, meaning to keep the kiss perfunctory. Professional. But when their lips met, her warmth disarmed him. Her mouth was soft and yielding, and the scent of her skin – vanilla and citrus – flooded his senses.

A business transaction. Nothing else.

Max pulled back, angry at himself for letting his control slip. Again. Her cheeks were pink, lips soft, breath unsteady. He turned to the desk where the marriage certificate waited for their signatures.

The scratch of pen on paper calmed him. Signatures, witnesses, dates. This was what mattered. The legal framework that would secure his inheritance, his reputation. A formality, as impersonal as filing a tax return.

But as Rowan signed her name with a flourish, the ring glinted. It sat on her hand like it had been waiting for her all along.

Nonsense, of course.

Slater produced a bottle of Drummond's Finest 18-year-old single malt. 'Traditional toast for the happy couple. All the best from the distillery team.'

Max accepted a glass, watching Rowan charm their small audience with her quick wit and genuine warmth. Her dress shimmered as she moved through the study to be congratulated. Mrs MacPherson was already looking at her with motherly approval, while Oliver suppressed a grin like a proud, grumpy uncle.

The liquid burned Max's mouth, but couldn't wash away the lingering taste of her lips.

'Time for a proper toast in the drawing room,' Mrs MacPherson declared.

'Well then, husband,' Rowan said with a cheeky smile. 'Shall we?'

Max offered his arm because that was what was expected. Her fingers settled in the crook of his elbow. Together, they left the study – his father's former domain, now the site of this peculiar ceremony – and stepped into their new reality.

The ring felt heavy. But not, Max realised with growing unease, as heavy as the weight of what they had done.

In the drawing room, Mrs MacPherson distributed champagne with precision. Light caught the rising bubbles in each crystal flute, forming tiny constellations. Rowan's hand remained tucked in Max's elbow. Her fingers pressed a fraction harder than necessary.

'To the happy couple.' Mrs MacPherson raised her glass. She seemed to buy into it. 'May you bring each other what's needed, in ways neither of you expect.'

He felt Rowan's quiet inhale at those words. She fit against his side as naturally as if they had rehearsed it. Which they had, somewhat. Everything was calculated.

Time for the next act.

'A toast to my wife.' Max raised his glass. 'Your strength and spirit are extraordinary. The way you challenge everything, question what others take for granted. I've never met anyone like you.' He paused. There was a truth to it that even he couldn't deny. 'And now here we are. To my best acquisition ever – my wife, Lady Rowan Drummond of Dunmarach.'

'Hear, hear!'

She leaned into him, a soft weight against his side.

'The dress suits you perfectly,' Mrs MacPherson said. 'As if it were made for you. But it was made for Lady Margaret in 1925. I'm so glad I found it in good nick.'

'Oh yes, it's gorgeous! Thank you so, so much, Mrs MacPherson.' Rowan smoothed the vintage silk and smiled at her.

The way it lit up her face caught somewhere in his chest. He ignored it on principle. She was striking in her own way, but her looks didn't matter. Or they shouldn't. Still, he was only a man, and she was…his wife.

The small talk drifted around them like leaves. Polite, inevitable, random. Max answered questions about salmon crudités, Drummond's Finest, love at first sight (as expected), and honeymoon arrangements (there weren't any) while attuned to every movement Rowan made. The shift of her weight. The way she tucked a rogue strand of hair behind her ear. Was he afraid that she might do something unpredictable? Possibly. He didn't know her after all.

She was a risk. A risk he had to take.

'Thank you all for sharing this special day with us, but I believe it's time I took my wife to dinner.' It came out smoother than he felt, calibrated for their audience. 'Just the two of us.'

'Oh, I can't wait,' Rowan murmured through a smile, and only Max caught the dry thread in her tone.

After everybody said their goodbyes, he guided her toward the door, eager to escape the pressure of expectations and tradition. And all those curious, prying eyes.

But as they stepped into the corridor, her hip bumped against his, and it dawned on him that being alone with her carried a different kind of risk.

The Torridon Hotel rose from the Highland landscape like something from a fairy tale, all stone turrets and glowing glass. Rowan's nose almost touched the car window. The silk of her wedding dress hissed softly over the leather seats as Ollie navigated the winding drive.

Beside her, Max sat with the confidence of someone who belonged in five-star hotels. His cufflinks glinted in the fading light. She glanced down at her ring.

Holy shite. I'm a respectable woman now. Haha.

As soon as they arrived, a man in a suit – clearly the one running the show – led them through the restaurant like royalty, past tables of diners who pretended not to stare. She concentrated on not tripping over the dress, hyper-conscious of Max's hand hovering near the small of her back.

Their table overlooked the loch, silver in the gloaming. Rowan counted three forks and suppressed a nervous giggle. Her usual dining experience involved takeaway curry and Netflix. On special days, maybe Paesano's or Spuntini's.

'The wine list.' The sommelier materialised beside Max, who accepted it with natural ease.

She took in her freshly-minted, old-money husband over the rim of her water glass. He looked so at home among the starched linens and polished silver, as if he'd been born knowing which fork to use first. Which he had. Meanwhile, she felt like an impostor in borrowed silk. Which she was.

'Do tell,' she said when the sommelier glided away, 'is this the jaunt where you bring all your fake wives?'

The line of his jaw drew taut. 'I chose it to be seen with you.'

Of course. This was all part of the ruse.

'And for the Michelin star, I'm sure.' She unfolded her napkin. 'I wouldn't have said no to pizza, though.'

'This maintains appearances.'

Her mind drifted back to the ceremony, to Max standing there like the modern incarnation of some brooding Celtic deity in a perfect suit. To the weight of centuries in that simple band of gold and amber.

And to that kiss… Christ, that kiss.

She'd expected detached efficiency, like signing a contract with lips instead of ink. But he'd kissed her like she was made of ice and gunpowder, like she might either dissolve or explode.

A business transaction wasn't supposed to feel like that.

The working girl in a borrowed dress, marrying the laird in his castle. Except in proper fairy tales, the bride didn't have to fake it, and the groom's touch didn't leave her skin buzzing like she'd licked a battery.

Silence stretched between them, delicate as a soap bubble on the verge of bursting. She turned the water glass between her fingers, watching condensation bead on the crystal.

'What's your favourite comfort food?'

He blinked. 'I beg your pardon?'

'You know, what do you eat when you're sad or stressed? Everyone has something. Mine's mac and cheese.'

He assessed her, checking for traps. 'Shepherd's pie.'

'Are you serious?' His answer surprised her. She'd expected something posh, like caviar or quail eggs. Or the sautéed hearts of his rivals.

'The school cook used to make it.' His voice took on a shade more ease. 'On Wednesdays.'

'Boarding school, right?' She caught something flickering across his face. 'From what age?'

'Twelve.'

She imagined a boy with stormy eyes, sent away from home so young. A pang shot through her heart. 'That must have been so lonely.'

'It was character-building.' His tone was brisk, but his fingers drummed against the tablecloth.

A tell she was learning to recognise.

Their first course arrived, something delicate involving

scallops and foam. She kept her attention on using the correct fork, knowing full well that he was watching her.

Thank the universe for Pretty Woman.

'What about university?' she asked between bites. 'Let me guess – Cambridge? Hence the jumper.'

'Cambridge.' He took a sip of wine. 'Economics.'

'Makes sense.' She grinned. 'Bet you were president of the rowing club or something equally posh.'

'No. Not much of a people person, as you might be able to tell.'

The conversation flowed a bit easier with time like a stream finding its path between rocks. His answers remained measured, but occasionally she caught glimpses of the man behind the polished facade. The way his eyes crinkled when he was amused. The enthusiasm in his voice when whisky came up, a passion so natural he didn't even notice how it softened him.

Max Drummond was a puzzle of broken pieces and concealed layers, each one more confounding than the last. A man who loved shepherd's pie, but navigated haute cuisine on a daily basis. Who'd been sent away at twelve but spoke about it with practised indifference.

She was warming up to him.

'Ready for the wedding night, Mrs Drummond?' His tone was light, but something lurked beneath the words.

'Are you trying to seduce me, Mr Drummond?'

'I wouldn't dream of it.' But his eyes lingered on her lips for a heartbeat too long. 'I'm tired. Since we need to keep up appearances, we will have to share a bedroom tonight. Mine.'

What was his bedroom like? A sterile marble-and-leather mausoleum? Whips and paddles – full Mr Grey? Or a pod filled with a nutrient solution?

'In his capacity as the trust's representative, Blackwood is staying the night,' Max declared.

'Seriously? Is he camping next to our bed?'

'Don't be silly. He's next door, in the former valet's room.'

'Oh, do I have to fake an orgasm to make it real? I'm rather good at it.'

'That's not the brag you think it is,' he said. Then, after a beat, 'With me, you never have to fake it.' His face looked even broodier than before.

Whew, Drummond.

'You can talk all you want, we'll never find out anyway.' She got up and her dress rode up her shins.

'Rowan?'

'Yes, darling?'

'Are you wearing your Doc Martens?'

The silk swished around her ankles as she peeked down at her feet. 'Yeah, the shoes Mrs MacPherson put out were too small.' She wiggled her toes in the well-worn boots. 'Besides, they're my something old. And the dress is long enough so you don't see it. Win-win.'

'Unbelievable.' He offered her his arm. 'Ready?'

'To non-consummate our fake marriage? Anytime, hubby.'

Max's bedroom was a surprise. Modern and masculine, but not cold. Charcoal walls, leather armchairs, and white linens on a huge bed that dominated the room.

'Nice lair you've got for someone who's never here. Very Ralph Lauren meets Highland bachelor pad.'

He ignored her and busied himself with his laptop at a desk by the window. His shoulders formed a rigid line under his shirt.

She grabbed her overnight bag and retreated to the ensuite. The bathroom was more spacious than hers, with a rainfall shower that could easily fit two people. Not that she was thinking about that.

Why would she on her wedding night?

She changed into her usual sleep shirt, another old Taylor

tee. It was cosy and familiar and that was what she needed. When she came out of the bathroom, Max's head snapped up.

'You need proper pyjamas.'

'What, this not fancy enough for you? The contract didn't say anything about sleeping in posh granny gowns and—'

'It's inappropriate.' His took on a darker edge. 'Put on bottoms.'

'Or what? You'll write me up for dress code violations?'

'Rowan.' Her name came out like a warning. 'It's not covering your bum. I promised not to touch you, but I'm only a man. Don't make this more difficult than it has to be.'

'Och, fine.' She dug through her bag for sleep shorts. 'I didn't know you were such a Victorian prude.'

'You have no idea what you're talking about. I'm being respectful.'

'You're being daft. I've shared sleeping bags with male friends before.'

'I'm not your friend.'

The words landed like pebbles in still water. She pulled on shorts, suddenly aware of the bed looming behind them.

'I can sleep on the floor,' he offered.

'Don't be silly. The bed's big enough. We'll be fine for one night.' She laughed. 'Unless you snore? Please tell me you don't snore.'

'I wouldn't know, I've never slept next to anyone. Not since school.' Max disappeared into the bathroom.

Was he being serious?

Rowan heard water running and slid between sheets that felt smooth against her bare legs.

When he walked in wearing navy silk pyjamas ten minutes later, a subtle awareness tingled low inside her.

Definitely in the top thirty of Hot Hubbies under Thirty.

He moved with contained grace like a predator pretending to be tame. The bed dipped under his weight as he lowered himself on the other side, keeping a precise distance.

'Want a bedtime story?' she quipped in an attempt to diffuse the tension.

'Go to sleep, Rowan.'

He switched the lights off, and darkness settled around them like a cloak. She lay still, her body keyed to Max's magnetic presence next to her. He smelled amazing. So woodsy and warm that it made her want to bury her face in his neck. The thought was dangerous. Forbidden.

But she also felt safe. Despite the rigid control he wore like a shield, something about his presence made the chaos in her head quieten.

'Max?'

'Hm?'

'Thanks for not making this too weird.'

His quiet laugh held no humour. 'Night.'

Rowan stared into the darkness, counting heartbeats. Sleep felt impossible with him, so close yet untouchable. Her husband. A total stranger.

Chapter Nine

All night, Max had been attuned to Rowan. Her breathing, the dip in his mattress, her scent that shredded his self-control. The inches between them had felt like miles and yet impossibly close, his body reacting to her every tiny movement until dawn.

Now, she sat across from him in one of the new outfits the stylist had sent over – no, not Hugh Grant – a cashmere jumper in a soft sage that brought out the depths of her eyes. The cut was classic but relaxed, draping just so across her collarbones. She had paired it with high-waisted cream trousers that skimmed her slight figure before tapering to show off pristine white trainers. The whole ensemble walked that perfect line between polished and comfortable.

But that wasn't what pulled him in. It was the way she carried herself. She could have worn a bin bag and looked like a duchess.

Her hair, still damp from the shower, curled against her neck in a way that pulled at his gaze and refused to let it go. How had he become a man who fixated on such things?

He blamed sleep deprivation.

'Coffee?' Mrs MacPherson appeared with the silver pot, her practical presence a welcome distraction.

'God, yes!' Rowan's enthusiasm made the housekeeper smile. 'I mean, yes, please. That would be very kind.'

Steam rose from the Spode china as Mrs MacPherson poured. The scent of fresh coffee mingled with toast and bacon, but Max's appetite had vanished the instant Blackwood entered.

The solicitor sat like a gargoyle in a tweed suit at the far end of the table, spreading jam on his toast while radiating disapproval. A glint flashed across his glasses as he inspected them over the morning paper.

'Sleep well, Mr Blackwood?'

Rowan's innocent tone set off warning bells. Fascinating, how he had only known her for a couple of days, and yet he already sensed when she was up to something.

And right now, she *was* up to something.

'Adequately.'

Max reached for the *Financial Times*, determined to maintain a veneer of normalcy.

'Oh, I'm so glad to hear that.' Her eyes danced with wicked amusement. 'You see, my husband was *tireless* last night. Relentless, really. But I suppose that's what they mean by marital bliss and a wonderful wedding night, isn't it?'

Blackwood's toast paused halfway to his mouth.

'In your role as our watchdog, you must be thrilled. We did try to be quiet – but, well, you know how it is. Or…maybe you don't?'

Coffee sloshed over the rim of Max's cup.

'Perhaps we could discuss the trust paperwork,' the solicitor suggested stiffly.

Rowan speared a strawberry with delicate precision. 'I mean, you *did* camp out next door to monitor our wedding night.'

'The trust requires—'

'Audio verification?' She popped the strawberry into her mouth.

Max lowered the paper. 'Rowan.'

'What?' She blinked. 'Just keeping things transparent for our dear friend here.'

'Mr Blackwood is performing his duties,' Max ground out.

'As were we. So many times, *tiger*.' She turned to the solicitor with a disarming smile, the kind that could charm the clouds into parting. 'Tell me, is eavesdropping on intimacy in the job description? Is that why you studied law?'

Blackwood's fingers locked around his coffee cup. 'I merely—'

'Though I suppose it's better than watching.' Rowan tapped her chin. 'Unless you're into that sort of thing.'

Part of Max – the part not occupied with damage control – admired her ability to wield awkwardness like a dagger. To baffle people into submission. Blackwood looked ready to combust. It was a joy to watch.

'The trust requires verification of cohabitation,' the solicitor said.

Rowan's smile was pure Christmas morning wonder. 'And what's the verdict?' She got up and sauntered around the table, trailing an index finger along the rim. 'Getting sufficient material for your report?'

She was magnificent when she went for the jugular. The thought ambushed Max before he could suppress it.

'I think that's quite enough discussion of—' Blackwood choked on his coffee, spluttering as he set the cup down with a sharp clink. He dabbed at his mouth with a napkin before finishing, '—private matters.'

'Private?' Rowan perched herself on Max's lap as if it were her throne.

Her casual claim on his personal space should have triggered his defences, yet his body betrayed him, shamelessly responding to her fire.

'Nothing about this is private. But I'm sure you're merely conducting your due diligence. Do you need to see the sheets? No blood stains, I'm afraid. That ship sailed ages ago.'

This time it was Max who choked.

Her audacity was a weapon. The way she turned discomfort into an attack, precise and merciless, made his pulse pound against the stiff line of his shirt. Every calculated word dripped with enough honey to make the sting worse, and watching Blackwood squirm stirred something in Max's chest. Her weight on his lap felt dangerous, like holding lightning in a jar. And the scent of her hair eviscerated his restraint.

This woman was lethal. A loaded gun wrapped in cashmere and cheeky smiles.

Absolutely phenomenal.

He was so turned on by her right now.

No.

Max shifted in his chair to stop her from getting too close to the evidence of his…admiration.

Jesus. No.

'We should stick to business,' Blackwood suggested, composure hanging by a thread.

'But this *is* business.' Rowan's tone could have stripped paint, while her fingers followed Max's jawline, raising every hair on his neck. 'Making sure the newlyweds consummate their marriage? Doesn't get any more business-like than that.'

Her small frame radiated heat through his suit, and Max suppressed the urge to settle his hands on her hips to pull her closer.

'The trust has certain standards—' Blackwood began.

'Standards for love?' Rowan's laugh cut, clear as glass. 'Is there a manual? "Proper Procedures for Verifying Marital Relations"?'

He had to stop her. But hell, he didn't want to.

'That's enough.' Max's voice carried the authority to sever

the moment before it could spiral further. 'Mr Blackwood, I believe we have the last documents to review?'

'Yes, quite so.' The solicitor leapt from his chair. 'In the study, perhaps?'

Max watched Blackwood's hasty retreat with a wave of satisfaction. He had been reduced to a shell by a small woman with a cutting tongue.

A tongue, Max realised, he would like to taste.

The sight of a shrunken Blackwood filled him with an unfamiliar lightness – a bubbling sensation that took him a second to recognise as joy. When was the last time he had felt...this? This spark of vindication mixed with something warmer, more profound. The knowledge that someone had his back, had chosen to fight his battles with wit and irreverence.

His wife.

These two words echoed in his mind like a bell tone. The thought that Rowan's presence in his life might be more than a business arrangement sent a flare of panic through his chest. Yet he couldn't suppress the smile pulling at the corner of his mouth. This feeling of having an ally. He had forgotten what that felt like since...

No.

'Time to let me up, *darling*.' Max's fingers flexed against her hip. Rowan's lips brushed his cheek. She slid from his lap and took her warmth with her. Only the faint trace of her shampoo lingered, making his next breath feel somehow incomplete.

He stood, straightening his cuffs. 'And try not to terrorise anyone while I'm gone.'

'No promises, *honey*.' She blew him a kiss that managed to be both mocking and intimate.

Flames climbed the back of his neck, biting at his skin as he followed Blackwood from the room. The solicitor's shoulders were rigid with indignation.

'Your wife is rather…direct.'

'Indeed.' Max kept his tone neutral, though something possessive flared in his chest at Blackwood's use of the word 'wife'.

'Some would even say crude. The trust may have concerns about her suitability.'

Max stopped walking. 'The trust's requirements said nothing about personality.'

'Nevertheless—'

'Nevertheless, she is my wife. And more than capable of handling herself, as you have just witnessed.'

Blackwood's mouth pinched. 'That's what concerns me.'

'That a woman can hold her own? I see how that could be unsettling for a small man with an antiquated worldview. I suggest you keep to the paperwork,' Max said, 'and leave my wife's suitability to me.'

They reached the study, but his thoughts remained in the dining room with Rowan. The way she had gone straight for Blackwood's weak spots while looking butter-wouldn't-melt innocent.

It was unspeakably, irresistibly sexy. Mesmerising.

To his surprise, he was increasingly curious about what she would be like in bed. What it would take to make her surrender…

Hold your horses, Drummond. She said no and that's that.

The marriage might be arranged, but his wife was proving anything but predictable. The thought should have worried him more than it did. Heaven help him, but he was looking forward to whatever chaos Rowan created next.

As long as she directed it at someone else.

The study door clicked shut behind them with the finality of a prison cell. Max sauntered to his usual position by the window, needing the illusion of escape. Blackwood stood at the desk, needing the illusion of importance.

Max kept his focus on the distant hills. 'The final documents that the marriage is valid?'

'In a minute.' Papers rustled. 'First, I think we need to discuss your situation.'

'My marriage, you mean?' He turned, leaning against the windowsill with calculated casualness. 'I wasn't aware that needed discussing beyond the legal requirements.'

'Come now, Maxwell.' Blackwood removed his glasses and polished them. 'You didn't even have a girlfriend five days ago. Then suddenly you're married to a stranger? I'm not stupid.'

'Not a stranger.' The lie rolled off his tongue. 'We know each other.'

'Really?' Blackwood's eyebrows rose. 'How convenient that no one knew about this relationship until the trust's deadline loomed.'

'My private life is exactly that. Private.'

'A secret romance? With a woman who conveniently appeared out of nowhere, just when you needed a bride?'

Max's fingers stilled on the windowsill. 'I saw her, and I knew.'

'Knew what?'

'That she was the one. I mean, you've met her. She's gorgeous. Brilliant. Unexpected.'

At least that part wasn't a lie.

'The heart wants what it wants, Blackwood. Which is impossible for you to know, since you don't have one. No offence. Now, those documents—'

'Tell me, what did she cost?' Blackwood's glasses threw back the study's dim light and turned his pale eyes into empty mirrors.

The words shot like ice through Max's veins. 'Excuse me?'

'Your arrangement.' Blackwood's voice dripped with

disdain. 'How much are you paying her? Or did you find some other way to convince a who—'

Max moved before conscious thought caught up. His hands grabbed Blackwood's shirtfront, throwing the older man against the wall behind the desk. Fury blazed through his veins, hot and foreign.

'If you dare finish that sentence,' Max's voice went deadly quiet, 'I will make your life extremely fucking unpleasant.'

'Struck a nerve, have I?'

Max's grip hardened. 'Listen carefully, you pompous shit. That woman is my wife. My wife! You will treat her with respect, or I will personally destroy everything you've built. Your practice. Your reputation. Your insignificant life. I'll grind it all to dust and make you eat it. Are we clear?'

'Chivalry.' Blackwood wheezed. 'Almost convincing.'

'Unlike your piss-poor attempts at intimidation.' Max released him with a disgusted shove. 'You're out of your depth, Richard. That's why you're lashing out.'

Blackwood straightened his tie. 'The trust won't be fooled by this charade.'

'The trust's requirements have been met. The clause in my father's will is satisfied.' Max's tone could have frozen whisky. 'Unless you would like to explain to the board why you're harassing the primary beneficiary and his lawfully wedded wife?' He closed the distance between them again, letting his height advantage work for him. 'And questioning its validity without proof could be seen as slander.'

'You wouldn't.'

'Try me.' Max smiled, all teeth and threat.

'I will find out what's really going on, Maxwell. This isn't over.'

'Oh, I think it is.' Max moved to the desk. 'Now, shall we review those last parts?'

'At least that trash is Scottish,' Blackwood said. 'The trust might appreciate that small mercy.'

'I changed my mind. Get out before I hit you.'

'The papers—'

'Can wait, my assistant will arrange for it via email.' Max's knuckles went white against the desk's rim. 'Get. Out.'

The door closed behind Blackwood, leaving Max alone with the thundering of his pulse and the echo of rage in his bones. What the hell had just happened? He never lost control like that. Never let emotion override strategy. He had built his reputation on never letting feelings cloud his judgement.

Losing it now, over an insult that should have rolled off him, felt like a crack in his foundation.

Yet the moment Blackwood had implied... Jesus. The memory alone made his hands shake. The need to defend Rowan had bypassed all his barriers. It made no sense. Their marriage was what Blackwood accused – a paid arrangement. He had no claim to righteous anger, no right to feel protective of a woman who was essentially his business partner and in no need of protection.

But Blackwood's vile insinuation had felt like a physical blow. To both of them.

And Max couldn't bear it.

He crossed the study's length, trying to analyse his reaction. The violence of his response disturbed him. One word against Rowan, and he had been ready to put it all on the line by nearly assaulting a solicitor.

Footsteps in the corridor made him freeze. He recognised Rowan's light tread. His body tensed, anticipating her presence. She passed without stopping and her steps faded toward the library. Max released a breath.

What was happening to him?

The morning light glinted off his wedding ring and made the gold gleam. He rolled it under his thumb, the unfamiliar weight a constant reminder of how she had infiltrated his ordered world.

Not even twenty-four hours married, and already she was

disrupting everything. His discipline, his plans, his peace of mind. Her presence felt like static in his signal, crackling with interference that made it impossible to think straight.

Blackwood's parting shot reiterated in his mind. *'I will find out what's really going on.'*

Max's molars ground hard. Let him try. He had faced worse threats than a greedy small-town solicitor with delusions of grandeur.

But as he stared out at the Highland landscape, he couldn't shake the feeling that defending Rowan's honour was the least of his problems. The real danger lay in how instinctive that defence had come – and what that meant.

The trust might accept their marriage as legitimate, but Max was beginning to suspect he had underestimated the true cost of this arrangement. Not in money or legal complications, but something far graver. The true danger might not be losing his inheritance. It might be losing his control. Himself.

And that should have scared him.

But it didn't.

He scrubbed a hand over his face. Two days down. Three hundred and sixty-three to go.

Chapter Ten

R owan lay still and let her mind adapt to the bizarre reality that this wasn't some hallucination brought on by too much caffeine and too little sleep. Her four-poster bed could have slept a family of five.

Lady Rowan Drummond.

'Time to face day three of this circus.'

She swung her legs over the side and pulled on her running gear: basic leggings and a faded t-shirt. The contrast between her clothes and the room's opulence made her huff.

She'd barely opened her door when the sight hit her like a rogue frisbee to the face.

A naked male chest greeted her with all the subtlety of a centrefold piece.

Max emerged from his room opposite hers, straight from the shower, with only a towel slung low on his hips.

Holy mother of—

Her thoughts splintered into a thousand incoherent fragments. Water droplets ran down his chest, following the defined lines of muscle like they were rivers between mountains and valleys. Max's torso looked like it belonged on the cover of some pretentious art book – *The Human Form: Volume*

One, Peak Perfection. And those shoulders? Broad enough to make her hands itch with the urge to measure their span. His skin held a warm golden tone and a line of dark hair disappeared beneath the towel, drawing her attention down to—

'Good morning.' His voice was sleep-rough.

Her gaze shot up; a traitorous flush bit into her cheeks and set her ears on fire. 'For God's sake, put some clothes on! There are rules about this sort of thing.'

'In my own home? In front of my own wife?'

He lifted an eyebrow, and good grief, even that was irritatingly attractive.

'Our home,' she corrected. 'Temporarily, at least. And yes, rules like "don't parade around half-naked when your fake wife might bump right into your pecs". Christ, I could get a bruise.'

'I wasn't parading, I'm not a circus elephant. The water pressure cut out mid-shower, and I'm checking the control panel. Didn't realise I needed a formal invitation to step into my own hall.'

Water dripped from his hair onto his shoulder. Another droplet slid down his chest.

'Also, you're staring, Rowan. I feel objectified by your female gaze.'

'I am most definitely not!' She turned her eyes to the ceiling. 'I'm averting my female gaze from this inappropriate display of muscle and masculinity.'

'Right, that's why you're blushing.'

'It's warm in here. And all that...that...' She gestured at his torso. 'The whole muscles situation. Very try-hard. Bit desperate.'

He arched an eyebrow. 'Desperate?'

'Oh, aye.' She nodded. 'Let me guess – personal trainer? Protein shakes? Probably one of those blokes who grunt at the gym.'

'I row and box, when I find the time.'

Was there a glint in his eyes? No, that couldn't be. He was made of stone. Perfectly chiselled stone was still stone.

'Whatever.' She straightened her T-shirt. 'I'm going for a run. Try to be dressed when I get back.' Hot pressure surged through her, creeping up her chest like flames licking at dry wood. 'Ugh. Just…get dressed!'

She fled down the corridor. Her heart thrashed, and she wasn't even running yet. The castle's entrance hall stretched before her. Morning light streamed through stained glass windows and painted the floor in jewel tones. Her trainers squeaked against the polished surface as she headed for the door.

'Mrs Drummond?'

Rowan kept walking, her mind clouded with the memory of Max's grin. Unexpectedly boyish. Cute, even. There was more lurking beneath that posh power suit than a boardroom ego and overpriced shirts.

A body that could moonlight as a statue in this very castle, for example.

'Mrs Drummond?'

It took three more steps before the name registered, hitting her like ice water down her back.

'Oh, right. That's…me.' She spun around to find Mrs MacPherson emerging from a side corridor, a knowing smile playing at her lips.

'That'll take some getting used to,' Rowan said. 'Makes me sound like I should be organising church fêtes and judging people's scones.'

Mrs MacPherson smiled again. 'You'll get there. No rush.'

'The dress…' Rowan wrung her hands. 'I wanted to thank you. It was perfect. Exactly what I would have chosen. And the earrings… So very pretty. Thank you, Mrs Mac.'

Mrs MacPherson's eyes crinkled. 'I thought they'd suit you.'

Guilt twisted in Rowan's stomach. 'I can't keep them. Not when this is all...' She caught herself. 'I mean, we've only known each other such a short time.'

'Nonsense.' Mrs MacPherson's tone was gentle, but firm. 'You're the Lady of Dunmarach. Those pearls belong with you now.'

Rowan shifted. 'You've been so kind, helping arrange everything. I feel like I'm taking advantage.'

'Not at all. I've known that boy since he was in short trousers. Never seen him look at anyone the way he looks at you.'

Another surge of fresh guilt stabbed through Rowan. If only Mrs MacPherson knew the truth. This was all a ruse. Apparently, a convincing one. She didn't dare correct her, though. The more convincing this thing seemed, the better.

'I'm not...I mean, we're not like...'

Mrs MacPherson patted her arm. 'Love comes in all shapes and speeds. Neither way's wrong.'

The kindness in her voice made Rowan's eyes sting.

'Now then, will you be wanting breakfast after your run? The cook can have something ready when you return. Porridge, or a full Scottish?'

'No, I couldn't possibly... I can make my own...' Rowan was about to refuse, then remembered she was living here now. Had to do what was expected. Blend in. 'Actually, yes. A bowl of porridge would be lovely. If it's not too much trouble.'

'Trouble?' Mrs MacPherson's laugh was genuine. 'Not at all. In the dining room or—'

'Kitchen's fine!' Rowan said. 'No need for all that formal stuff. Unless... Is that not allowed?'

'It is allowed if you say it is. So the kitchen it is. Mind, the path's slippery after the rain.'

'Thanks, Mrs Mac!'

Morning air hit her like a shot of clarity, washing away the lingering image of Max's sculpted chest. Mostly. Sort of. The gravel drive crunched under her feet as she started her warm-up jog. Ahead, the grounds sprawled in that artful mess only the truly wealthy could afford – rolling greens, tree clusters, and pockets of wilderness so carefully curated they probably had a gardener on standby to ruffle the grass just so. She picked up her pace, following a path that wound through rhododendron bushes taller than houses.

Running had always been her reset button, her way of processing things when life got overwhelming. And currently, life was breaking the overwhelm-o-meter.

She'd married a stranger. A ridiculously attractive stranger with abs you could grate cheese on, but still a stranger. For money. She thought about the reasons she'd agreed to the whole thing. For her gran, for her mum, for rent that wouldn't pay itself. For a chance to dig into a story. She needed access to the archives, as Max had promised. The path wound around an ornamental lake, where a pair of swans regarded her with aristocratic disdain.

The king can keep his angry birds.

By the time she returned to the castle, her legs burned and her head felt clearer. She found her way to the kitchen, where the cook, Mr Calder, had laid out fresh coffee, porridge, and fruit.

'You're a saint,' Rowan declared, then dropped onto a stool at the central island and dug in. 'An absolute angel.'

Mrs MacPherson smiled. 'Mr Drummond is in his study. He asked to see you when you returned, at your leisure.'

Rowan's good mood dimmed as she licked creamy porridge off her spoon. 'Did he say why?'

'No, not to me.'

'I'd better be off then.'

But not before a shower.

Why do I even care if he sees me in my stinky state?

After a quick dip, Rowan changed into a crewneck jumper in a peach tone and slim-cut dark denim jeans. She made her way to Max's study, rehearsing arguments about archive access in her head, wishing she'd had time to dry her hair. But showing up with wet strands was a lot better than keeping Maxwell Drummond waiting any longer than she already had.

She knocked twice, firm and decisive.

'Come in,' he said. 'No need to knock.'

'What do I know? You could've been watching porn.'

Max's pen skidded across the page, leaving an inky slash through his notes. Jesus, she was like a spark in a powder keg. He looked up as she approached, irritation colliding with a pull that was reckless, volatile.

'You summoned me, husband?'

The outfit she wore emphasised the lean strength in her narrow shoulders, the sleek lines of her frame. Those skinny jeans hugging her slender legs weren't helping his concentration, either.

'My birthday,' he stated, 'is in two days.'

'Okay, well, mazel tov.' She perched on the corner of his desk, scattering his papers.

'Get off and listen,' he said. 'There will be a party.'

She ignored him. 'Since we're convening here so cordially, you promised me access to the archives. It was one of my conditions.'

He leaned back, fingers drumming against his armrest. 'The birthday party takes precedence.'

'Over our agreement?' She crossed her legs, making herself far too comfortable. 'Access was part of our deal.'

'And you'll get it. After we convince the trustees that this marriage is legitimate.'

'By throwing you a party?'

'It's tradition. The castle always hosts a gathering for the laird's birthday each decade.'

'"The laird".' She rolled her eyes. 'Listen to yourself.'

'This isn't a joke.' He stood, needing to regain some control over the situation. 'The trustees will be here. If we can't convince them—'

'Then you lose everything, I know, I know. Why is this place so important to you? I mean, as far as I know, you've rarely ever been here until now. You live in London, right?'

Max turned to stare out the window, where mist was rolling in from the loch. How could he explain what Dunmarach meant? The weight of centuries, of promises made and broken? The ghost of his brother, laughing in these halls?

'It's my life's responsibility,' he said.

'That's not an answer.'

'It's the only one you're getting.' He faced her again. 'Don't worry, Mrs MacPherson and my assistant will do the planning. But the party needs to be perfect. Every detail matters.'

'And I suppose I'm another detail to manage?' A hard note crept into her voice. 'Another asset to be controlled?'

'That's not—'

'I won't be managed, Maxwell.' She slid off the desk and advanced on him with that fierce grace that made his pulse stammer. 'I won't be steered or directed or handled.'

'I'm trying to protect both our interests.'

'By keeping me away from the archives? That's not protection, that's control.'

'The archives are private.'

'I'm your wife.'

'Temporarily.'

'Still counts. Or is that only when it's convenient for you?'

'Row—'

'No, I get it. I'm good enough to wear a ring and smile for your solicitor, but God forbid I actually do something with my time here.' With simmering impatience, she cut across the study's length. 'What's so terrible in those dusty old papers that you can't let anyone see?'

'Careful, Rowan.'

'Or else?' She moved closer, anger making her heedless. 'You'll divorce me? Go ahead. I won't sit around looking pretty while you—'

Max's hands itched to grab her shoulders, to shake some sense into her. Or pull her closer. Both impulses were equally infuriating. 'This discussion is over.'

'Like hell it is!' She matched his stance, lifting her chin even higher to meet his gaze. 'I'm not one of your employees you can dismiss with a wave of your hand.'

'No.' His voice roughened. 'You're my wife. And you will respect my decisions regarding this family's privacy.'

'Make me.'

'Don't test me.'

'Or what?' Her voice carried a challenge. 'What will you do, Max?'

For a moment, he thought he might kiss her. His gaze dropped to her mouth as her lips parted on a half-drawn breath, and his world narrowed to that tiny movement. The fragile space between them felt charged with possibility, with the unspoken certainty that one slight shift would bring her mouth against his. His muscles tensed with the effort of restraint, every fibre screaming to grab her hips and yank her against him. To devour that defiant mouth until she melted. The wanting clawed at his chest, leaving him struggling for air that didn't taste of her.

When had simple breathing become so difficult?

Then he stepped back and collected himself by straightening his cuffs. 'What I'm afraid of is you writing some exposé that destroys everything we're trying to achieve.'

'First of all, what *you* are trying to achieve. Secondly: is that what you think of me?' The hurt in her voice was masked by rage. 'That I'd betray you the first chance I get?'

'I don't know what to think of you. You're unpredictable.'

'Good.' She poked his chest with one finger. 'Maybe that's what you need.'

That touch set off a heat that wasn't anger. Her finger lingered for a second too long, and the study felt too small, too warm.

'The party.' He stepped back. 'We need to present a united front. No arguments, no sarcasm, and no taking the piss out of solicitors.'

'So you want me to be tame and boring?'

He wanted the exact opposite. But he would rather eat mud than tell her that.

'I want you to be convincing.' He ran a hand through his hair. 'These people aren't idiots. They'll catch on to your little rebel girl routine in a minute.'

'Then let me help.' Her tone lost its bite as frustration gave way to something softer. 'Let me learn about this place, its history. How am I supposed to play the devoted wife and Dunmarach's lady or something if I don't understand what makes it special?'

This bloody smartass.

Max examined her face, searching for any sign of deception. But all he saw was genuine curiosity and that damned determination.

'Limited access,' he said. 'One hour each morning, supervised.'

'Four hours, minimal supervision.'

'Two hours, I check in regularly.'

'Deal.' She grinned, triumphant. 'When do we start?'

'After the party.' He held up a hand to stop her protest. 'That's non-negotiable. We need to focus.'

'Fine.' She sighed. 'So that's how it is being in a power couple? Underwhelming, I have to say. And what does one wear to a laird's birthday soiree? Should I break out my plastic tiara?'

'I'll organise something appropriate.'

'Appropriate,' she echoed. 'There's that word again. Tell me, Maxwell, what's appropriate about any of this?'

He stared at her mouth again, wondering what it would feel like to kiss that sardonic smile off her face. To bend her over his desk and—

'Well, then.' She stepped back. 'I'll let you get back to your brooding. Lots of important laird things to do, I'm sure.'

He straightened his jacket. 'I have meetings all day. Please don't turn the house upside down.'

'House. You're funny. I might reorganise your sock drawer.'

A muscle jumped in his jaw. 'Rowan.'

'Or colour-code your ties.'

'Get out.'

She was already backing toward the door and flashed him a grin. 'Have fun at your meetings, darling husband.'

She was almost gone when he called out, 'Rowan.'

'Yes?'

'Wear the pearls.' He didn't know why he said it, but something in him needed to see his family's legacy against her skin. 'The ones from the wedding.'

'As you wish, my laird.' And then she curtsied.

He wanted to slap her. Kiss her. Put some respect into her. *Dammit.*

The door closed behind her, but her presence clung to the room. Max sank into his chair, his world tilting beneath him.

Two days until the party. To convince everyone their marriage was real – and himself that it wasn't. He had to ignore the way his skin burned where she touched him, had to resist the urge to push back when she met him head-on, just to see what would happen. Had to stop himself from reaching out, from testing how her hair would feel around his fist and…

He was so screwed.

Chapter Eleven

The mirror reflected a stranger. Someone polished and elegant, with her hair somehow turned into soft waves. The hired stylist had worked miracles, though Rowan suspected actual witchcraft might have been involved.

The little black Alaïa-dress was a study in contradictions. Classy enough to scream 'respectable wife', but short enough to whisper 'bit of trouble'. It was made of some textured fabric that felt way fancier than anything she'd ever worn. The high neckline was sleek and minimalist. Without sleeves, it showed off her shoulders in a way that felt powerful, not prissy.

'Right, MacKay. I mean, Drummond.' She fiddled with Max's great-grandmother's pearl earrings. 'Time to convince Scotland's finest that you belong in their tax bracket.'

The day had been a whirlwind of last-minute preparations. She'd spent the morning helping Mrs MacPherson direct an army of caterers, making sure the champagne was chilled and the canapés were arranged just so. The housekeeper had tried shooing her away – apparently, ladies of the manor didn't pitch in hands-on with party prep – but Rowan had ignored the protests and rolled up her sleeves.

Max had been absent all day. No brooding presence at breakfast, no chance encounters in corridors. Even his study door had remained shut when she'd walked past... Three times, but who was counting?

Her reflection stared back, eyes bright with nerves she refused to acknowledge.

The bodice hugged her like a second skin – which made her boobs look bigger than they were – cinching at the waist before flaring out into a skirt that was short, wide, structured, and ridiculously fun. It had that perfect dramatic swing, the kind that made you want to twirl to see it in action. Though she'd die before admitting she'd tried it in front of the mirror.

The shoes were pure temptation. Cute strappy sandals in emerald suede that purred luxury. The delicate ankle strap added elegance to balance the drama of the flared skirt. The heels were high enough to make a statement, but still comfortable and solid.

Minimalist, sophisticated, but with a dash of audacity. It was maddening how Max had nailed it. Every detail – from the clean, powerful neckline to the wicked flare of the skirt – felt like it had been plucked straight from some hidden part of her she didn't even know he'd noticed. It wasn't just that he had impeccable taste, though he did, it was the unnerving sense that he'd been paying attention. To her. Like he'd pieced together the bits she tried to hide and turned them into a dress that didn't just fit her body, but her personality.

Like she wasn't playing dress-up in someone else's life for money, so her gran could get the best care there was.

I suppose there are worse sacrifices.

Even though right now, Rowan felt as if she was about to dive into a shark tank after shaving her legs with a flint stone.

She grabbed her lipstick and swiped on the red, putting her best game face on. 'You've got this. Smile, nod, and try not to swear and hiss.'

But why was her stomach doing backflips at the thought of seeing Max?

Nothing had changed.

Except something had.

Maybe it was the way he'd looked at her in his study like he was fighting the urge to—

'Nope.' She capped the lipstick harder than needed. 'Not going there.'

Music drifted up from downstairs. She took one last look in the mirror. 'Showtime.'

The grand staircase stretched before her as Rowan held the bannister. Voices floated up from the hall below. Cultured accents, no doubt discussing stock portfolios and how to best profit from rising energy prices.

Her heels clicked against the first step, and she made herself move with grace. No stumbling allowed, not in front of Scotland's financial elite. The dress swished around her upper thighs with each step.

Then she saw him.

Max stood at the foot of the stairs, one hand in his pocket, radiating that effortless authority that had made her want to punch him and now... Well, snog his brooding, chiselled face off.

But not only had he made it abundantly clear that she wasn't his type, but it would also complicate their arrangement times a thousand.

But wowza, Max cleaned up far too nicely.

His dinner jacket fit like it had been poured over his shoulders. He glanced up, and something flickered across his face. A glimmer of unchecked appreciation that made her steps break for a second. He took in the heels, the pearls on her ears, the dress. When their eyes met, the quiet storm in his expression knocked the breath from her lungs.

'Happy birthday,' she said as she reached the bottom step, still above his eye level. 'Will I do as a prop for your little performance?'

His Adam's apple bobbed. 'You…' He paused, searching for words. 'Extraordinary.'

The simple honesty in his voice hit harder than any elaborate compliment. A flush rolled over her chest and up her neck.

'The dress was a good choice,' she said, trying to recover her equilibrium. 'Though I still think you had help picking it out from Hugh Grant's stylist.'

'No. I simply knew what you needed.'

The air hung heavy around his words, brimming with meaning neither of them was ready to face.

Max stepped closer, and she let him guide her toward the growing noise of the party.

What terrified her most wasn't the prospect of facing board members or the trustees or posh pals. It was how natural this felt. Her hand on his arm, their steps falling into sync, like they'd been doing this for years instead of days.

The ballroom took Rowan's breath away. Not because of its size – it was way smaller than she'd thought before she'd walked in for the first time – but because of how the space vibrated with excitement, warmth, and history. Crystal chandeliers cast honeyed light across wood floors that had known centuries of dancing feet.

The guests turned as one to watch their entrance, a sea of old money. Max's arm stiffened beneath her fingers. She pasted on her best 'of course I belong here, fuckers' smile.

'If anyone asks me about hedge funds, Max, I'm pretending to faint.'

His mouth curved. 'I'll catch you.'

The simple statement shouldn't have made her stomach lurch. She blamed the champagne she hadn't drunk yet.

They moved through the crowd, Max introducing her with

polished ease. 'My wife, Rowan Drummond.' The words rolled off his tongue like they belonged there, like this wasn't all elaborate play.

She shook hands, smiled, laughed at the right moments. But her mind kept circling back to those two words.

My wife.

When Max stepped forward to address the room, Rowan watched him transform. His posture straightened even more, and his voice filled every corner of the space with natural authority. He thanked the staff, praised Mrs MacPherson's dedication, welcomed his guests, and then…

'…finally, I must thank my beautiful, captivating wife.'

A shallow inhale stuck in her chest as he turned to face her. His eyes softened with something that looked a lot like affection. So effortless that it seemed utterly real.

Oh, he's good.

'Your spirit and determination have brought new life to these old walls.' His voice carried, but the words felt intimate. Personal. Meant only for her. 'Thank you for choosing to share this journey with me.'

He was fantastic at this. Too fantastic. Because for a moment, she almost believed him. Her pulse wavered. It was an act. She knew that. And yet… It didn't feel as scripted as it should have, it slotted into place a little too well. Like they'd been designed to clash, but somehow still meshed together in all the ways that mattered.

In a parallel universe, they could've made sense. Hell, she might even have let herself enjoy it. Him.

But not here. Not now.

Not ever.

Music started again and twenty seconds later, Max appeared at her side, hand extended. 'Dance with me? It's in the contract, you know.'

Rowan hesitated. They hadn't practised this. But refusing wasn't an option, not with every eye in the room on them.

She'd never thought she'd be this glad for the annoying dancing lessons her gran had made her take in her teens. Because that was how her gran had met Joe, her one true love, in the Barrowland Ballroom. 'Ye need to ken how tae dance,' she had declared. 'That's how ye find oot if a lad is right for ye.'

So Rowan placed her hand in his, and her world swerved.

Max drew her close. Not inappropriately so, but close enough that she felt his strength, and the muscles she now knew were hiding there. His hand came to rest at her waist, warm through the fabric of her dress. They began to move, and her feet remembered what to do.

'You can dance,' she said.

'Don't sound so shocked. I had lessons.'

'So did I.' She tried to regulate her breathing, which shouldn't have been this difficult. 'Let me guess, you squeezed them in between fencing and brooding 101?'

'I'm surprised you let me lead you, Mrs Drummond.' He spun her out and back and her skirt flared.

'Show-off,' she muttered as she returned to his arms.

'You love it.' The words ghosted across her ear.

And that was the problem, wasn't it? She was starting to love too many things about this arrangement. It was so much more than free breakfast and fancy soap. It was the way his hand rested on her back. The way his eyes crinkled when he almost smiled. The surprising gentleness beneath all that rigidity.

The music came to a close, and Max's expression shifted. Rowan recognised that look now. It meant he was about to do something that would complicate her life.

He lowered his head, and time stretched like treacle. His jaw locked tight like a part of him was battling the very thing he was about to do. But then his lips – God, his lips – were so firm and soft. He tasted like potent Scotch, like a secret he hadn't meant to share. Raw masculine energy, sheathed in restraint, but underneath… Underneath was something she had no business craving.

His kiss was careful, contained, perfectly appropriate for their audience.

And yet it hit her like starlight bursting inside her chest.

Without her permission, her fingers clutched at his lapels. His mouth shifted, the soft glide of lips over lips, like he needed to know how she fit, how she'd let him have her, if… For three heartbeats, maybe four, the rest of the world ceased to exist.

Wow. Oh God. What the—

Then applause broke out, splintering the moment. Max drew back, his eyes darker than usual. Rowan's lips burned, and her heart performed an impressive triple axel.

Right. Just for show. All part of the dramaturgy.

But it didn't feel like a performance to her. How his lips had moved against hers had felt real. Too real.

And she didn't know what to do with that.

Over two hours later, Rowan leaned against a pillar, watching the crowd through the golden fizz of her third glass of champagne. She had mastered the art of nodding at lobotomisingly boring stories about exclusive mooring spots and shooting grouse, when a statuesque blonde materialised beside her, exuding Chanel No. 5 and casual superiority.

'Victoria Thorne,' the woman purred and extended a manicured hand. 'I simply had to meet Max's mysterious new wife.'

Something in her tone made Rowan's hackles rise, but she accepted the handshake. Victoria's grip lingered a beat too long.

'Rowan…erm…Drummond. Though you probably already know that.'

'Oh, everyone's talking about you, darling.' Victoria's

smile was a precision-cut diamond. 'You've certainly captured Max's attention. I've never seen him look at anyone quite like that.'

'He doesn't seem to look at people much in general.' Rowan followed Victoria's gaze across the room. Max stood with a group of trustees, but his glance kept finding her through the crowd. Whenever their eyes met, her pulse kicked hard in response.

'He seems different with you,' Victoria continued, swirling her champagne. 'More intense. Though he's always been intense in certain situations.' Her pink lips twitched. 'In particularly memorable situations.'

The penny dropped with an almost audible clang.

'Oh, so you're trying to tell me you slept with my husband.' Rowan kept her voice breezy, though her grip firmed around the stem of her glass.

'Ages ago, yes. It was nothing.' Victoria waved. 'But my goodness, what a night. He has particular talents. Unforgettable ones. But of course, you already know that.'

The champagne turned acidic on Rowan's tongue. She pictured Max's hands on Victoria's perfect skin, his mouth on her—

No.

'How fascinating,' Rowan drawled. 'Perhaps we could talk about your obvious desperation, instead of my husband's "talents"?'

So much for keeping herself in check.

Victoria's nonchalant composure crumbled. 'I beg your pardon?'

'No need to beg, *darling*. Your attempt to mark your territory is noted, if painfully transparent. See this ring?' Rowan held up her hand and wiggled her fingers. 'Max put it there. Couldn't wait, actually. So, I don't care if you or everyone slept with my husband. It only made him the *incredible* artist he is now.' Her smile was pure Glasgow steel wrapped in silk.

'And you know who's benefitting from that each night? This girl right here. Cheers.'

She clinked her glass against Victoria's stunned silence and turned away, her exit unhurried despite her thundering pulse.

But Victoria's words echoed in her head, painting pictures she couldn't shake. Across the room, Max caught her eye again. A shadow crossed his features as he read something in her face, and he cut through the crowd toward her.

By now, the party had reached that phase when crystal glasses clinked a little too enthusiastically and laughter carried a touch too much warmth. Just before the first guests were announcing their departures.

'There you are.' Max's voice carried a whisky-tinged timbre, slower and richer, with a rasp that snagged like wool against bare skin. His fingers circled her wrist.

'Dance with me again.' Not quite a question, not entirely a command.

'Shouldn't you be entertaining your other admirers?' She let him pull her closer. 'Victoria's been sharing some fascinating stories about your specific talents.'

His laugh rolled through his chest. 'Jealous, Rowan?'

'You wish. Though I must say, you've collected a fan club. That ex-model by the piano has been eyeing you like a gull spotting chips on the pier all night.'

'I can feel your pulse, your heart is racing. Don't start a scene. Play nice.'

His thumb traced circles on her inner wrist, tiny flames licking up the skin of her arm. That should have been illegal.

'You're doing so well tonight, Rowan. Being so very…*good*.'

His words seeped down her spine like honey, settling low in her belly. She fought to keep her voice steady. 'Careful there. Or I might think you actually like me.'

'Maybe I do.' His eyes held that dangerous softness again.

'You're nothing like them, you know. Nothing like anyone here. Nothing like anyone.'

'Max—'

'That kiss earlier.' His tone deepened. 'You liked it. You felt it, too.'

She should step back. Should make a joke about his ego. Instead, she heard herself say, 'Felt what?'

'Don't play coy. You're too clever for that. It doesn't suit you.'

'Neither does this dress, apparently. Since you can't seem to stop staring.'

'The dress is perfection on you.' His look roamed over her body, languid and appreciative. 'Though it's making it very difficult to respect the terms of our arrangement.'

He was tipsy, the alcohol loosening his tongue. Still, a traitorous warmth unfurled beneath her sternum.

'Poor husband. Such hardship.'

'You have no idea how hard. If you weren't my wife… I would move behind you…' With that, he stepped behind her and wrapped one arm around her stomach. His other hand claimed the back of her thigh, tucked between them, hidden from view. Only his thumb moved in searing, knowing strokes. 'Then I would let this hand work its way underneath that *scandalously* short skirt of your dress. Right where you felt my kiss earlier.' His breath was hot on her neck. 'And then I would tease you. Until you came right here, in front of everyone, without so much as making a sound.'

Rowan's breath suspended like a held note. A throb gathered between her thighs like her body was already making room for him. The space around them faded into colours and sounds. All that mattered was the man behind her. Her skin hummed as if kissed by static. She almost felt his hand sliding higher, fingertips slipping beneath lace, palming her swollen sex like he had every right to be there.

'But since you're my wife, not an affair, and since this is a business deal, I can't. And I won't. As I told you, I won't touch you unless you want me to.'

That was the thing, though. *Did* she want to?

This was Maxwell Drummond. The walking embodiment of everything she despised about the elite – privileged, entitled, accustomed to the world bending to his will. She should despise him. Shouldn't crave him like this, shouldn't feel this gnawing hunger scraping at the edges of her self-control.

Yes, fine. He was stupidly gorgeous. That she could admit. The kind of mouth that begged to be ruined, pecs that could take a bite. But this? This raw, visceral full-body need that pulsed through her like a bass drop? She'd never felt anything like it. Not once. Not even close.

Because he's not just hot, is he? whispered a voice in the back of her mind. Not just the ridiculous face and the body built for sin. It was the way he owned every space he stepped into, that quiet, unwavering authority wrapping around him. The sharp mind behind those knowing eyes, the strength that met hers. Challenge for challenge, fire for fire.

It was the way he saw her. Really saw her. Like her sharp edges didn't scare him. Like they made him *want* to get closer. No one else ever had. Not truly. She'd spent her whole life standing on her own two feet, proving she didn't need a man.

And now she wanted to fall back into him, let him catch her, surrender to his hands?

The fuck I will.

Rowan pulled in a steadying breath. If Max thought he could throw her off balance, he had another thing coming.

She half-turned, glancing up at him over her shoulder. 'And if you weren't my husband,' she murmured, voice dripping with sin, 'I'd take you by the hand, lead you into your study, and give you a birthday present you'd never forget. The kind you'd think about for the rest of your life.'

She rolled her hips back, brushing against the hard ridge pressing into her.

Oh. *Oh.* Victoria had not been fibbing.

'Here's something you should know about your wife, Maxwell...' She turned fully now and rose onto her tiptoes, letting her lips hover just a breath away from his. 'She doesn't have a gag reflex.'

His intake of breath was as gratifying as his strangled voice. 'Rowan.'

For a fleeting second, she thought he might haul her back, consequences be damned. For another fleeting second, she thought *she* might.

Instead, she dotted a quick kiss to his cheek and let her lips linger long enough to feel him tense. 'Happy birthday, hubby. I'm withdrawing to my chambers now. Feel free to watch me walk away.'

She slipped from his grasp before he could react, but his touch didn't let her go. It clung, a smouldering brand on her flesh, a tease of possession that shouldn't have thrilled her.

The hem of her dress danced high on her thighs as she wove through the thinning crowd, and God, she felt him. That gaze, hot and unrelenting, raking over her like a rough hand between her legs.

What the hell was she doing? This wasn't part of their deal. This thing between them – this spark that threatened to ignite every time they got too close – it was dangerous. Messy. Complicated.

And Christ help her, but she wanted more.

Chapter Twelve

Research was meant to be an escape. Rowan stared at the ledger until the spidery handwriting blurred. Nine days in the archive, and her most significant discovery was that burying herself in centuries-old accounts did nothing to banish thoughts of Max.

The library's panelled walls seemed to trap the August heat. She'd stripped off her cardigan, leaving her in a thin cotton vest.

'Righto, Dugald Drummond.' She tapped her pen against the leather-bound volume. 'Show me how a Glasgow merchant bought himself a castle.'

The numbers were fascinating. In 1835, Dugald had swooped in like a savvy vulture and snatched up Dunmarach for what seemed like a pittance. The previous owner, drowning in debt, had given it away.

But her mind kept wandering to other, more dangerous territories. Like the way Max's voice had dropped half an octave when he'd pressed against her at the party.

'Stop it. He's made it clear he regrets the whole thing.'

Max had left for London right after the party on a four-day business trip. Which was for the best, considering how close they'd come to pushing the night past the point of no return. As a nice side effect, it also left her with unsupervised access to the archive. But the castle had felt different without him. Quieter. Emptier.

Not that she'd noticed.

The past five days since his return had been an exercise in avoidance. Max had retreated behind his work, emerging only for brief check-ins that left her frustrated. Gone was the man who'd whispered a wicked promise against her neck. Was it guilt? Or did he regret letting the lines of their deal blur?

She should've expected it. She *did* expect it. Things never lasted. Not with her useless dad, not with Ben, and definitely not with a posh git she'd married for money.

Rowan exhaled and rolled her shoulders, shaking it off.

Not that she cared. Much.

It wasn't like she caught herself listening for his footsteps or missing the way he loomed around all broody and annoying. Definitely not.

She was halfway through an interesting section when the library door opened. Her heartbeat sprang up like a deer startled in an open field.

'How's the research?' Max's voice was neutral. Too neutral.

Rowan didn't miss the slight pause before he spoke, or the way his jaw shifted. 'Riveting. Your great-great-whatever-grandfather had expensive taste in chandeliers.'

'Anything useful?'

'Define useful.' She stretched, knowing her vest would ride up. Taunting him was dangerous. Of course, this could backfire. Her speciality.

'I've learned that Dugald Drummond was either brilliant or ruthless. Probably both.'

Max moved closer, and his cologne wrapped around her like a physical touch.

'Interesting. Show me.' He leaned over her shoulder and his exhale stirred her hair.

Who is taunting who, I'm beginning to wonder.

'See here?' She pointed to a column of neat figures. 'He swooped in when the MacLeods were in dire straits, offering just enough to clear their crippling debts but nowhere near the estate's value.'

'Smart business.'

'After the MacLeods had lived here for centuries? Cold-blooded, more like. Must run in the family.'

A muscle ticked in his cheek. 'Don't push it.'

'Or what? You'll avoid me even harder?'

'I've been working.'

'Crap.' She spun in her chair to face him. 'You've been hiding.'

'Don't.' His voice held a warning.

'Don't what?' She stood, forcing him to step back or stay too close. 'Don't notice how you hardly look at me? Don't remember what you said at the party?'

'I was drunk.'

'Liar.' She advanced on him, and a zing of satisfaction zipped through her as he retreated. 'You were in control. You're *always* in control. So much so that it's annoying. Do you ever stop holding the reins so tight?'

His back bumped into a bookshelf. 'Rowan.'

'Say my name again.' She moved into his space. 'Say it like you mean it.'

His hands balled at his sides. 'I can't be near you like that.'

'Why not?'

'Because I might do something I will regret!' The words exploded from him like shrapnel.

'Here's another thing you don't know about me...' Reckless flames surged through her bloodstream. 'I *live* for regrets.'

The colour of his eyes shifted from glacier to thundercloud, pupils expanding until only a thin ring remained.

'Testing me like that is unwise, little writer.'

She splayed her fingers across his chest, cataloguing each beat beneath the cotton.

He grabbed her wrist and moved her hand away. 'This isn't part of our deal.'

'Neither was that kiss. Or that boner against my arse.'

'A mistake. Don't worry. It won't happen again.'

He strode from the library before she had a chance to reply, leaving her buzzing like she'd touched a dodgy wire.

'Coward,' she said to the books surrounding her.

But she wasn't sure which of them she meant.

Max pushed into the study, his body thrumming with an energy that made his skin feel too tight. Rowan's touch lingered on his chest. She was insufferable. Brazen. Impossible.

And brilliant.

Stunning.

No!

Max slammed the study door with enough force to rattle the ancestors in their frames. He strode to the window, jerking it open to let in a blast of Highland air.

It wasn't her stubbornness – though that could drive a saint to drink – it was the way she made him feel exposed. Like she could see straight through to the parts of himself he had spent a lifetime hiding. Like she had slipped a hand inside his ribcage and rearranged something vital. No one else dared. Not his board, not his acquaintances. Rowan, though? She ploughed through his defences with a raised eyebrow, iron will, and a wicked tongue.

Jesus. The way she had looked at him. All challenge and fire and...

His mind betrayed him, dragging him down paths he had no business treading. Hadn't he spent days fighting this? And yet, every minute, there she was.

Rowan, on this desk. Her wild red hair spilling over polished wood like a goddamn wildfire.

Rowan, on her knees. His hands pulling that hair, guiding her closer, closer. Until her lips hovered against his zipper, warm breath teasing the promise of ruin.

Rowan, riding him. Right here, in his father's leather chair, her nails biting into his shoulders.

His chest heaved with the effort of suppressing the groan building in his throat, and his palms left prints on the windowpane as he leaned against the cool glass.

Max turned away, yanked at his tie, and tossed it onto the desk. The afternoon sun slanted through the windows, catching dust motes that danced like sparks.

The Johnson portfolio waited on his laptop, demanding attention. Three hundred jobs on the line. The numbers were clear, the subsidiary was bleeding money. Cutting it loose was the only logical choice. He opened the file, forcing himself to concentrate on cold, hard data instead of the way Rowan's vest had ridden up, revealing a strip of skin that begged to be…

'For Christ's sake.' He ran a hand down his face.

Usually, decisions like this came easily. Remove emotion, analyse data, execute. All for maximum profit. But now his mind kept circling back to the human cost. Three hundred families. Three hundred lives upended because some numbers didn't align.

When had he started caring about that?

You know when.

His phone rang and Blackwood's name flashed on the screen.

'What is it?' Max bit out, nonetheless grateful for the distraction.

'Bad time?'

'Every time you call is a bad time. What do you want?'

'Thought you would like to know what our investigator found about your charmingly authentic bride.'

Max's grip turned to iron around the phone. 'Investigating my wife? How spectacularly stupid of you.'

'The trust has concerns—'

'The trust can get fucked.'

'Language, Maxwell.' Blackwood tsked. 'What would your father say?'

'He's dead. Get to the point.'

'Very well.' The shuffle of papers filled the pause. 'Your wife worked at a rather unsavoury establishment in Glasgow. The Last Drop. Ring any bells?'

Max pinched the bridge of his nose. 'And?'

'Not the sort of place a Lady Drummond should have connections to, wouldn't you say?'

'Is there a point to this character assassination?'

'She was arrested.'

'Fascinating.' Max's tone could have extinguished a bonfire. That piece of information caught him off guard, yes. He should have done a background check. But he would rather eat glass than let it show. 'Do tell.'

'Involved in a knife fight,' Blackwood said. 'It seems that she disarmed the attacker herself. Paints a rather vivid picture, doesn't it?'

What the…

A knife fight. A bracing sting ran through him. Then a startled laugh escaped Max. Of course she had. Of course, his fierce, impossible wife had waded into a knife fight. The mental image was so perfectly, absurdly Rowan that something in his chest loosened.

'I fail to see the humour,' Blackwood said.

'No, you wouldn't see it. Tell me, what did you expect this revelation to accomplish?'

'Surely you see that this sort of background—'

'…makes her even more remarkable? A woman who would risk her safety to protect others? Who has survived things? Did you honestly believe this would shock me?'

Blackwood paused, weighing how far he could push. 'The timing is unfortunate, of course. But you can't deny she's drawn attention. Questions. Certain trustees felt it prudent to ensure the marriage aligns with our standards.' His voice oozed self-satisfaction. 'The trust wouldn't want any ugly surprises.'

'The trust,' Max said, 'can review my extensive legal team. The marriage requirements said nothing about social status or background or arrests or reputation. You're grasping at straws, and you know it.'

'Maxwell, listen. I—'

'No, you listen.' Max's voice went deadly quiet. 'You will cease this investigation. You will destroy whatever sad little file you've compiled. And you will never, ever attempt to use my wife's past against her. Because if you do, I will bury you so deep in litigation that your great-grandchildren will be paying crippling legal fees. Are we clear?'

'You can't—'

'Watch me.' Max smiled into the phone. 'And Richard? The next time you want to play detective, remember this: I *chose* her. I *want* her. She's precisely who and what I need. So back the fuck off.'

Max ended the call and tossed the phone onto the desk. Energy surged through his veins, making it impossible to sit still. He prowled the study's perimeter, thoughts racing. The trustees were circling like vultures, waiting to strip him of everything. And now Blackwood wanted to weaponise Rowan's past, to rip apart the only good thing he hadn't planned for.

The Last Drop. He knew the place by reputation. A neon-lit haven for Glasgow's cheap party scene on Sauchiehall

Street. Mostly students. And Rowan had worked there. The image landed in his mind like a body shot: Rowan, younger but just as fierce and fuelled by rightfulness, refusing to back down from a blade. His fingers dug into his palms at the thought of her in danger.

But she had handled it, hadn't she? Like she handled everything, with wit and that remarkable fearlessness that left him both awed and unnerved.

Well, and she knew jiu-jitsu.

He laughed.

The Johnson portfolio sat in front of him. He stared at the numbers. There had to be another solution. Something less destructive. Less cold.

Max's phone pinged again. Probably Blackwood with more threats. Let him try. The thought of anyone using Rowan's past against her made his blood run hot. The idea of someone tearing her down felt intolerable. He would never let anyone make her feel like less than the extraordinary woman she was.

She was his wife.

And God help anyone who tried to hurt her.

That truth should have sent him running. Instead, it pulled him in. Even the study felt different somehow, less oppressive. As if Rowan's presence in his life had begun to chase away old ghosts.

'Quite the woman you've married,' his brother's voice seemed to whisper from the corners.

Yes, Max thought. *Quite the woman.*

He closed the Johnson file without signing. Tomorrow, he would find another way. A better way. One that wouldn't make Rowan look at him with disgust and disappointment.

Because somehow, without quite knowing how or why, that was becoming the one thing Maxwell Drummond couldn't handle.

Chapter Thirteen

Rowan was getting used to the castle. The all-encompassing quiet had become her friend. So when her phone rang, slicing through the hush, she almost dropped it.

'Hey, love.' Her mother's voice filtered through the speaker. 'How's married life?'

Rowan slid down the wall to sit on the floor. 'Och, you know. It's *Downton Abbey*, except with fewer dramatic deaths.'

'Still can't believe you went through with it.' Her mum sighed. 'You're my daughter right enough. When are you coming to visit? Gran keeps asking.'

'Soon.' Rowan breathed through the guilt. She should go. She wanted to. 'Maybe you could come up here first?'

'Aye, as soon as I have more than one day off.' Another pause. 'You sound a little different.'

'Different how?'

'A wee bit more serious. Did marriage finally make you grow up?'

Rowan managed a laugh. 'Must be all the fancy living. The silk sheets are going to my head.'

'Right love, you take care.'

After saying goodbye, Rowan headed to the library. Over the past week, the room had become her sanctuary. A few ledgers lay across the oak table where she'd left them. She eased into what she'd started thinking of as *her* chair and flipped to her marked page. The handwriting detailed business transactions from the 1810s.

And there it was.

Dugald Drummond hadn't just indirectly profited from the enslavement of human beings by trading in sugar and cotton; he'd actively invested in it, buying shares in Caribbean plantations. Or 'the West Indies', as they used to call it.

This entire place was tainted.

'Fuck.' She dug her fingertips into her temples, tracing small circles. It shouldn't be a surprise, Glasgow's Jamaica Street had that name for a reason. But seeing this hit differently, literally too close to home.

But she kept doing it. Because someone had to.

The compensation records from the 1830s made her stomach churn with nausea. Dugald Drummond and his son had received thousands of pounds – the modern equivalent of millions – for the 'loss of property' when slavery finally had been abolished.

He'd used that money to buy Dunmarach.

Rowan stared at the ledgers until the numbers danced. The castle's luxury, which had seemed like a fairy tale at first, now felt suffocating. Every gilded frame, every crystal decanter, every thread in the rugs… All of it bought with human misery.

And here she was, married into it.

She had to talk to Max.

Part of her wanted to storm straight to him, demand answers, and make him face his ancestors' sins. But what if he already knew? What if he didn't care? He was a sharp-suited

London finance player, after all. A cold fist wrung her insides. She had to see how he'd react when faced with the reality of the legacy he was so fixated on protecting, even to the point of marrying her.

The library's silence weighed on her ears as she stood, stretching muscles stiff from hours of reading. Outside, the Highland twilight painted the hills in shades of purple and gold. Beautiful and brutal, like everything else about this place.

Rowan gathered her notes, her mind already on the conversation with Max. 'Sorry, Dugald, but your bloody laundry's about to get a public airing.'

Whatever happened next would change things. This marriage, this story, maybe even her understanding of herself. But that was what she did, wasn't it? Stir up trouble. Ask questions.

Was it easy? Hell, no.

The scent of ageing paper wafted around her as she stretched higher, searching for the year 1834.

There – a flash of something newer wedged between two ancient volumes. As she gently jimmied at it, the folder slipped free. Manila, unmarked, corners soft with age. The kind of folder that shouldn't have caught her attention at all.

Which was why it did.

Someone had tucked it between old financial records far enough to avoid casual discovery. It didn't belong with dusty ledgers from the 1800s. It had been hidden. Not for safekeeping, but to keep it out of sight.

The folder felt light, its intentional lack of labels setting off her journalist instincts. She sat down again. 'Aren't you a suspicious little bugger?'

The first page was a newspaper clipping, yellowed and creased. *The Scotsman*, thirteen years ago. The headline punched her in the gut:

TRAGIC LOSS OF DRUMMOND HEIR IN HIGHLAND
CRASH
Martin Charles Drummond, 20, killed. Younger brother Maxwell,
17, in critical condition…

'Oh Christ.' Rowan's fingers trembled as she read on. The article painted Martin as the golden child. Head boy at Fettes College in Edinburgh, now at Oxford, 'beloved by all who knew him'. The kind of young man who seemed destined for greatness.

The police report lay beneath, its clinical language somehow worse than the newspaper's flowery prose.

23:47 – A87, near Fort Augustus. Porsche 930 Turbo. Male driver (17) lost control on wet road. Vehicle impacted passenger side. Fatal injuries sustained. Death pronounced at scene by attending paramedics.

A Porsche? That was a dangerous car in inexperienced hands – like those of a seventeen-year-old boy with a brand-new license, just two and a half weeks shy of his eighteenth birthday.

Max.

The insurance report completed the triptych. Max had spent a month in hospital. Multiple surgeries and physical therapy. The dry language couldn't hide the severity of his injuries or the miracle of his survival.

But he'd lived.

And Martin hadn't.

'Oh no.' She bit into her thumb. The words melted together as she followed Max's name in the report.

The rain would have come suddenly. It often did on Scotland's west coast. One moment of hesitation, one overcorrection…

'That's why you're such a control freak,' she murmured, as the pieces clicked into place.

Because the last time he'd lost control, his brother had died.

She gathered the documents with unsteady hands. The folder seemed heavier now, weighted with understanding. Max didn't just carry his family's legacy. He carried his brother's ghost. She should put it back. Pretend she'd never found it.

I can't unknow this.

The sky had darkened while she read, heavy clouds gathering over the hills. Rain spattered against the windows, each drop an echo of that long-ago night.

Knowledge was power, her journalism professors had preached. But this felt less like power and more like responsibility. The weight of understanding why Max had become the man he was.

For a flicker, Rowan could almost see them. Two boys in a sleek car, one golden and bright, the other eager to measure up. Brothers. Best friends.

She tucked the folder back where she'd found it, but its contents had already carved a space inside her. Some mysteries only led to painful questions. And some wounds never healed. They got buried under expensive suits, power, and control.

Should she bring it up? Confronting him about his family's dark history was one thing. This, though… This was so personal. Traumatic. But the knowledge had already rooted itself in her, making it impossible to ignore.

She'd start with Dugald Drummond and see where it led.

The library felt colder as she gathered her notes. Strange, how one instant of lost control could echo through decades.

And somewhere in Dunmarach, her husband was shouldering that weight alone.

Chapter Fourteen

Rowan found Max at the distillery. He stood by the ageing barrels, silhouetted against the rain-streaked warehouse windows, long after everyone else was gone. The tumbler in his hand glowed in the low light. The hoppy scent of malted barley hung thick in the air.

'Your family bought this place with blood money.' The words slipped out before she could soften them.

His shoulders stiffened. 'Excuse me?'

'Dugald Drummond. Slave trade investments. Caribbean plantations.' She stepped closer, heart thundering. 'That's how he bought Dunmarach. With compensation money from losing his human…property.'

'So you've been busy.' His words hit with the bite of an ice bath.

'That's all you have to say?'

'What would you like me to say? That my ancestors were bastards? They were. Welcome to the British upper class.'

'And that doesn't bother you?'

His spine went rigid, and Rowan thought he might deny it.

Instead, he huffed out a harsh laugh. 'Of course it bothers

me. But what do you want me to do? Rewrite history? Undo centuries of greed and cruelty? I wasn't there, and I can't change the past.'

'No, but you can acknowledge it. Make amends.'

'By doing what? Writing a cheque? Selling the estate? Would that satisfy your moral outrage?'

She advanced on him. 'Don't you dare make this about me and my values!'

'What else did you find to feel upset about?'

The pain in his voice made her flinch. 'I didn't mean—'

'Didn't mean what?' Max's voice cut like frost. 'To pry into things that don't concern you? To use my family's history for your exposé?'

'That's not—' Her chest seized up like it was trying to crush her heart. 'I'm trying to understand.'

'Understand what?'

'You!' The word shot out of her chest. 'This place. Why you're so determined to keep Dunmarach when it makes you miserable.'

'You know nothing about what makes me miserable.'

'Because you won't bloody tell me!' She gestured at the rows of barrels lining the dimly lit space. 'You act like this is some sacred duty, but I've never seen you enjoy a single moment here. So why? Why tie yourself to a legacy built on suffering – personal and otherwise?'

'It's not that simple.'

'Then explain it to me!' She moved closer and refused to let him retreat behind that wall of icy restraint. 'Help me understand why you're willing to marry a stranger but won't talk about what matters.'

His laugh was bitter. 'And what matters to you, Rowan? Getting your story? Solving the mystery of the brooding laird?'

'Fuck you.' A sting pricked behind her eyes. 'You think that's all this is?'

'Isn't it?' He loomed closer, using every inch of his height to make his point land harder. 'The journalist who married for access and money? Don't pretend you're here for any other reason.'

The words hit like slaps. 'Right, because you're such an expert on my motivations. At least I'm honest about what I want and need, Max.'

'Are you?' His smile was almost cruel. 'Then tell me, little writer. What do you want?'

'I want…', the truth caught in her throat, '…you to trust me. I want you to let me in. I want… I want you to stop being such a stupid coward.'

His eyes turned arctic. 'Watch your mouth.'

'Or you'll shut me out harder? Push me away more effectively? Newsflash, you absolute weapon – I'm your wife. I'm not going anywhere.'

'This marriage is purely business.' But something shifted behind his mask.

'Sorry, but no. It isn't. Not anymore. You're reaching out, but you're terrified of letting anyone close. Of losing control for even a second. But guess what? I'm already here. I already know about Martin—'

The crystal tumbler hit the floor, shattering on the stone tiles. Rowan jumped, heart thundering.

'Get out.' Max's voice was lethal.

'No.'

'Get. Out.'

'Make me.' She spread her arms wide. 'Go on. Show me how good you are at pushing people away. But I won't make it easy.'

He closed the gap between them, backing her against a barrel of ageing whisky. 'You want to know why I keep this place?' His breath fanned hot against her face. 'Why I tie myself to duty? Because it's all I have fucking left!'

'Max—'

'What do you want from me? A confession? Fine. I killed my brother.' The words fell between them like ash after a fire. 'I killed him. All of this should have been his, and keeping this godforsaken castle and distillery is the only way I can make any of it right. So don't stand there with your righteous judgement and tell me what I should do or feel about my legacy.'

She reached for him, but he jerked away. 'You didn't kill anyone. It was an accident.'

'Was it?' His laugh was hollow. 'I lost control of that car, and he died. Cause and effect.' His chest met hers as he crowded closer, the wood of the barrel digging into her back. His body was a wall of tension that left no space to breathe.

'You wanted the truth, and that's it. I woke up in hospital to learn I had killed my best friend, my brother. That every-thing – absolutely everything – was my fault.'

The raw hurt in his voice cut through her anger and left only the weight of his words. He wasn't carrying guilt, he was drowning in it. She reached for his cheek again, but he stiff-ened and leaned away.

'Don't.' The word scraped out of him. 'Just...don't.'

'You were seventeen.'

'Old enough to know better. Old enough to live with the consequences.'

'Young enough to make a mistake.' She caught his wrist. 'A horrible, tragic mistake.'

'Let go.'

'No.' She strengthened her grip. 'You've been carrying this alone for too long.'

'Rowan.'

'I'm not afraid of your guilt.' Softly, she put her palm to his chest, feeling his heart race. 'Or your pain. Or your past. Do you want to spend your whole life punishing yourself? Pushing away anyone who might care?'

'I don't need your pity.'

'Good, because I don't pity you. I'm furious with you. For keeping this to yourself. For not letting me…'

Help you. Hold you.

The fight seemed to drain from him all at once. He slid down the wall and sank onto the distillery floor. Rowan followed, settling beside him.

'Martin was drunk.' The last syllable came out fractured. 'So bloody drunk he couldn't even stand.'

'Tell me,' she said. 'I want to hear it. I'm here.'

Max stared at his hands. 'He had nicked Papa's Porsche. Wanted to impress some girls at Tobias Featherstone's party. I told him it was mental. That car… They call it the Widow-maker for a reason.' He swallowed. 'But Martin laughed. Said I needed to loosen up and drove us there in two hours instead of three.'

Rowan found his hand and threaded her fingers through his. This time, he didn't pull away.

'We couldn't stay the night. Martin had this thing early the next morning, something about shadowing our father at the distillery. First proper step toward taking over, whether he wanted to or not. Didn't matter that he was heading back to uni. He knew how his story would end, it was already written. And he was okay with it. But he said he needed to feel a bit of freedom.'

Max's hand clasped hers tighter like he was testing if she'd hold on even if it hurt. 'The party was a riot. I spent most of it watching Martin get plastered. He wouldn't listen to me. When it was time to leave… Jesus, I had to carry him.' He closed his eyes. ' Yes, Martin could be a reckless idiot, but he was also the one who could make me laugh even when I didn't want to. The one who believed in me when no one else did. And we had to get home. So…'

'So *you* drove,' she said softly.

'What choice did I have?' The words held thirteen years of agony. 'And that idiot wouldn't wear a seatbelt. Said it wrinkled his jacket. Kept fiddling with the radio, telling me to go faster.' He ran his free hand through his hair. 'I was terrified. The rain, the dark, the single-track road. And then that bloody car…'

'It wasn't your fault.'

'You weren't there.' Max's glassy eyes fixed somewhere beyond the copper stills, staring into the past. 'One moment we were fine. The next… I hit the gas too hard coming out of a corner. The back end…went. I tried to correct, but…'

He shuddered. Rowan shifted closer, pressing her shoulder against his.

'The tree came out of nowhere. Passenger side.' His voice faded to a near-whisper. 'When I woke up in hospital, my parents couldn't even look at me. My father was just staring past me. Like he couldn't believe I was the one who survived.'

'What did he say?'

'Nothing.' His fingers flexed against hers.

'What? Why?'

'No idea. Grief turned them into strangers. Or maybe it revealed who they had always been. People who valued the family name more than the sons who bore it. Martin was perfect in their eyes. I was the difficult one. Too quiet. Too serious. Not enough of a "people person" to run the business, the estate. Not the heir, just the spare.'

Her stomach dropped. '*Those* were his words?'

'No, he was more subtle. "Perhaps Cambridge would suit you better than Oxford, Maxwell." When I finally got out, they sent me straight to university, to get rid of me.'

'You let them blame you. You didn't tell them he was drunk.' Understanding spread like ink in water. 'To protect Martin's memory. Shit, Max. That's… God.'

'I couldn't… He was their favourite. The ideal son. The heir. I couldn't let them know he had been irresponsible and rash. Stupid. Drunk.'

A sting shot through her. 'So you carried it alone.'

'Seemed fitting.' His laugh was jagged. 'I lived. He died. The least I could do was preserve who he was to them.'

'Listen to me.' She shifted until she faced him. '*Martin* took that Porsche without permission. *Martin* got steamin'. *Martin* refused to wear his seatbelt.' She gently tapped his chest with each point, punctuating the words. '*You* were trying to get your pissed brother home in a dangerous car. In the rain. On Highland roads.' The edge in her tone eased. 'The only thing you're guilty of is trying to be a good, loyal brother.'

His shoulders slumped forward. 'I tried to never lose control again.'

'Oh, love.' She let go of one of his hands and found the nape of his neck, threading through the short hairs there. 'It's okay.'

'I don't know how to stop being careful. Being controlled. I don't know if I can survive without it.'

'We'll figure it out.' She rubbed slow circles on his back. 'It wasn't your fault,' she said again and again. 'It wasn't your fault.'

They sat tangled up together on the floor in his family's distillery, surrounded by shadows. He didn't pull away, he didn't let go. And neither did she.

'I haven't touched a steering wheel since that night. I had just got my full license a few weeks before the accident. Now...' He exhaled, the sound catching like fabric on thorns. 'That's why I hired Oliver when the London job started paying proper money. Everyone assumed it was some posh git thing, the finance boy too important to drive himself.' A wry pull played at the corner of his mouth. 'Easier to let them think that than to admit I still wake up some nights choking on blood and petrol.'

The vulnerability in his voice felt like someone had shoved a fist under her ribs. She imagined seventeen-year-old

Max, trapped in a cage of crumpled metal, while his brother's life bled out beside him.

'You lost control once, and it cost you everything. So now you micromanage every detail, every interaction, trying to prevent another catastrophe.'

'Amateur psychology?'

'Common sense. And maybe a bit of projection. Growing up without my dad, I went the opposite way. Figured if I had no expectations, nothing could hurt me.' Her lips quirked. 'Didn't work so well.'

Max was quiet for a beat. He lifted his hand and let his knuckles graze her cheek. 'That must have been lonely and tough. You, your mother, and your grandmother deserved better.'

Her swallow stuck halfway. 'Agreed. But that's a story for another day. One trauma at a time.'

'I've never told my story to anyone,' he murmured. 'Not the whole thing.'

She scooted closer on her knees. 'Thank you for sharing it with me.'

His arms came around her, pulling her in, and something shifted between them.

Sometimes, she thought, *healing starts with being held.*

Eventually, she pulled back and stood, joints popping after too long on the cold floor. While they'd talked, the distillery's shadows had darkened. Barrels loomed heavy in the dim light, and the copper stills threw back a dull gleam like they were waiting for something.

Dwelling on it too much at once would only drown him. Max needed a lifeline, something to remind him that life didn't have to be all ghosts and guilt.

And Rowan was determined to give it to him.

She held out her hand. 'Up you get, Drummond.'

'What now?' he asked, but he took it.

'We're spending this evening together, not alone.' She

hauled him up. 'I *am* your wife. Looking after you when you're being miserable is literally in the contract.'

'Is it?' Some of the shadows lifted from his eyes.

'Page twenty-three, subsection B,' she said, already moving towards the door.

His steps faltered as she tugged him along. 'I'm not sure—'

'Come on, Max. Let's go back and see where the night takes us. We're young, we're broken beyond repair, and we're alone in a castle. Let's live a little.'

His lips hinted at something that wasn't a smile but held the promise of one. 'And where do you suggest we start?'

'Fancy a dram with your wife?'

For a second, she thought he'd refuse.

'Lead the way, little writer.' His voice held a warm note she'd never heard before.

As she pulled him from the distillery back up to the castle, neither mentioned how their fingers remained intertwined. Some truths, after all, were better left unspoken.

For now.

Chapter Fifteen

Dunmarach's small music room held shadows like secrets. Max's great-grandmother's Bösendorfer grand piano dominated the space. Its ebony surface reflected the light. The instrument, worth more than most London flats, now sat unused.

Vintage jazz records filled the cabinet beside the modern turntable, his father's concession to the twenty-first century. Max could almost hear the scratch of a needle on vinyl, John Coltrane's smooth sound drifting through summer evenings. Jazz was the one thing Murdoch and Max Drummond had ever had in common. It was one of the few memories untainted by distance or failed expectation or unspeakable grief.

Rowan had scattered candles across various surfaces. He watched her light the last one, fascinated by how the flame teased out the burnished bronze in her hair. 'Care to share what you're trying to achieve?'

'Creating ambiance. Unless you'd prefer to sulk in darkness?'

'We have electricity. And I don't sulk.'

'Sure, and I don't swear.' The candlelight melted into the

room's corners, pushing back the shadows. 'Now, where's that fancy booze collection I've heard so much about?'

He pointed at a cabinet. 'Third shelf. But—'

'Nope.' She cut him off. 'No buts. Tonight we're drinking the good stuff. Talking. Like a normal couple.'

'We are *not* a normal couple.'

'Ha! But you admit we *are* a couple.' She turned, brandishing two glasses. 'Scotch? That's a rhetorical question, obviously.'

'You don't like whisky. Or so I thought.'

The truth was he didn't know that much about her. Shame wedged itself under his skin like grit after a fall. He had done more recon on business rivals than on his own wife.

'No, I don't.' She poured two fingers into each glass. 'But tonight's about you and pure honesty.' She handed him the drink.

'Is that what we're calling it?'

'Better than "emotional bloodletting while surrounded by dead people's furniture".' She sat down on the piano bench, patting the space beside her. 'You're going to tell me about Martin while we drink.'

'I don't—'

'What? Share? Feel? Let anyone see past that snazzy suit? Too late for that, I'm afraid. The trauma bottle is open; now we need to empty it.' Something warmer crept into her voice. 'What I mean is… You don't have to carry all of this alone. Just start somewhere.'

'You're not going to let this go, are you?'

'Not a chance. I'm your wife. Let me carry some of your weight.'

'It's not that simple.'

'See, you keep saying that. But nothing ever is. I'm stubborn and surprisingly strong and I'm not going anywhere. At least for another 348 days.'

Max ran a finger along the piano's edge, muscle memory drawing him to the bench.

'You play?' She angled her head, and the faint glow of the candlelight danced in her eyes.

'Used to.' He took his seat on the bench and the wood creaked. 'Before.'

'Play something for me?' She nudged his shoulder. The request held no pressure.

He stretched his fingers, remembering endless hours of practice at his mother's insistence. The discipline of scales, the mathematics of rhythm. Repetitive. Safe. Predictable.

'Hey. We can just sit.'

'No.' His fingers rested on the keys. The ivory felt both familiar and foreign. 'Martin was terrible at it. Could barely manage *Chopsticks*. But God, he could charm anyone with his voice. You should have heard him sing *The Rowan Tree*.'

'Och, that bloody weepy tune. You know how many times I got serenaded with it at school?'

'He used to throw a hand over his heart and belt it out like he was leading the clan into battle, like carrying on the name was some grand, noble calling.' Max huffed. 'I never knew if a part of him bought into it or if he just liked the applause.'

She exhaled a quiet laugh. 'Sounds like a character.'

'That he was.' Max's chest locked up. 'Everything came easily to him. Sports, business, people, parties. Life, I guess.'

Light from the candles glanced off the crystal, painting the keys in amber.

She took a small sip. 'Must have been exhausting.'

Her thigh touched his on the narrow bench and radiated warmth through his trousers. She was finding ways in, quiet and persistent as roots breaking pavement.

'I suppose that's why he had to let off steam sometimes.' Max spread his fingers over the keys, muscle memory taking over. The opening notes of *Someone To Watch Over Me* filled the room, and the piano's resonance travelled up through the pedals into his feet.

She leaned closer and hummed along, slightly off-key. Each small movement, the brush of her knee or the touch of her shoulder, sent his pulse hammering in places he'd rather not acknowledge.

'Tell me something good.' She leaned her head on his shoulder. 'A happy Martin memory.'

'He...taught me to swim, down there in the Loch. It was freezing, but fun.' A good memory. Rare. Enough of that for one night. 'Okay, your turn. Tell me about *your* family.'

Rowan stared into her glass as if debating whether to speak. Then, in a low voice, she said, 'My gran's in cognitive decline. Dementia. I might have mentioned that. She's forgetting and confusing more and more things and people. Sometimes, she asks where my mum is, even when she's sitting right there. And soon...' She took another swig. 'Soon she won't know me at all, and I don't know if my heart's going to survive that.'

Max's fingers halted on the keys. 'I'm so sorry.'

'Aye, well.' She shrugged, but he saw the shimmer in her eyes. 'At least I had her growing up. After my dad fucked off when I was two, my gran raised me.'

Even after the accident, Max had had wealth, education, opportunities. While Rowan...

'Why?', he asked.

'I don't know. He just left and I don't remember him. Mum worked hard to keep us fed. So my gran took care of me while my mum was working. Taught me to read, to cook, to swear. Proper wee Weegie granny.' Her smile wobbled. 'And now she's slipping away, bit by bit.'

'That's tough.'

'Believe it or not, Maxwell Drummond, loss, pain, illness, and trauma don't give a toss about money and titles. We all have to dig through our own shit. Some just have bigger shovels. And yes, that does make a difference.'

He couldn't help but grin. 'Martin would have liked you. He always said I needed someone who wouldn't put up with my stoical nonsense.'

'Your brother was an intelligent man.' She set her glass down and turned to face him. 'You're still wound too tight. Let me help you with that.'

The piano bench creaked again as she inched closer. The air snagged in his chest as she reached for his tie.

'What are you doing?', he asked.

'Helping you breathe.' The silk whispered through her fingers as she loosened the knot. 'When was the last time you relaxed?'

The first button surrendered to her touch and his pulse thudded against the confines of his shirt.

'Come on, Drummond. Let some oxygen in.'

Heat and cold warred beneath his skin as she worked another button free.

'Last one.' Her knuckles brushed the ridge of his shoulder. 'There. Human again.'

The candlelight painted shadows in the hollow of her throat. Max fought the urge to trace them with his tongue.

She didn't have to be here. Not like this. Not lingering past what their deal required. She should have walked away from his ghosts, his baggage, all the jagged edges he didn't know how to smooth out. But she was still here. Not just tolerating him but enjoying his company. Not his money or power or…

'Better?'

The world narrowed to the heat of her fingertips.

'Rowan…' His heartbeat roared in his ears.

Her touch sank through the thin cotton of his shirt, straight to the bone, striking a charge through him he had never felt before. That scent of hers cut off rational thought for good.

'I need—' The words lodged somewhere between his heart and his mouth.

'What do you need?' Her voice was a low murmur.

'…to kiss you.' The confession tore from his chest. 'Rowan, I need to kiss you.'

The soft catch in her breath sent a searing bolt of want through him.

'Then why don't you?'

Jesus.

'I told you I wouldn't touch you if you don't want me to. Do you *want* me to touch you, Rowan?'

'Yes. God, yes.'

She was his wife.

His wife.

His.

And she wanted him. All of him. Even the sides of him he had never shown anyone.

He took her chin between his thumb and forefinger, lifting her face to his. 'Last chance to run.'

'Not going anywhere.' She wet her lips.

It shouldn't have sent blood rushing south like a tidal wave, but here he was, iron-hard against his zipper, one second away from losing the last shred of control. The restraint that had ruled his every move, the carefully calibrated distance he had kept from her, from this – obliterated. None of it mattered anymore. Not when she looked at him like that. Not when she was so sweet. So close. So willing.

'Good. Because I'm going to kiss my wife now. And then I'm going to fuck her until she knows she belongs to me.'

Her pupils went wide, green gone molten. There it was. That blush. That blush that made him want to ruin her.

'Promises, promises.' But the quiver in her voice betrayed her.

That was it. That was all he needed.

Max surged forward, sealing his mouth over hers, claiming. Devouring. Her breath shuddered into him, and he drank it up. His fingers tousled her hair, angling her head, forcing the kiss deeper, wilder. Because that was what she did to him.

She unleashed his wild side.

Her hot little tongue was so eager to meet his, it was unbearable. He slid his hand down to the slim column of her neck, gripping it just enough to keep her where he wanted her. A sound caught in her throat, part moan, part challenge, and it shot straight to his cock. She nipped his bottom lip, the sting making him growl against her mouth.

He pulled back. 'Careful. I can only hold back for so long.'

It had been ages since he last had sex, but it had never felt like this. Nothing had ever felt like this. She was the one who made him feel things. She was the one who got under his skin.

She was the one…

'Then don't hold back,' she said. 'Let go. You know I can take it.'

Max snapped. One second, he was on the bench. The next, she lay on the grand piano, lifted with the force of his need, sheet music scattering like fallen leaves. He had to make her feel the same powerful rush he felt.

'I need to…make you mine. I need to—'

'And I…need to see you try.' Her chest heaved in shallow, uneven breaths.

'You want to see what happens when I let go?' Max rolled his hips against her core and let her feel how desperate he was for her. She didn't shy away. No, she pushed back.

Of course she did.

Her lips teased the corner of his mouth. 'Hell yeah.'

That single phrase undid him.

He grabbed the fabric of her vest and pulled it up. The sight of her perched on the piano… This woman called to every dark, buried part of him.

She was a drug. Clouded his judgement and made him crave the taste of her skin. Her lips. Her everything.

But he refused to rush.

She deserved more. He would give her everything she didn't know she needed. He would savour her. Every sound she made, every move. He would make her feel the same roaring intensity he was feeling. And by the end of the night, he would have her exactly where he wanted her.

Where he had wanted her the moment he had laid eyes on her.

In his bed.

Willing. Surrendering. Begging for more.

Completely his.

Chapter Sixteen

They were kissing. Holy fuck, they were kissing.

Or they had been. Five seconds ago, Max's mouth had crashed onto hers. For real this time.

The scrape of stubble, the press of lips – soft, then savage. Like he'd go hungry without her. Stealing her breath. Scrambling her thoughts. Rewiring her brain.

Now Rowan was pinned against a piano. Its smooth surface was cold against her spine, but he was burning her up everywhere else. His hard length pressed through the fine wool of his trousers, a grinding tease right where she ached for him.

His breath came fast. Rough.

This wasn't the Max she knew. Not the man who guarded himself at all times.

His grey eyes snared hers and held. A promise. A warning. A challenge.

One she was about to lose. Because there was no going back.

This wasn't some cocky fuckboy fumbling in the dark. No, Max was a man.

In his eyes, she saw her own hunger staring back. She

needed him. Like oxygen. Like coffee on a Monday morning. And she'd never needed anybody. Not like this.

He let out a sharp breath. 'This wasn't supposed to happen.'

'What…wasn't?'

His hands – those strong hands – trailed up her ribcage. His touch was a contradiction, just like him. Gentle and commanding.

'You, Rowan.'

A laugh caught in her throat. 'Aye, well…join the club.' Then she pressed into his touch, let him feel how little fight she had left. 'Guess we're both fucked, then.'

'Very.' Max reached behind her, found the clasp of her bra, and flicked it open like he'd been undoing *her* his entire life. He pushed the lace up and rubbed his thumbs over her hardened peaks. 'God, look at you. You're exquisite.'

'I bet you say that to all the girls with tiny boobs.'

He bent down, his face inches from hers. 'No, Rowan. I normally don't talk during sex.'

'Then… Why are you talking to me?'

Why, out of all the women he could have – polished, sophisticated supermodels and socialites – was he here with her?

His lips brushed the shell of her ear, sending a throb of need straight between her thighs. 'Because you're my wife, and you deserve to hear how stunning you are.'

He lowered his head, and a gasp punched from her lungs as his mouth closed around her nipple. A testing, teasing flick – then he sucked hard enough to make her jolt.

'Ah! God, Max…Your mouth–'

He soothed the sting with a slow, wet lap. 'Do you want me to be gentle?'

'N-no?' Her cheeks burned, as if she'd stepped too close to an open flame. 'I…like it.'

A groan rumbled up from his chest as he dragged his open mouth over her skin.

'Is that right?' He bit down, and her spine arched clean off the piano. 'Does my wife like getting fucked up by her husband?'

'Yes,' she whispered. 'God, yes.'

She felt it. The wetness rushing between her thighs, the desperation to have him inside her. Her hips jerked against his, seeking release. She couldn't remember the last time she'd been this needy.

Never, that was when.

But Max was in no hurry. He pulled back, his eyes burning into hers. This man – this powerful, dark, complex man – wanted her as much as she wanted him.

When the hell had that happened?

She leaned back on her elbows, and he slid his hands down her sides until he found the zipper of her jeans. Her breath stuttered as he hooked his thumbs in the waistband, lifted her hips, and pulled the denim down her thighs and calves.

'You know...' He skimmed the seam of her panties. '...I almost fucked you when you walked into my bedroom on our wedding night in that excuse for a shirt. And I was seconds away from fucking you in that tiny dress on my birthday. You got so close twice, Rowan.'

A single touch. A firm, electrifying circle over her clit, right where she needed it.

'Shit, Max... Just like that. Just like that.'

'And judging by how wet you are right now, you would have let me. Both times.'

Oh, Yes. Very much so.

Max hooked his fingers into the waistband of her thong and peeled the lace down. The fabric hit the floor without a sound.

'Open your legs for me. Let your husband see you.'

He settled onto the piano bench and gripped her thighs. Spreading her. Holding her in place. The vulnerability of it should have made her feel exposed, bare.

But no.

Because she saw what she was doing to him. His heaving chest, his huge pupils. He traced the crease where her thigh met her hip.

'So pretty. Dammit, Rowan. Why do you have to be so perfect?'

'You're only now realising that?'

His response was a growl. 'Cocky.'

'You love it.'

'As a matter of fact, I do.'

Before she could retort, he ran his tongue over her sex in one long, languid stroke.

'Oh, fuck!'

Pleasure crashed through her. Her feet hit the keys in a resounding chord vibrating through the wood, through her, through every inch of her soul.

She had *not* meant to do that.

He kissed her mound before straightening up. Her hips tilted in desperation as he drew one teasing, tortuous circle around her entrance.

'So delicious. So wet for me.'

This was too much and not enough.

'Would you kindly fuck me already? I'm so wet for a reason.' She was done with the teasing, done with the games. She needed him inside her. Needed to be one...with her husband.

Yeah, that was a surprise.

'Patience, Rowan. We have all night.'

She opened her mouth to argue, to demand more, now, right this second, but he was already moving. His middle finger eased inside. Slow, painfully slow.

'So tight and hot. I can't wait to feel you.'

'Then—'

'Shhh…' He pushed deeper.

Her lids slid shut on a sigh as pleasure washed over her.

'No.' His voice slashed through the moment. 'Eyes on me.'

Her lids flew open again. She couldn't look away if she wanted to. He added another and her body took over, pushing back against him.

'Oh, m-my God!'

'You're all over my wedding ring,' he whispered into her ear. '*That's* how wet you are for your husband.'

A pulse of mind-melting pleasure blasted through her. She was close, and the look in his eyes told her he knew it. He'd got her there so easily, it was almost humiliating.

'Oh! Max… I'm coming. I'm co—'

'Not yet.' His voice brooked no argument.

And then he stopped.

Her hips twitched, but he held her still with his other hand. Why was he so strong? She let out a whimper. A plea, a protest, a broken mess of both.

'You're so pretty like this, all flushed.' His tongue brushed over her lower lip, soothing, like he wasn't destroying her from the inside out.

'Max, stop it. I… I need you in me.'

'And I need a proper taste of my wife.'

He lowered himself onto the piano bench. Then his mouth was on her. Hot, slick pressure. The fast flick of his tongue. Skilled torment that sent her reality spiralling.

'Fuck. Jesus Christ. Oh… Yes! Yes! Make me come, make me come, please…'

He sucked her clit between his lips, just enough to wrench out a sound she hadn't even known she could make.

Overwhelming. Too much. A million per cent right.

Yes, he was eating her pussy as if he had a Master's in Cunnilingus Studies.

Rowan's voice reached her ears from somewhere outside

her body. Her thighs trembled around his shoulders. Every muscle tightened, her body strung tight, ready to snap.

Max glided his broad palm over the mess he'd made of her, each pass coaxing out more, more, more.

'Christ… I'm losing my… I'm… Ah! Max!'

Her hips rocked against him, chasing friction, pride be damned.

But just as quickly, he eased off. 'On your knees, Rowan.'

Her brain short-circuited. 'What?'

'On your knees. I want my birthday present.'

Rowan's pulse thrashed as he lifted her off the piano and sat her down with a grip possessive enough to leave a mark. Her legs wobbled as she stood before him, but she lifted her chin and held his stare as he loosened his belt. The clink of the metal buckle lit a sparkler in the pit of her stomach, tingling through her veins.

He shoved down his designer briefs, and her breath caught.

Rowan was as far away from being a virgin as Scotland was from the Virgin Islands, but…

She had *not* been ready.

Not for this.

Thick. Heavy. Demanding.

Max closed his hand around the base, giving himself a lazy stroke. 'Show me what a lucky man I am that I married you.'

A skein of defiance and desire warred in her chest. She was not one to be commanded. But the challenge in his voice, the need… She wanted to prove to him she could take whatever he dished out – and then some. That she could wreck him just like he had her.

So Rowan sank to her knees. Heat pulsed between her legs.

She had never understood the appeal of surrender.

Until now.

'Open your mouth for me. That's it. Nice and wide.'

She leaned in and flicked her tongue against the head of his cock.

Max hissed in a breath, his hips jerking forward. Rowan was the one on her knees, but she held the power. And they both knew it. She curled her hand around him, steel sheathed in warm velvet, and pumped him with a firm grip.

'Stop teasing,' he growled.

'Patience,' she echoed his earlier words. 'We have all night.'

His eyes blazed with desire and admiration. That flicker, that thrill, when she pushed back – it lit him up.

And it left her drunk on him.

She took him inch by inch. He groaned, hand tangled in her hair. But she refused to be rushed.

Her mouth. Her rules. Her pace.

'Fuck…' His fingers flexed, not pulling, just holding on. Like he needed a lifeline. Like she was the only thing keeping him tethered to the ground. He was shaking. Not much, just a tremor at the base of his spine.

Because of her. Because he couldn't help it. Because he was starting to understand what this could mean.

And so did Rowan.

'You feel that? You're doing this to me. I've never been as hard as I am for my wife.'

A pause. Like he wasn't sure if he should say the next words. 'Let me feel the back of your throat. Make me yours.'

Her pulse surged. She had never let herself belong. And now, kneeling before the man who was her husband, she was consumed by the need to change that.

She relaxed her jaw, pushed her head forward, and took him. Took him until her eyes watered, until his breath turned ragged above her.

'God, Rowan. Fuck yes!'

His head dropped back. He was losing control. She felt it

in the way he trembled, the throb against her tongue. He was close. She wanted to push him over the edge. Wanted to reduce him to nothing but need.

Wanted to make him hers as inevitably as she was becoming his.

Max stared down at her mouth stretched around him. His cock pulsed in time with the racing drumbeat in his chest. Lips shiny, cheeks flushed, eyes wet from the effort.

'You're enjoying this, aren't you? The power you have over me.'

Her tongue flicked out to lick him off her lips. 'Obviously.'

He hoisted her up, spun her around, and bent her over the piano bench.

'You undo me, Rowan. And you know it. And now...' He pushed against the soft heat where her thighs met.

'Oh, do I finally deserve to be fucked? What's the verdict?'

He lowered his mouth to her ear. 'Yes. You're a good wife for keeping your promise and taking me all the way. You deserve to be fucked precisely how you like it.'

'How do you know that I like what you're doing?'

He ran his palm over the slight rise of her ass and slipped his fingers between her legs.

Wet. Hot. Soaked for him.

Oh God.

'Because your pussy is screaming for me so loudly, the whole village can hear it.'

'Then what are you waiting for?'

'Do you want me to put on a condom?'

'No. I need...to feel you.'

'Fucking my wife bare? That's how it should be.' Max dug his fingers into her hips. 'Birth control?'

'Yes, yes. I'm on it. Clean?'

His breath shuddered against her neck. 'Tested. You?'

'Yes! Same.' Her hand reached behind her, desperate to pull him into her. 'Now Max. Please, please!'

A groan tore out of him. 'Jesus. Fuck.'

He gripped his base and pushed in, sinking into her impossible heat. He couldn't move. Couldn't breathe. Every nerve, every thought, funnelled down to this.

'M-more.' Her needy moan cracked something inside him.

Each inch was a battle for control he was doomed to lose.

'OH! It's so much… That's a lot of… Oh my God.'

Her body took him in slow, impossibly snug and slick. 'You're so tight. You're squeezing me. Like you never want to let go.'

'Maybe I don't.' She glanced over her shoulder, mouth kiss-bruised, eyes glittering. 'I need you so bad… All of it…all of it… I want all of it…'

He drove into her with one smooth thrust, wringing a helpless cry from her, forcing her to stretch around him until there was nothing left between them.

No arrangement. No contract. Just her. Just him. Just this.

She took him beautifully, bravely. Like she was made for him.

Maybe she was.

Maybe he was made for her, too.

Her hands scrambled for purchase on the grand piano, breath breaking into little cries that stole his sanity.

'Is this what you wanted? For me to take you like you're mine?'

'Yours? I thought…this was a…marriage of convenience.'

He leaned over her. 'This is…the opposite of convenient. This is necessary.'

'Are you telling me…that you…need me?'

The truth crawled up his throat. Something he had never, ever let himself feel before.

He was lost in her.

And he wanted to stay here.

'What does it feel like to you, hm?'

A moan rolled over her lips, her body arching into his. Not an answer. A surrender. 'Max… oh God… I-I need you—'

His blood was too hot. Pressure coiled at the base of his spine, his balls pulling tight, but it wasn't enough. He needed her to know that this – whatever it was – was irreversible.

He slowed to a deliberate grind. Let her feel it. The way he stretched her, filled her, owned her. Her body trembled. He felt the sharp inhale, her thighs shaking.

'OH! Max… What are…you doing?'

Holding back had never been this painful. He needed to come so badly it hurt. But not until she knew. Not until she felt what he felt.

He did it again. And again. Slow and deep.

Her hips bucked back, but he held her in place. 'You're so perfect for me, Rowan. So fucking perfect.'

She turned enough to find his mouth in a feral kiss. Teeth. Tongues. A clash of need. She kissed like she fought. Like she lived. Without restraint, without apology.

With all her heart.

He slid his hand between her thighs and rolled his thumb over her clit. 'Now come for your husband.'

'Make…me.'

His lungs burned. His vision blurred. It was as if he was having a heart attack. But it wasn't a heart attack. It was something worse. Something he had never experienced, and yet he knew what it was. He knew.

He was falling for her.

And then he fucked her like he needed it imprinted on her soul. He gave her everything he had.

Everything that was supposed to belong to no one.

All hers.

She shattered beneath him with a raw cry. Her body

locked down around him, pulling him deeper, taking him under with her. There was nothing left to break his fall. His balls drew tight and a shockwave shot up his spine, each burst a hot pulse travelling up his shaft. His body collapsed over her back, muscles wrung dry, breath ragged against her damp skin. His heart raged inside him like it was trying to break free.

'God, Rowan.' His voice was nothing but a low, broken rasp. 'I made you mine. Whether you like it or not.'

She looked over her shoulder, and her satisfied smile stole the last piece of him. 'I kind of do like it. And I don't know if you noticed, but you're mine, too. For better or worse and all that.'

Max pulled back, turned her around, and gently scooped her up into his arms. Her body was soft and pliant against him. He kissed her hot, damp forehead. She felt small, almost fragile, but oh, he knew better.

This woman was a force of nature.

His only equal.

She looped her arms around his neck, her head nestling into the crook of his shoulder like she trusted him. He hitched her up higher and kissed her temple.

'Where are you taking me?' she murmured.

'Into our bed. Where you belong.'

She melted against him, her breath warm against his skin. A strange feeling took root in his chest, something quiet but vast. Humility. Fierce protectiveness. The bone-deep need to keep her safe. He fastened his hold as if he could shield her from the world.

Because that was what husbands did.

And that was what he would do for Rowan. Every second. For as long as she let him.

Chapter Seventeen

The first rays of dawn crept through the bedroom window, painting silver stripes across Max's torso. Rowan blinked away the remnants of sleep. A well-earned ache throbbed between her thighs – proof of activities that would've rattled even Queen Victoria's corset.

And she'd been a right horn-dog for Albert, that was common knowledge.

Everything had changed last night. Their marriage was no longer just a contract.

Or maybe a contract with benefits?

The bed stretched around them like an ocean of Egyptian cotton, yet somehow they'd gravitated to its centre, sharing the same patch of warmth.

Max lay on his back, one arm flung above his head, the other resting across his stomach. The sheet had slipped to his waist, revealing the lean planes of his chest. His torso rose and fell in the steady rhythm of deep sleep.

No snoring. Thank God.

'Oh, Drummond,' she whispered. 'You absolute work of art.'

Sleep softened the angles of his face and smoothed the

furrow between his brows. A lock of dark hair fell across his forehead, making him look younger. His dark lashes cast shadows on his cheeks, and his mouth – that clever, talented mouth – had lost its stern set. A tiny scar marked his bottom lip, almost invisible unless you knew where to look. Which she now did.

Her fingers itched to trace the strong cut of his jaw, dusted with one-day stubble, to follow the path her lips had taken hours before. But she didn't want to wake him up.

The thing was, he looked vulnerable. Like someone had stripped away his armour of expensive suits, leaving just… Max. A man who carried the weight of generations. Who'd lost his brother too young and learned to guard his heart behind walls of duty and discipline.

Life had a way of leaving its marks, even on those born with silver spoons in their mouths. Money couldn't shield you from loss or loneliness. It couldn't fill the empty spaces where love should be.

Quite the pair we make, eh? Both of us pretending we don't need anyone.

But… She needed him now, didn't she? Not his money. This. The way he saw through her sass to the girl underneath. How he matched her spark with his own, didn't try to dim her light.

Aye, she was falling for Maxwell Drummond. The man who'd basically bought her – and now looked at her like she was a puzzle he was dying to solve.

You're such a romantic bampot, Rowan.

She half-arsed a list of all the reasons this was a terrible idea. He was a rigid, emotionally closed-off posh git. She was chaotic, independent, and allergic to rules. They were from different planets. No, dimensions.

Except…

Beneath his refinement and her rebellion, they burned with the same flame, drawn from the same fire. The same drive to prove themselves. The same loyalty to family. The same resistance to bend to anyone's will. Ever.

Perhaps that was the problem. Two flames that close together could consume everything in their path – or each other.

His breathing shifted, and she froze. But he only turned, seeking her. Still sleeping, he slid his arm across the sheets until he found her hip. His instinctive touch sent a hum through her, and Rowan let his breathing lull her. She'd face reality later. Their deal, their boundaries, their limited time.

For now, she'd allow herself this slice of peace. Of belonging.

Even if it was based on a contract.

She drifted off with a small smile, her body aligned with his. As if the restless part of her soul had found its harbour. Her last conscious thought was that she'd never slept better than she did next to Max.

The rich aroma of fresh coffee teased Rowan from sleep, pulling her from a dream about swimming in Scotch.

She blinked against the light. Max sat on the edge of the bed, two steaming mugs in his hands, wearing nothing but tight black boxers that left very little to the imagination.

Not that she needed to imagine anything. Not since last night.

'Morning.' His hair stuck up at odd angles, soft and rumpled.

He looked…cute?

Yes, cute. Really, really cute. He wasn't supposed to look this relatable. Now, he was just a man with messy hair and drowsy eyes.

'You brought me coffee?' The simple gesture loosened something in Rowan's chest. Her gran's voice echoed in her memory: *'Yer grandda never missed a mornin'.'*

She had to blink a tear away.

Max handed her a mug. 'Apparently, marriage comes with certain obligations.'

'Who are you, and what have you done with my uptight husband?'

'Uptight?' He took a sip from his coffee. 'That's not what you were saying last night. It sounded more like "Thank you for making me come a million times, husband".'

'Well, erm… It was a spur-of-the-moment thing.' She sat up and clutched the sheet to her chest. 'Wait. Were you sitting here, watching me sleep like some creepy vampire?'

'Yes.' The honesty in his voice caught her off guard. 'And you talk in your sleep.'

'I do not!'

'Something about swimming in Scotch?'

'Oh God. What else did I say?'

'Nothing coherent. Though there was an interesting bit about my—'

'If you finish that sentence, I'm divorcing you this instant.'

His rare laugh was different this morning, lighter. It did funny things to her insides. And if that wasn't enough, the coffee was perfect. Strong and sweet, exactly how she liked it.

'I see you've been paying attention to my coffee tastes.'

'I pay attention to the things that matter.' His gaze skated over the small curve of her shoulder.

She blew across her mug. 'Aww. You're almost human in the morning.'

'Don't tell anyone. I have a reputation to maintain.'

'Your secret is safe with me. All your secrets are.'

'Speaking of my reputation: I have a call with London soon.' Letting out a grunt, he turned and bent to grab his socks from the floor.

Rowan's playful mood evaporated.

Silvery scars crisscrossed his back like a map. Pale, raised lines telling a story of metal and glass and pain.

She reached out and hesitated, her hand hovering over his back. This wasn't her place. Or was it? These scars weren't just physical; they were part of the fortress he'd built. She wanted to scale that wall, to touch the part of him he hid from the world. Her fingers moved before her brain caught up, tracing the largest scar with a feather-light touch.

Max went very still.

'I'm sorry,' she said and withdrew her hand. 'I shouldn't—'

'No.' His voice was hoarse. 'It's fine.'

'The accident?'

'Yes. My spine was… I'm lucky I can still walk.'

'Does it hurt?'

'Not anymore.' His voice was tight. 'Not physically.'

'They're part of your story, Max. They're beautiful.'

He turned, his eyes so dark it made her pulse skip. 'Beautiful?'

'I mean…they suit you. They make you more…you.' She explored each scar with careful fingertips, his history written into his skin.

And she needed to be closer.

So she shifted, letting the sheet slip away as she wrapped her arms around him from behind, bare skin meeting his. Soft to solid, heat to heat. His muscles tensed as her breasts pushed against his back. She wasn't trying to rub against him. She wasn't *not* trying either. What she was trying to do was make him feel whole.

His breathing grew uneven. 'Drink your coffee before it gets cold.'

But he didn't move, and she didn't point out that his own mug sat forgotten on the nightstand. The weight of the moment pressed down on her, so she did what she did best – lighten the mood before she did something daft.

Like cry.

'Come here.' She tugged his shoulder. 'Your brooding is disrupting my morning caffeine ritual.'

He resisted for a beat, then let her pull him back against the pillows. 'You're impossible, woman.'

'Mhm. Just the way you like it.'

'How do you know what I like?'

She let her hand wander down his stomach until she found his hard arousal. 'Because your dick is screaming for me so loudly, the whole village can hear it.'

He laughed as she climbed on top of him.

It was a wonderful sound.

Rowan straddled him, sinking her knees into the plush mattress. He was hard, and she was sore. But the hunger – God, the hunger for this man – only burned hotter.

She needed this.

He needed this.

He followed the length of her spine with his hand like he was learning her by touch alone. 'You're so soft.'

'Is that your way of saying I'm not as firm as your ego?'

He let out a low chuckle. 'Always ready to pounce, aren't you?'

'Mmm.' She hummed, a non-committal sound that wasn't yes but sure as hell wasn't no.

Heat rolled off him as he moved lower down her back and palmed her ass. He followed the curve of her hip, then eased between her legs, teasing and testing, coaxing a shameless little moan from her.

Handy that she hadn't even bothered with underwear.

She leaned in to kiss him. 'I'm right here,' she whispered. 'I'm right here. I want to feel you.'

His groan was ragged like she'd dragged it from the depths of his chest. Then he pulled his briefs down.

Hot. Hard. Hers.

She reached between them, closed her fingers around him, and guided him where she needed him most.

'I love that my wife takes what she wants.' He let her find the angle, let her set the pace as she worked him inside.

'Oh, that feels good… that feels good… ooh, that feels so fucking good…'

The stretch was still a challenge, a sweet burn that made her hiss through her teeth. She felt every unrelenting inch of him, and it still wasn't enough.

'Rowan. Oh, damn.'

The way he said her name when he was inside her? She never wanted to hear it from anyone else. His gaze held hers as she began to move. She felt beautiful. Powerful. Whole.

This thing between them was something else. Something she hadn't signed up for. Something she couldn't get enough of.

She leaned forward and braced her hands against his chest, her fingers tracing the hard planes of muscle. She caught his bottom lip between her teeth, scraped along his jaw, and kissed the spot between his neck and his shoulder that smelled the most like him.

He wrapped his arms around her and held her flush against him as he moved, each thrust a soul-shattering grind.

'Oh my God, you're so deep. Max… So deep. I can feel you everywhere.'

'Yeah, you do.' His breath singed her ear. 'Your pussy is like you. So fucking brave. No one else could take me like this. No one else could handle me the way you do.'

Oh. Oh, holy fucking fuck.

Max's hands came up again, cupping her tits in a firm grip. His fingers worked her to stiff points, sharp tugs sending heat raging between her legs.

'Yes,' she whimpered. 'More.'

The gleam of his wedding ring caught in the morning light.

My husband.

Mine.

The sight sent a scorching thrill up her spine and made her body clench around him in an instinctive squeeze.

'Say it,' she breathed, voice breaking. 'Say my name when you come.'

'First, I'll make you say mine.'

He drove hard and fast, and her body went taut. Then she was screaming his name, pleasure hitting in wild, rolling waves, drowning everything else.

Everything but him.

'Max,' she sobbed against his mouth. 'Max, Max, Max—'

His grip on her hips hardened so much it hurt. His breath staggered, his entire body locking up. 'Rowan...' His voice was coarse, desperate. 'Rowan. Rowan!'

He pulsed inside her, the hot rush of him spilling in powerful bursts.

For a moment, neither of them moved. Their bodies fused, their breath one.

This was real.

She'd entered this castle as Max's wife in name only, but now? Now she was his in every way that mattered.

Max should have gotten ready for the call by now, it was almost nine. But he preferred tracing idle patterns on Rowan's bare shoulder. Her head rested in the crook of his arm, red hair spilling across his chest like flames. Slipping back into bed after a shower? He had never done that. But she made him want to try new things.

'Are you one of those pricks who owns a private jet?' Her voice held that blend of sass and genuine curiosity that never failed to catch him off guard.

'What?' He huffed out a laugh. 'Where did that come from?'

'Well, you're minted.' She propped herself up on one elbow, a sly gleam lit her green eyes. 'Super rich people have private jets, don't they? Helicopters.'

His fingers found a soft patch of skin at the base of her throat. 'Private jets are for wankers with more money than sense.'

'Says the man who owns a literal castle.'

'The castle owns itself. I merely pay the heating bills.' He shifted to see her better. 'Which are astronomical, by the way. Have you any idea how much it costs to heat stone walls in winter? Not to speak of the roof repairs.'

She patted his chest. 'Must be tough, being a castle-owning millionaire.'

'The distillery barely breaks even most years.'

'But you won't sell it.'

It wasn't a question. Max's hand stilled on her skin. 'No.'

'Why not?'

The quiet acceptance in her voice loosened something in his chest. 'It's complicated.'

'Try me.'

He stared at the ceiling, pulling up thoughts buried for thirteen years. 'My father... He was different there. Almost happy sometimes, when he worked with the master distiller. Testing new blends, arguing about barrel selection.' The words snagged, reluctant to come out. 'It's the only place I remember him laughing.'

She spread her palm over his heart. 'And now it's yours.'

'For whatever that's worth.'

'It's worth everything.' She rose. 'It's your heritage, your family's legacy. Your roots. Of course, you have to protect it.'

Her understanding struck him like a well-placed body shot, but in a weirdly good way. 'Even if it's not profitable?'

'Some things matter more than profit.' She smiled. 'Though I bet admitting it physically pains you.'

'Deeply.' But his lips pulled at the corners.

'Good thing you married a financially irresponsible writer then.' Her ring flared in the sunlight as she gestured. 'I can teach you the art of making terrible decisions, business and otherwise.'

Max took her hand and brought it close to examine the gold band on her ring finger. The one *he* put there. 'About that.'

'About what?'

'This.' He aligned their hands, wedding rings glinting. 'Us. I don't...' He paused. 'A year seemed reasonable at first. For the trust.'

'And now?' She interlaced her fingers with his, both rings touching.

'Now I'm not sure about anything. Except that I enjoy having you here. In my bed, by my side.'

'To my own surprise, I don't *hate* being here. With you. Even if you don't own a helicopter.'

He brought her closer, as close as he could, and hid his smile in her hair. 'Stop fishing for luxury vessels, little writer.'

He kissed her, rolling them until she lay beneath him, laughing that bright, infectious laugh that shifted his entire world into focus and sent everything falling perfectly into place.

For the first time since Martin's death, the weight on Max's chest eased.

His mobile vibrated next to the pillow where Rowan dozed. The screen displayed Blackwood's number. Max tensed, but he kept his voice neutral.

'Richard.'

'I have it.' Blackwood's smug tone carried through the speaker.

Max's fingers stilled in Rowan's hair. 'Have what? Mad cow disease?'

'The contract. Your little arrangement with Miss MacKay. Or Mrs Drummond, as she calls herself these days.'

Ice crystallised in Max's veins. Rowan's copy of the contract was in his safe, he had seen it there last night. His copy was with his law associates in London. Also in a safe.

So this was nonsense.

But doubt niggled. Had Blackwood somehow accessed his study? Maybe when he stayed at Dunmarach after the wedding, while Max and Rowan were out for dinner. Or during the birthday party?

If Martin were here, this wouldn't even be a conversation. He would have laughed at Blackwood. But Martin wasn't here, and the burden of potential failure fell on Max.

No reason to show his cards, though.

'You can't have what doesn't exist. There is no contract beyond our prenuptial agreement.' Max kept his tone bored, dismissive. 'Which you drafted, old chap.'

'Come now, Maxwell. We both know better.' A faint shuffle of pages. 'Shall I read the relevant sections? The part about monthly payments?'

Rowan stirred against him. Max gathered her in, tucking her against his side.

'You're talking rubbish.'

'Am I?' Blackwood's laugh was biting. 'The trust won't look kindly on fraud, Maxwell. Especially from a London city boy who has no connection to his lega—'

'Thin ice.' Max's tone fell to a dangerous whisper.

'You'll threaten me again? Punch me? I'm not some hedge fund manager or little gangster you can intimidate with your antics. I knew your father, Maxwell. You're not even half the man he was.' More rustling. 'Even a non-disclosure agreement. Tell me, how much did it cost to buy a council estate wife? Was she a bargain?'

How did that piece of shit…?

'Drop the act.' Max set his teeth against the anger rising in him. 'You want to sell the distillery to cash in. A percentage of the sale profits and consulting fees from restructuring the estate, isn't it? Richard, you're a transparent, pathetic little man.'

'And you're finished. The board meets for the quarterly review next month. I wonder how they'll react when they learn Maxwell Drummond arranged a sham marriage with a wh—'

'I told you before, and I'm telling you again, if you finish that word, I will end you.' The warning cut through the air like a blade.

Rowan opened her eyes. Concern creased her brow.

'We both know what this is, Maxwell. A losing hand played by a spoiled boy who would rather hire someone than face reality.' Blackwood's tone dripped acid. 'The distillery is dying. It's time to let go and sell.'

'Never.'

'Then you leave me no choice but to inform the other trustees about your fraudulent marriage. The trust will take over and sell. I'll see you at the quarterly review meeting in four weeks. Bring your so-called wife. It should be entertaining.'

The line went dead.

Max's pulse rushed hot through his skull. Blackwood was bluffing. Had to be. As a lawyer, he knew enough about high-stakes financial agreements to make semi-educated guesses. But that sliver of doubt...

There was another paper trail, of course. The transfers to Rowan's account. He should have covered his tracks better, been more thorough...

'What's wrong?', she asked.

'Nothing.' He pushed off the bed, spine rigid.

'Max, don't be a dick. Let me help.'

Her offer landed like a punch to the sternum. He couldn't. Involving her would only make things worse. For her, for them. He had to protect their arrangement, protect his wife.

'I have to handle something.' He pulled on his trousers, movements clipped and precise. 'An urgent business matter.'

She sat up. 'That was Blackwood, wasn't it? I heard—'

'Leave it.' The words came out harsher than intended.

Hurt flashed across her face before she masked it. He hated it.

'Of course. Wouldn't want to muddy the waters of your pristine, mysterious business dealings.'

Max's hands stilled on his shirt buttons. He burned to tell her everything – about Blackwood's threats, the board meeting, his fears, the noose around his neck. But the words stuck. She had already seen too much of his mess, and knowing more would only endanger her. Better she remained innocent of whatever measures he took to protect them both.

Plausible deniability.

He knew what he was doing. Skirting the edges of legality was second nature to him. That was how the world of finance operated. Never criminal, just flexible. It wasn't something he wanted her mixed up in.

But that wasn't the real problem, was it?

She was making him impulsive. Undisciplined. Careless.

Every moment he spent with Rowan, he lost ground.

His life was built on strategy and calculated pragmatism. But with her? He acted on emotion. Snapped when he should have stayed cool. Gave away tells he never should have shown. Rowan had become the variable he hadn't accounted for, and that vulture Blackwood had smelled it.

That disgusting prick had found his weak spot.

It was *her*.

'I'll see you at breakfast.' He slipped into his jacket, armour against vulnerability.

'Max, wait—'

But he was already striding from the room, each step

widening the space he had fought so hard to keep – until she had slipped past his defences, making him forget the reality of their arrangement.

What was at stake.

The way she was looking at him. Like she saw something worth holding onto. That was more dangerous than anything Blackwood could throw at him.

Max clung to what he knew. The practical. The controllable. Blackwood was likely posturing. Max knew that. But he also knew there were financial traces to erase, contingency plans to set in motion in case Blackwood's poking triggered an investigation. That was what mattered now – keeping Dunmarach. The distillery. His legacy.

Not Rowan. Not the way…

No.

Time to remember why they were really here. Because this couldn't be real. No matter how much he wanted it to be.

Chapter Eighteen

Rowan hunched deeper into Max's Cambridge jumper, squinting at Dugald Drummond's looping handwriting until the letters swam across the page. Her phone sat beside the ledger.

Go on, coward. Call your gran. Maybe she has a good day. Maybe she remembers.

Three days of Max's moping and Rowan was done. He'd been all broody and silent, like a wounded stag. Retreating behind work and one-word answers. Avoiding her during the day, then showing up at night, all rigid muscle and unspoken tension. Not touching her.

And she had no idea why.

But since Blackwood's phone call, there was a distance.

At night, Rowan often woke up to the shape of his back. Broad and unmoving, as if she weren't there. He would reach out to her, sometimes, when he was fast asleep. But never consciously.

It was a miracle he still let her sleep in his bed.

No idea what's wrong with him. Was it something I did or said or didn't say or didn't do?

All he'd told her was that this had to do with 'business' and that was it.

Rowan had never been good at knowing when to stop trying, so she pulled out all the stops. She pushed, she argued, she demanded – nothing. Talking went about as well as teaching a rock to dance. Eventually, she tried backing off, and that felt the worst of all.

There was only one tool left in her box. And she was about to use it.

Rowan's finger hovered over her gran's number. She'd made sure the phone was mounted on the wall next to her gran's bed in the care home so she could always get it. But the daily calls had become a minefield of memory lapses and redirected conversations, each one chipping away at Rowan's heart.

She answered on the sixth ring.

'Hi, Gran, sunshine of my life. Are you busy?'

'Hello, ma wee treasure! Naw, I just couldnae find my phone.'

'Quick question – what's in your shepherd's pie? The one you used to make for me?'

'Oh aye, that old thing.' A pause stretched between them. 'Now let me think… There's mince. Tatties. And…carrots? Naw, that's not right. Did I put carrots in?'

A knot formed in Rowan's chest, pulling tighter every second. 'I think so, aye.'

'The recipe's in ma wee green book. The one with the… the…' Her voice wavered. 'It was there a minute ago.'

'Don't worry, it's okay.' Rowan had known this could backfire. 'Maybe we could talk about something else? How's the garden club?'

'What garden club?'

'The one with Mrs Henderson?'

'Who?' Her gran's voice held a thread of panic. 'Oh, aye. The blond lass. I'm a daftie.'

After hanging up, Rowan stared at the ledgers. The words taunted her with their permanence. Centuries of preserved history, while her gran's mind slipped away like water through cupped hands.

Her thumbs flew across the phone screen:

> ME (13:21) Hi Maw! Need Gran's shepherd's pie recipe. The proper one. Emergency levels of comfort food required. x

Rowan opened her notebook, determined to immerse herself in work. Yet the page remained blank while her mind kept circling back to Max, to the way his shoulders had bunched up during Blackwood's call, how his voice had dropped to a glacial chill.

Aye, his walls had slammed back up so hard and fast she'd heard the drawbridge chains rattle.

What had that creep Blackwood said to spook him?

The thing was, she'd started to see past Max's exterior. Cracks in his façade that made her want to dig deeper. Maybe that was the problem. Maybe she'd pushed too hard, asked too many questions.

Story of her life. Always poking at things better left alone.

She wanted to ease the tightness in his jaw with her fingertips. To comfort him.

But the truth was, she needed his comfort just as much.

'Shite.' She slumped forward, forehead touching cool wood. 'When did this get so complicated?'

Her phone vibrated with a text from her mum:

> MAW (13:23) Everything awright? Recipe incoming. Don't burn down the fancy kitchen. xx

The recipe came in segments, peppered with warnings about browning the mince and not skimping on the Worcestershire sauce.

ME (13:24) Thanks! Trying to do something
nice for The Laird. He's been stressed and
won't talk about it.

Three dots appeared, disappeared, then:

MAW (13:24) Men are always a bit weird.
Feed him and see what falls out of his mouth.

Rowan snorted out a giggle. Trust her mum to cut through
the bullshit with a bread knife.

The afternoon sun slanted through the library's tall
windows. She'd come to Dunmarach to write a story about
Highland heritage and whisky traditions. Instead, she'd
found the bloody history of oppression and exploitation and
then stumbled into a different narrative altogether, one with
no clear ending and too many complicated emotions.

'Get it together.' She shoved the chair back from the desk.
'You're not some lovesick teenager. You're an aspiring journalist who happens to be temporarily married to an incred-
ibly fit but emotionally stilted whisky heir.'

*Who, inconveniently, happens to conjure up an entire green-
house full of butterflies in my stomach with a single touch.*

Rowan gathered her notes and tucked them into her backpack. The shepherd's pie was a silly idea. Domestic gestures
weren't her forte. She'd once managed to burn pasta. The pot
still bore the scars.

And yet.

Worth a try, right? Even if it meant potentially poisoning
her interim husband with botched mince.

Rowan squared her shoulders. 'Your family's not the only
ones with steel in their spine,' she told the nearest ancestor
portrait. 'Aye, I know. Not quite what you pictured for the
next Lady Drummond. But here we are.'

She'd be damned if she'd let anyone dead or alive – including Max – decide she wasn't enough.

Rowan paused at the library door, her hand resting on the smooth brass handle. Through the window, she saw Dunmarach's grounds stretching out like an oil painting. Muted greens and greys under the Scottish August sky. This place had its own gravity, pulling at something in her chest. Or maybe that was just its owner.

'Righto,' she said to the empty room. 'Time to feed the beast.'

The kitchen smelled of browned mince, warmth radiating from the Aga's black iron belly. Rowan prodded the shepherd's pie with a fork and examined the peaks of mashed potato. Browned, but not burnt.

Victory!

She'd given the cook half the day off. Mr Calder had looked worried – like a man leaving his prize carrots in the care of a starved rabbit – but she'd sworn not to burn the place down. Reluctantly, he'd left.

Max's footsteps echoed in the corridor. The scent must have lured him here. Part one of her master plan? Check. He paused in the doorway, shirt sleeves rolled to his elbows, and took in the scene.

'You…*cooked*?' His words held a note of scepticism.

'Allegedly.' She pointed at the pie with her fork. 'Though I make no promises about its edibility.'

'Brave of you to test it on the lord of the manor.'

'Well, if you kick the bucket, I inherit everything, so…' She grinned. 'Kidding. Mostly.'

Max crossed to the Aga and peered at the pie. 'It looks…competent.'

'High praise indeed.' She hip-checked him away from the

cooker. 'Go sit down before you hurt yourself, trying to compliment my culinary skills.'

He dropped into a chair at the kitchen table, stretched his legs out, and crossed his arms. 'I didn't think you would take marital duties seriously.'

She scoffed. 'Glad all that brooding didn't steal your sense of humour. We're not in the fifties anymore. And that's not a duty, that's me showing you some care. Don't expect it to happen again anytime soon.'

Rowan plated their food, placed his portion in front of him, and sat down. She blew on her fork and tested it with the tip of her tongue.

Max took his first bite and his eyebrows shot up. 'This is…' He paused, searching for words.

'If you say "edible" I'll throw my fork at you. And I was our pub's dart champion.'

'Not bad.' He took another bite. 'Consider me impressed. I can taste the love.'

Rowan's fork clattered against her plate. 'Sorry, what was that? Did the mighty Maxwell Drummond make a joke?'

'Don't expect that to happen again anytime soon.'

It wasn't the first bite. Or the second. But somewhere between Max's third forkful and the way his shoulders softened – imperceptibly at first, then definitively – Rowan knew. The walls were coming down. Not with a dramatic crash but a quiet crumble. She held her breath. Max didn't do intentional openness, but his body was giving him away.

He realised it, too. And for a moment, he seemed to fight it.

But food reached places words couldn't.

'My gran would be chuffed,' she said, testing the waters. 'Wooing Laird Maxwell Alexander Drummond of Dunmarach with nothing but mince and mash.'

A small huff, almost a laugh, slipped out.

Her gran's shepherd's pie had done what days of talking,

touching, and prodding could not. Magic, that. Absolute bloody magic.

'No one has ever cooked for me before,' he said. 'Not for me...specifically. And you made my comfort food. You *remembered.*'

'Aye, well. I used my gran's recipe. Worked for me all these years, so...'

'How is she?'

'Some days are better than others.' Rowan jabbed at a potato peak, she didn't want to talk about it. 'Today wasn't great.'

He nodded without pushing for details. But his knee rested against hers under the table.

After they'd finished eating, Max stood to clear their plates. He set the dishes in the sink and turned. For a second, he assessed her with a look that cinched around her like a wire drawn tight. Not like he was deciding something, but like the decision had already been made, and he was bracing himself for it. Then he crossed the kitchen in three long strides, pulled her up from her chair, and kissed her.

Just like that.

His mouth tasted of wine and him and home. Relief swept through her first, a hard, breath-stealing thing. Then the elation. Then something heavier, unfurling inside her like it planned to stay.

For days, she'd felt him slipping through her fingers, and she hadn't known how to hold on. Now, he was kissing her like she was something he never wanted to lose.

When he pulled back, his forehead touched hers. 'I thought... It's my duty to protect my legacy *and* you.' He sighed. 'But staying away from you was never going to work.'

'I'm glad you're finally seeing the light.'

'Rowan... I'm not a good man. You must know that you can't fix something that has been broken this long.'

'I don't need protection. And I'm definitely not trying to

fix you, because I like the man you are,' she said. 'But if I *were*, I would succeed. Naturally.'

'Naturally.' He exhaled, rough, almost like a laugh. 'Thank you. For this.' He gestured at the kitchen, at them.

Her heart stumbled. 'Aye, anytime.'

His answering smile held promises that made her breath catch. And when he lifted her onto the counter, his touch was tender enough to make her believe them.

'You might not think of yourself as a good man,' she said, nuzzling his neck, 'but you've been such a good husband, finishing every bite.'

His lips curved into a lopsided smile. 'And I know how to thank you for cooking.'

Her pulse kicked into a sprint. 'What do you have in mind?'

Max's voice was a husky whisper against her cheek. 'I'm going to make you come for dessert, of course.'

'That's a hell of a thank you. What about a bit of kissing first?'

He caught her mouth with his, still smiling. The first slide of his tongue was slow, teasing – then deeper, hungrier. A firm hand at her jaw, a quiet growl in his throat, like stopping wasn't an option. He reached for her jeans, popping the buttons with ruthless efficiency. Hot fingers dipped past lace, past every layer, and—

'Fuck!' She gasped.

'Oh, Rowan.' He brushed over her clit with gentle precision. 'You really want your dessert, don't you?'

'I think...I earned it.' She bit down on the edge of her bottom lip.

'You think cooking for me earns you an orgasm?' His voice was low and hoarse. 'Rowan, you could burn down the kitchen and I'd still be on my knees for you.'

Heat rushed to her core, a pull of want so intense it sent her thighs clenching.

His breath left him in a staggered burst like he felt it too. 'I don't even have to work for it, do I?' he said with a smug grin.

'Sure you do.' Her head tipped back, her hips canting forward to feel more of him. 'Like that…'

'You know how to make me happy.' His face was serious as his finger pushed in knuckle-deep. 'How to make me forget everything else.'

Her hand fumbled for him, clawing at his suit trousers until she found him. Thick, hard, burning through the fabric.

'That's a good wife. Taking care of me even when I don't deserve it.'

Then he added another digit, his teeth scraped her neck, and her whole body fucking pleaded. A desperate flutter, a slick, involuntary pulse.

'Jesus, Rowan.' His lips brushed her ear. 'Are you there already?'

Nothing existed but the press of his palm against her clit, the pressure of his fingers inside her. 'Max, p-please—'

'Shhh. I got you.' He stroked that spot that made her world detonate.

'Oh my god, oh my god.'

And then he destroyed her. Sharp flicks of his wrist, the hard press of his palm.

'Ah! Max! You… Oh, fuck, Max—'

Her orgasm cracked her open, tearing her apart and piecing her back together in the same breath. She screamed his name, over and over, tightening around him like she was never letting him go.

Max groaned, his temple against hers as he worked her through it, whispering something she couldn't hear over the roar in her ears. His fingers were still inside her, owning every aftershock.

She reached up and cupped his cheek. 'I—'

He stopped her with a kiss. 'You're welcome.'

Her laugh was shaky. 'Cocky much? But aye, thank you. That was better than a lava cake.'

'You *did* earn it. You *do* deserve it.' He tucked a strand of hair behind her ear.

'What, for cooking?'

'For being you. I can't resist you, Rowan. I can't. You're the only real thing. The only one who cares for me. The only one.'

Bright joy lit up inside her. Like popping the cork on a shaken bottle. She hadn't expected *this*. Not from him. Not after the past few days. Not so freely given.

But it was everything she wanted.

She ached to freeze this moment, hoard it, live inside it forever.

He lifted her into his arms – a girl could get used to that mode of transport – and carried her out of the kitchen.

'Let's go to bed. Because you see, wifey,' he said and gently nipped her earlobe. 'I haven't had *my* dessert yet.'

Chapter Nineteen

The flagstone floor chilled Rowan's bare feet as she padded into Dunmarach's kitchen. Max's white shirt shifted around her thighs, still holding traces of his cologne. Her legs threatened to give out. No wonder.

Who knew that being married meant having so much sex? It was as if their bodies connected in a way that they couldn't fully understand yet.

And this new life fit her better each day.

Three weeks ago, she'd needed a map to find the kitchen. Now she navigated these halls in the middle of the night by muscle memory, knowing which floorboards creaked.

She reached for a glass. The pipes grumbled as she filled it at the sink like the castle itself was commenting on her late-night wandering. 'Next thing you know, you'll be embroidering his initials on handkerchiefs.'

Moonlight spilled through the tall windows across the worktops. Her reflection in the window caught her eye – hair mussed, lips swollen from Max's kisses.

The truth crackled beneath her skin like electricity. She'd gone and done the one thing she'd sworn to avoid. The one thing she hadn't even thought was possible. Because it made zero sense.

She'd fallen for Maxwell Drummond. Hard and fast.

For Moody MacDarcy, with his suits and scars and elegant hands. The way he touched her like she might shatter, then held her together when she did. The quiet strength in his arms when he'd carried her upstairs earlier, refusing to let her walk on legs that were useless beneath her.

'You've fallen in love with your husband. Bit backwards, but when have you ever done anything the normal way?'

Husband.

The word felt not awkward anymore.

Her phone lay forgotten by the fruit bowl, its screen dark.

'Some plan that turned out to be.' She picked up the phone, smiling. 'Marry the grumpy heir, write the story, keep it professional, move on. A1 execution there.'

The phone's screen blazed to life, its blue glow harsh in the moonlit kitchen. Seventeen missed calls. Nine texts. Three voicemails.

What the…?

Rowan's fingers went numb as she scrolled through the messages, each one more pressing than the one before. The words spun into a kaleidoscope of nightmares: Fall. Stairs. Blood. Hospital. Come now.

'No, no, no.' The glass wobbled in her grip, water splashed across her feet. The cold barely registered.

Her gran had wandered downstairs at some point before midnight. Confused and partially undressed. Found face-down at the bottom of the care home stairs, trousers tangled around her ankles. Head trauma. Currently unconscious at The Queen Elizabeth in Glasgow.

The kitchen reeled out of focus. Rowan grabbed the counter, her wedding ring clicking against marble. She'd been here in the Highlands, playing house and tossing around in expensive sheets while her wee gran lay bleeding on institutional linoleum.

'Fuck. FUCK!' The word echoed off ancient stones, splintering in the silence. 'I should've been there. I should've—'

But she'd been here instead, pretending to be someone she wasn't.

Would never be.

Her breaths shrunk with every second. The moonlight seemed to strobe and the muscles in her legs seized, balance teetering on the edge.

Her mother's last message glowed accusingly:

MAW (2:01) Where are you??? Are you ok??

'Living in a fake fairy tale while she's dying. God.' Rowan's voice frayed as she darted out of the kitchen.

The word 'dying' hit her like a physical blow. Memories flooded in. Her gran teaching her to make Scottish macaroons with mashed tatties, singing off-key to the radio. She could still picture her gran's hands sewing her torn school blazer. 'Ye're ma wee fighter,' she'd said with a wink, the needle flashing in the lamplight. 'Never let any wanker grind ye doon.'

And now her gran was lying in hospital and Rowan hadn't been there to accompany her.

'Please,' she prayed to whatever goddess might be listening. 'Please. Please don't take her. Not like this. Not yet. Not yet...'

Adrenaline kicked in. She needed clothes. Her bag. A quick way back to Glasgow.

Why did I marry the only Highland millionaire without a helicopter?

Rowan bolted for the stairs. She took the steps two at a time, her breath coming in frantic gasps that sounded like sobs.

She barrelled into the bedroom and fumbled for the light switch. The bedside lamp cast harsh shadows across the rumpled sheets where Max lay sleeping, his dark hair tousled against white cotton.

'Max! Wake up. Please wake up! Please!'

He jerked upright, one hand rising to shield his eyes. 'Rowan? What… What's wrong?'

'Gran fell.' The words tumbled out. 'Head trauma. She's in hospital, and I wasn't—' Her hands fumbled with a jumper, dropping it twice. 'I was here playing princess while she was—'

She yanked open drawers at random, searching for clothes. 'I need to go. Now.'

Max sat up. 'Calm down. Tell me what happened.'

'I can't calm down!' Rowan stood by the bed, struggling to get dressed as the room around her warped. 'She's hurt and unconscious, and I wasn't there and—' Her hands shook as she tried to button her jeans. 'Shit!'

'Stop.' He caught her wrist. 'Take a breath.'

She wrenched away. 'Don't tell me to breathe! My gran's dying, and I've been too busy shagging you to even check my bloody phone! Oh God…'

'She's not dying.' His tone was annoyingly metered. 'You're panicking. Catastrophising.'

'Catastrophising?' Rowan whipped around. 'She cracked her skull on care home stairs! While I was here letting you fuck me!'

'Let me help you calm down, look at it logically.' He swung his legs over the bed's edge.

'No!' She spun away. 'I don't need logic, we need to get to Glasgow. Right now!'

'I'll have Oliver bring the car around so he can take you.' Max reached for his phone. 'At three in the morning, the Maybach will be faster and safer than a taxi. That could take hours – if they would even send one out here.'

'What do you mean, he can take *me*? What about you?' she asked.

'I have to stay,' he said, typing out a text like this was just another problem to be managed, not her entire world cracking in half.

She didn't need a plan. She didn't need his driver.

She needed him.

'That's your solution? Send the help?' Her laugh cracked. 'You're going to send me off with your chauffeur?'

Max's thumbs paused over the screen. 'Would you prefer to drive yourself? It's the middle of the night and these roads—'

'I'd prefer my husband to come with me! But that would require actual emotional investment, wouldn't it? And that's not in your portfolio.'

'Rowan.' His voice held a warning note. 'I have an important online meeting first thing tomorrow that can't be postponed. It's an informal hearing and involves sensitive documents that I can't carry around in public, so I need to be here. Missing this meeting would only fuel the trustee's doubts. Blackwood and the trust—'

'Oh, fuck the trust!' She yanked a jumper over her head. 'My gran is dying, and you're worried about meetings? There are things more important than stupid meetings.'

'I'm not a doctor. There's nothing I can do in Glasgow except sit in a waiting room. And she's not dying.'

'I know you have a god complex, but you're not God, and you don't know she isn't! But hey, at least the trust won't be inconvenienced.'

He frowned. 'You're being unfair and irrational.'

'Unfair? Irrational?' She spun to face him head-on. 'You're dismissing my emotions. That's fucking insulting.'

'This situation isn't my fault.' Max rose to his full height, raking a hand through his hair. 'But I'm handling it.'

'Handling it is not the same as showing up!' She forced

her feet into her boots, not bothering with the laces. 'But I forgot, you don't do messy emotions, do you?'

'I told you, you can't fix me. You know who I am.' His voice darkened. 'Don't pretend otherwise.'

'Aye. My mistake for believing there was more.'

He glared down at her. For a second, just one second, she saw it. Not indifference, but fear. The kind that looked like coldness because he didn't know what else to do with it.

And if she weren't already drowning, maybe she'd have the strength to carry his fear, too. But not right now. Not when everything was splitting open, and he was just...standing there.

'What do you want from me?' he asked. 'I'm arranging transport, ensuring you have everything you need—'

'I want you to care! I want you to come with me!' The words exploded from her chest. 'God forbid you truly show up for someone.'

He was right.

This was who he was.

Silence fell between them like cooling embers and soot. Max's face turned to stone. That perfect mask slid back into place.

'You're upset. We'll discuss this when you're calmer and the situation has cleared.'

'No. We won't. Because I won't be here.'

'The contract stipulates—'

'Screw your contract! My gran might be dying, and you're quoting legal documents at me?' She zipped her bag with force. 'What are you going to do? Sue me? Have me arrested for breach of contract? Go ahead, I dare you.'

He reached for a t-shirt, pulled it over his head, and straightened it. By the time the fabric settled over his skin, so did his expression. Impassive. Untouchable.

When he finally spoke, his tone was clipped. 'Three days. That's how long you have before you breach the contract.'

Rowan's chest closed up. An hour ago, he'd kissed her there, everywhere. Now he spoke of legal terms.

She grabbed her bag with numb fingers. 'Thanks for clarifying where we stand.'

'Rowan…'

The syllables held more than her name. A plea or an order, she couldn't tell. Something unfinished.

She shouldered past him, vision all blurry. 'Message received. Loud and clear.'

'Where are you going in Glasgow, which hospital?'

'Queen Elizabeth.' Her hand closed around the doorknob. 'To be with my *actual* family.'

'And after?'

'I don't know. Maybe I'll breach your precious contract. Maybe I'll come back. Maybe I'll tell the world how Maxwell Drummond bought himself a wife and couldn't even pretend to love her.'

'That's enough.' His tone turned caustic. 'You're lashing out because you're upset. But don't say things you can't take back.'

She turned, locking eyes with him one last time. 'You know the worst part, Max? For a minute – for one stupid minute – I let myself believe you might feel something for me. That this had become something real.'

She didn't wait for his response. It didn't matter. It never had.

The door closed behind her with a click that punched through her chest.

She ran down the corridor. Dunmarach's shadows reached for her, but she was done playing princess in this fairy tale gone wrong. Time to return to the real world, where grandmothers fell down stairs and love wasn't enough to bridge the gap between fantasy and reality.

Did he come after her? Of course he didn't.

Behind her, Max's silence spoke volumes in a language she

no longer wanted to understand. The old beams creaked as the castle settled.

Or maybe that was the sound of her heart breaking.

Chapter Twenty

The grandfather clock's ticking gnawed at Max. Seven hours and fifteen minutes since Rowan had taken off. A forgotten scrunchie on his desk taunted him with its casual intimacy.

He picked up his phone again. No messages.

'Goddammit.' The curse burst out on a harsh breath as he dropped into the chair.

The virtual meeting with the trust had been strained, yet manageable. Blackwood's vague hints at 'unusual expenditures' tied to Rowan's arrival were designed to plant seeds of doubt. Max had deflected, though this had only been Blackwood's opening salvo.

For now, the trustees seemed pacified.

That bastard knew what he was doing. Blackwood might not have tangible proof yet – otherwise, he would have thrown it on the table – but he was sure as hell looking for it.

Which was why Max had to make sure that there was no traceable record linking his finances to Rowan. That had kept him busy for a few days. Evidence erased, tracks covered, favours called in. Making sure that no one could follow the money. A textbook exercise in finance. His life's work.

So why did his hands feel numb and empty?

The study seemed heavy without the possibility of her barging in. When had this space begun to feel wrong without her sprawled across the antique furniture, asking impossible questions?

Max slid his hand on the spot where she had sat yesterday morning.

'This is pathetic.' He pushed the chair away from the desk, but couldn't flee the memory of her scent – vanilla and citrus, sunshine and trouble.

A stack of contracts waited for his signature. Important documents. Time-sensitive decisions. He stood there and stared at it until the words swam. All he could see was her face last night when she told him she needed him. And he didn't know how to be needed. He'd never learned.

How many messages had he sent? Too many.

Are you safe? Is your gran okay? Talk to me.

Yes, pathetic.

The walls inched closer, lined with Drummonds who had never let emotion cloud their judgement. Who had never compromised. Certainly not for a woman with wicked green eyes, a huge heart, and a laugh that cracked foundations.

Get it together.

The silence held no answers. Only memories of her voice filling these dusty corners with life. The way she had challenged him, seen through him, made him question everything he thought he knew.

Kissed him.

Summer rain drummed against the windows. Somewhere out there in Glasgow, Rowan was cursing his name. The thought tugged at something vital inside him.

His reflection fragmented across the window glass – a stranger with haunted eyes and too many shadows. The man she had begun to trust.

Your mistake, little writer.

The study clock struck one, its chime echoing through empty corridors. Another hour without word.

Without Rowan.

Mrs MacPherson's voice brooked no argument. She planted both hands on the worktop and fixed Max with the same stern look she had used when he was eight, refusing vegetables. 'When's the last time you ate?'

He hesitated. 'I had coffee this morning.'

'Coffee isn't food.' The kettle whistled, and she poured two cups of tea. 'And you're not seventeen anymore, running on caffeine and willpower.'

'I'm not hungry.' A day without food had left him light-headed, but the thought of eating closed his throat up.

She pulled out a chair. 'Please park yourself, Maxwell Drummond.'

The childhood echo in her tone made him comply before his brain caught up. Mrs Mac nodded once, satisfied, and turned to the Aga. The familiar sounds of her puttering about the kitchen pushed against his skull – metal against metal, water running, cupboards opening and closing.

A plate appeared before him. Plain toast with butter.

'That won't eat itself.' Her practical tone cut through his brooding.

The bread's yeasty scent turned his stomach.

'Small bites,' she instructed. 'And stop grinding your teeth. You'll wear them to nubs.'

Mrs MacPherson had always been more than the house-keeper. After his parents shipped him to university, she had been the only one who reached out. Her letters, filled with mundane updates about Dunmarach, had been a lifeline he had gradually ignored. Eventually, those stopped coming too, and he had told himself it was for the best.

He had spent years treating her like any other employee,

all while she had remained a constant in a life he had done his best to compartmentalise. So she was, in some unspoken way, the closest thing he had to an old friend.

Max made himself take a bite.

The ceramic mug clicked against the table as she set it before him. Earl Grey, a splash of milk, no sugar – just as he had drunk it since his Fettes days.

His fingers tapped against his thighs. Rowan would have noticed that tell. Would have called him out on it with that knowing half-smile.

'You're looking like death warmed over, if you don't mind me telling you,' Mrs MacPherson stated.

'I'm fine.'

'Are you?' She sat down across from him, her own tea cradled between weathered hands. 'Because that toast tells a different story.'

Max's fingers tapped against the table's scarred surface. How many meals had he eaten here as a boy, hiding from his father? From everything?

'Have you heard from her?' Mrs MacPherson's question held no judgement, only quiet concern.

'Her grandmother is stable.' The words clung to his tongue. 'According to Oliver.'

'That's not what I asked.'

'She won't answer my calls,' he said quietly.

'Can you blame her?'

'Pardon me?' His head shot up. 'Whose side are you on?'

'Marriage isn't about sides.' She took a sip of tea. 'It's about showing up. Being there. Even when it's messy and inconvenient and you don't have all the answers.'

Max stared at the tea in his hands. Showing up? What did that even mean?

'It's not that simple,' he said.

Her shrewd eyes fixed on him. 'Isn't it?'

'The trust could take everything if—'

'Everything?' She set her mug down. 'These stones have stood for centuries. They don't care about you. But that lass? She needed her husband. Not his driver. Not his money. Him. That's what marriage is about. Not money or a castle or that distillery.'

'How do you know—'

'My eyes are everywhere,' she said. 'And Lady Drummond texted me. Vague, of course. Just so I wouldn't worry. And Ollie called. Didn't take much to put one and one together.'

Lady Drummond.

His voice faltered. 'I couldn't—'

'Drop everything and go with her?' Mrs MacPherson leaned forward. 'You're not your father, if you don't mind me saying, and it's high time you stopped trying to be.'

The words landed like a stone dropping into the pit of his stomach. For a moment, he couldn't speak, couldn't breathe. He had spent so much of his life trying to hold it all together, to dominate every piece on the board.

Max pushed back from the table. 'You're overstepping.'

'Och, hush.' She waved off his protest. 'I've known you since you were knee-high to a grasshopper. I see more than you think.' His glare didn't so much as make her blink. 'That girl brought light back to these halls. Made you smile again. Real smiles. I haven't seen you smile like that since before Martin.'

'Mrs MacPherson—'

'Your family isn't around anymore, so I'm the one left to talk to you. Marriage isn't a business deal. It's standing by them when your spouse needs you, even if all you can do is hold their hand while the world falls apart. It's choosing them, every day. *Especially* when it's hard.'

His fingers dug into his thighs. Outside, rain lashed against leaded glass, each drop an echo of Rowan's parting words: *'For a minute – for one stupid minute – I let myself believe you might feel something for me.'*

Did he…love her?

Yes.

'I'm not sure… I mean, I don't know how to—'

'Be there? You start by showing up, day by day. The rest follows.'

Steam no longer rose from the tea. Like everything else lately, it had gone cold while he wasn't paying attention.

'What if I'm not—' He glanced away, biting his lip to stifle the unease. 'What if I can't be what she needs?'

'First of all, you're already married, so it's a wee bit late for that. And then it's not for you to decide what she needs. That lass is clever and has a good heart. She knows what and who she wants.' Mrs MacPherson stood and gathered his mug. 'Glasgow's only three and a half hours away. My Cameron lives down there, I visit him every month.'

'Thank you, Mrs Mac.' He had no idea why he used her childhood nickname.

She smiled fondly. 'Eat something proper first. You're no good to anyone running on empty.'

Mrs Mac left him in the kitchen alone with the growing certainty that he had got everything wrong.

Max's footsteps resonated through the study. The stag's head that had terrified him as a child and mocked him later, now watched with quiet understanding. It had become his space, shaped by late nights reviewing contracts and early mornings with Rowan claiming the space as effortlessly as his attention.

He traced the faint ring her tea mug had left. A tiny act of anarchy, soaking into the grain of his pristine world.

'Drummond, you fool.' The words were meant only for himself and the stag. 'She was never just part of an arrangement, was she?'

The moment she had looked at him, trying to tell him she had shown up to trim the trees... The moment she didn't yield a single inch. The moment she didn't see Laird Maxwell Drummond of Dunmarach, London financier and Highland whisky heir.

Just...Max.

All that cheek she had given him from minute one.

He never stood a chance.

And right from the beginning, Rowan had refused to fit into any boxes he had tried to put her in. Trespasser. Convenient solution. Contract wife. She had blown past every boundary.

The trust's latest report lay unopened on his desk. Paper and ink, nothing more. His father would have prioritised these documents over everything. Over everyone.

'I'm not him.' The words hung in the air, simple and true.

Mrs Mac was right. The revelation took hold in him with quiet certainty. He wasn't his father, but he also wasn't Martin, and Rowan most certainly wasn't another asset to be managed.

She was the woman who had brought warmth back to these cold halls. Who faced down his demons with nothing but sass, kindness, and unwavering faith. Who saw past his walls and scars to the man beneath – and opened herself up to him anyway.

Until he had failed her when she needed him.

The spare set of keys for the distillery's Land Rover lay in a bowl on the corner of the desk. Three and a half hours to Glasgow. To Rowan. To the only family alive, the only family that mattered.

Max picked up the keys. The trust could wait. The legacy could wait. Everything could wait. Right now, his wife needed him.

The study door closed behind him with quiet finality. His

steps echoed through Dunmarach's halls. He knew what he had to do.

The Land Rover's keys bit into Max's fingers as he approached the vehicle. Its hulking silhouette loomed in the gathering dusk, a beast of metal and memories waiting to devour him.

Thirteen years since he had sat behind a wheel. The door handle felt alien beneath his fingers, cold and unforgiving. He pulled it open and shut himself in with the scent of engine oil and mud.

His body remembered this – the subtle give of suspension, the dormant power.

Max's hand trembled as he adjusted the mirror. The ghost of that seventeen-year-old boy stared back. Every breath stuttered like he had forgotten how to inhale. The steering wheel's grip pattern dug into his palms. Rough and textured. Nothing like the Porsche's smooth leather.

Cold sweat gathered on his forehead.

'You can do this.' His voice sounded wrong in the enclosed space. Too tight. Rain drummed against the roof, its rhythm morphing into the screech of tyres on wet tarmac. The taste of copper flooded his mouth. Martin's laugh cut short. Blood on leather.

Max's fingers cramped around the steering wheel. Cold sweat trickled down his spine. The cabin walls closed in. He fumbled for the window control, desperate for oxygen that didn't taste of burning rubber.

Rowan's voice pierced through his panic. A memory, vivid and clear: '*Max, you're not made of stone. You just act like it.*'

The words anchored him to now. To purpose. To her.

He willed his mind back to the present. The rain wasn't metal. The air didn't reek of burning rubber. He wasn't seventeen anymore.

Three and a half hours to Glasgow. To redemption. To the only person who had ever seen past his walls to the scared boy beneath and loved them both.

He forced air into his lungs. The ignition key slotted home with a metallic click that echoed through each of his molecules. One turn. That was all it would take. One moment of courage.

Now he realised how much he had let fear govern him. His life.

He had passed his test, and his license had sat untouched in his wallet, valid but useless.

He shouldn't be driving alone. He shouldn't be driving. But if he stayed here, if he let fear root him in place again, he would lose her. She wouldn't wait forever. Not for a man too afraid to meet her halfway.

And losing her would be the only thing he couldn't survive.

'I choose her. I choose us.' He drew a shaky breath and turned the key. The engine roared to life, its purr drowning out the sirens in his head. Max's knuckles whitened on the steering wheel as he eased the Land Rover into first gear. He was ready.

Chapter Twenty-One

The thin hospital blanket chafed against Rowan's cheek as she pressed it to her nose, searching for hints of her gran's lavender soap beneath the antiseptic. Nothing.

She smoothed a strand of silver hair back from her gran's forehead, and her thumb skimmed against the bandage. She'd always been so put together. Rowan remembered standing on a kitchen stool as a kid, determined to style her gran's hair like the ladies in the magazines. It ended with half a can of hairspray and enough hair grips to set off a metal detector, but her gran had laughed and worn it the rest of the day like it was salon chic.

And the chin hairs... Christ, the chin hairs. Rowan had become a professional tweezers-wielder by the time she was twelve, plucking them out while her gran made jokes about ageing ungracefully.

Rowan had promised herself – no matter what happened, she'd keep showing up for her gran the way her gran had always shown up for her.

The monitors beeped their incessant rhythm, marking time in this liminal space. A black bruise bloomed across her gran's temple underneath her bandage. At least the doctors said she'd heal. Physically, anyway.

The dementia ward's brochure sat on the bedside table, its glossy pages promising 'round-the-clock care' and 'secure environments.' Such sterile words for such a heart-wrenching change.

'I met someone, Gran.' The words slipped out soft as a secret. 'He's irritating. Frustrating. Very wounded. And I bolted like a scared rabbit when things got real and I was in panic mode. You know me.'

Her phone lay silent in her pocket, heavy with unanswered messages. Max's last text burned in her memory: *'Talk to me.'*

'He's looking at me like he's reading a book with missing pages.' She smoothed a wrinkle from the blanket. 'But I don't know if I can handle his inherited damage.'

The night nurse passed by, rubber soles squeaking against linoleum. Through the window, Glasgow's lights over the Clyde painted the sky in shades of amber, purple, and regret.

'I miss him, Gran.' The confession sat heavy on her tongue. 'His stupid suits and the way he pretends not to smile at my jokes. How he knows what I need, except when it matters most. I just wish he'd be more emotionally available.'

A flash of hurt pierced her heart at the thought.

'You'd like him, I think. He's got Grandda's dark hair and light eyes.'

The door creaked, followed by the familiar tap of her mum's feet.

'Any change?' Her mother's voice was worn thin by worry and double shifts.

Rowan shook her head. The scans didn't show any severe or permanent damage. They'd said she'd wake up soon, but every hour stretched like it had its own gravity. And what if she woke up even more confused? For now, all they could do was wait.

'Want to talk? Maybe…tell me about him?' Her mum let herself sink into the other chair next to Rowan's.

'Och, I wouldn't even know where to start.'

'The beginning's usually good,' her mum said.

'Which beginning? The one where I broke into his castle or the one where I married him?'

'You broke into his castle? I don't think I ever got the whole story.'

'Technically, I scaled a crumbling wall to take a peek.' Rowan picked at a loose thread on the blanket. 'Which sounds more romantic and less criminal.'

'Christ, child.' Her mum's laugh held equal parts exasperation and fondness. 'Well, you never did anything by halves.'

'Says the woman who worked two jobs to put me through school and uni.'

'Ah, well. About that. See, I thought I was setting a good example. Show you that a woman doesn't need anyone. That being strong meant never asking for help.'

'You were brilliant, mum.'

'Naw, I was terrified.' Her mother's fingers closed around hers. 'Every minute of every day. Of not giving you enough, of not getting us through. But instead of admitting it, I worked harder. Pretended everything was fine.'

Rowan shifted in her seat. 'Fake it till you make it?'

'More like fake it till you break. And you learned that lesson too well, my darlin'. The whole "I don't need anyone, I'm better off on my own"-act.'

'It's not an act—'

Her mum folded her arms and shifted gears. 'This husband of yours. Tell me about him.'

A watery laugh bubbled up. 'He's thick-headed with a stick up his arse. Closed off. But he also…sees me.' The words peeled back layers she didn't know she'd been protecting. 'Even when I wish he wouldn't.'

'And?'

'What and?'

'There must be more to him. Why did you marry him?'

'For the money, mother.'

'Stop taking the piss, child.'

'I wanted the money so you can work less and Gran can get the best care. See where it got me?'

'Rowan, I don't… I don't know what to say. You married a man for his cash?'

'Hold your horses. I'm not the first person in history to do so, and I won't be the last.'

Her mum gave her the same look she'd always used when asking if Rowan had been smoking out of her room's window.

'I don't believe you, my darlin'.'

'What? Why?'

'Because I know my daughter. You're intrinsically motivated. You'd never, ever do anything for the money.'

'But I—'

'Aye, you might have told yourself that, but we both know that's not the reason you said yes.'

'Mum, I—'

'Be honest with yourself. Tell me why you like him.'

'What do you want to hear? He's got his own damage. Lost his brother in a car accident when he was seventeen.'

Rowan kept turning her wedding ring. She hadn't taken it off. Why not? It didn't mean anything, right?

'He hasn't driven since, that's why Ollie's here. Won't talk much about it. And sometimes I catch him watching me like…like he's afraid I'll vanish if he blinks.'

'I've heard of worse lads. So when things got difficult and too real, you ran.'

'I didn't—' Rowan stopped. 'Okay, aye. I absolutely did.'

'I know you did because that's what I would've done, and I was the one who taught you to do it.' Her mother's sad smile held decades of regret. 'Needing people isn't weakness, love. Neither is expecting them to show up when it matters.'

'Even if they kind of don't?'

'Especially then.' Her mum's palm rested against her cheek. 'I know where this is coming from. Your dad leaving… That wasn't about me or you being unlovable. That was about him being an arse and a coward and a lowlife.'

The truth of it stung like antiseptic on an open wound.

'Maybe,' Rowan said.

'Have a think about it. I should go check on your gran's chart at the nurses' station.' Her mum stood and kissed her on the cheek. 'I love you.'

'Love you, too.'

Rowan watched her mother walk out the door. Her words seeped in like summer sunrise, gradual but undeniable. She'd spent so long building walls, she'd forgotten how to build bridges instead.

Her phone beeped. One new message.

> MAX (22:34) I'm outside. If you want me to leave, I will. But I'm here.

Rowan stared at the screen. The message was simple, almost disarmingly so.

I'm here.

Why did he suddenly show up like a knight in tailored armour? Why now? Guilt? Obligation? The fear that he'd lose his estate without her? A thousand potential replies crowded her mind: sarcasm, deflection, anger, even a simple 'okay'. Instead, she reread the text for the fourth time. Her heart hammered against her ribs, that impulsive little thing.

Rowan chewed on her bottom lip. Maybe it was the way he'd worded it, offering her the choice. Briefly, she was poised to type something biting. Old habit. Instead, she typed:

> Institute of Neurological Sciences, ward 68, room 4

And then she waited.

Footsteps echoed down the corridor. Even before he appeared in the doorway, Rowan knew it was him.

Max knocked quietly and opened the door.

He filled the doorframe like a storm front. His suit jacket was gone, sleeves up to his elbows, collar undone, tie nowhere to be seen. Water clung to him in patches, soaking into the fabric.

He scanned the room, but he didn't linger on anything for more than a beat. The way his jaw flexed when their eyes met gave him away. He was trying hard to hold himself together. Max shot a quick, almost imperceptible glance toward her hands clasped in her lap.

He wants to see if I'm still wearing my ring.

It hit her square in the chest. For all his usual poise and power, he seemed like a man who had no idea how to fix what had broken between them.

'Jeez, you look like pure shite,' Rowan blurted.

'And you look worried.'

Her mum looked up from her crossword with a smirk. 'And who's this then, gallivanting in like Lord Muck?'

'Max Drummond, ma'am.' He stepped forward, offering his hand. 'Rowan's…husband. Mrs MacKay. I apologise for arriving unannounced—'

Her mother's eyes sparkled as she shook his hand. 'Did you bring a change of clothes? Because those fancy shoes are about ready for the bin.'

'Mum!' Rowan hissed, her cheeks fusing with heat.

'What? I'm making conversation with my new son-in-law,

whom I'm meeting over three weeks *after* the wedding, might I add.'

He absorbed the hit without a twitch. 'The shoes are replaceable. Other things aren't.'

A strange tightness pulled in Rowan's chest, as though her heart was testing its boundaries.

'Right, Mum. Weren't you going to…check Gran's charts?'

'Was I?' Her mother's innocent look wouldn't have fooled a toddler. 'Oh aye, suppose I was.' She gathered her handbag. 'You two sort yourselves out.'

She patted Max's arm as she passed. 'Welcome to the family. We're all mad here.' But then she paused at the door, fixing him with a look that could peel wallpaper. 'And son?'

'Yes, ma'am?'

'Next time my daughter needs you, maybe skip the chauffeur, aye?'

His throat worked. 'Noted.'

That's what you get when you tell your mum everything. Well, almost everything.

Max's attention landed on her gran's sleeping form with quiet concern. 'How is she?'

'Stable. The doctors say she'll recover. But she needs… The dementia ward has a space opening next week.'

'Ah.' He pulled the spare chair closer and sat down.

A waft of his cologne mingled with the smell of rain as he sat down beside her. 'Tell me what you need.'

A hundred responses crowded Rowan's head.

I need you to have been here yesterday. I need to know why you came now. I need to understand why my heart speeds up when you're near, even when I want to throw things at you.

Instead, she whispered, 'Just…stay?'

His hand found hers across the narrow space between their chairs, warm and solid and real.

'As long as you want.' The promise lingered between them, delicate as breath on glass.

'I'm sorry.' They spoke together, words overlapping.

Her laugh caught on the verge of a sob she refused to let out. 'You first.'

His shoulders caved slightly. He looked uncertain.

'Seriously, you first,' she repeated.

'Rowan. I'm…truly sorry.'

'Okay. And I'm still truly cross.'

'I would be worried if you weren't.' The hint of a grin teased at the corner of his mouth. 'But I'm here. No more excuses.'

She wanted to believe him.

'What if it's not enough?', she asked. 'What if we're too broken to make this work?'

'We'll figure it out together. We try. Even if we fall flat on our faces, I would rather fall with you than stand alone and pretend I don't care.'

The tension in her chest loosened, enough to breathe again.

'We need to talk about things, Max. But not before I've had coffee. I can't think straight.'

'Consider it done.' The scrape of his chair cut through the silence. At the door, he glanced back at her with a look that was almost too raw to hold. 'I'll be back.'

It felt like a vow.

A real one.

The door closed, and she looked down at her gran's hand, small and warm under hers.

'What do I even do with someone like him? He doesn't wear his heart on his sleeve, but I know he has one beating in there. You'd tell me to give him a chance, wouldn't you? You're such a hopeless romantic.'

Rowan bit the inside of her cheek. What if he was here out of guilt? Or worse, what if this was another of his moves? Max could charm a room full of suits without breaking a sweat. But she'd seen the fault lines, hadn't she? The way his voice had wavered, the hesitation in his step.

Perhaps he was as terrified as she was of what came next.

This was about their future. Whether they had one or not.

He was a rich finance guy who had an egg and a spreadsheet for breakfast. A laird! She was a starving writer, who spent more time arguing with editors over money than sleeping.

Yet somehow, they'd found the part in each other that made them feel complete.

Max wasn't afraid of her constant need to push. He didn't just tolerate her challenges and shenanigans – he met them head-on, matching her wit for wit until she was breathless with frustration or laughter. And when she pushed too far, testing boundaries to see if she could, he didn't waver. He pushed back, not to break her but to ground her.

Max wasn't intimidated by the parts of her that others found too much.

He *wanted* them.

The machines droned beside her. Her gran's mantra had always been the same: 'It isnae aboot the fall, it's aboot getting back up.'

And as much as she hated admitting it, Max was here now. Not with grand speeches or efficient solutions. Just here, messy and human and real. Was that enough?

The door opened.

Chapter Twenty-Two

The paper cup warmed Rowan's palms as Max passed it into her hands. Steam curled between them, carrying the burnt-coffee smell unique to hospital vending machines.

He sat down on the chair beside her and gripped his drink, but his hands wouldn't stay still.

'You're shaking,' she said.

'Side effect of driving through Scottish rain for hours.'

Her brain stalled. 'Wait. Ollie's at the hotel, so how did you—'

'I took Slater's Land Rover.'

The cup nearly slipped from her fingers. 'You *drove*? In a car? By yourself? The first time since—'

'Yes.'

'Oh God. Max.' Her voice wavered on his name.

'I had to be with you. Though hospitals still make me feel...' His jaw worked. 'Powerless.'

'That's so brave of you.' The words edged out, quiet but firm.

'I did it for you. Because you needed me.'

In that moment, she glimpsed the seventeen-year-old boy beneath the man.

'I should have come with you yesterday, Rowan. Not sent Oliver. Not quoted contracts at you. Been here, holding your hand.'

The fluorescent lights washed him pale, emphasising the dark circles beneath his eyes.

'Oh, aye. Not gonna fight you on that. You should've. But...I also shouldn't have stormed off like that. Or ignored your texts. I was scared for my gran, yeah, but also...' The truth lodged in her throat. 'I was...scared of depending on you. That you'd let me down if I let you get any closer.'

His hand found hers again. 'It was a family emergency. You were upset. You had to go.'

'Aye, but I didn't have to be such a weapons-grade harpy about it.'

A smile touched his lips. 'Your meltdown had remarkable range.'

'Och, fuck off.' But warmth bloomed in her chest. 'I'm trying to apologise here.'

'I know.' He bumped his knee against hers. 'So am I.'

'I shouldn't have shut you out,' she said and laced her fingers through his. 'That was me being a coward. A weird mix of self-preservation and emotional overwhelm.'

'No. You're the most fearless person I know.' His voice dropped lower. 'I lied. To myself. About this being business. About us.'

Her pulse skipped. 'Max—'

'But I didn't lie to Blackwood when I told him I knew you were the one the moment I saw you. I *knew*. That first day in the kitchen, when you stood there like you belonged. Like you weren't scared of me, or this place, or any of it. And I...' He swallowed hard. 'I wanted to keep you.'

He gathered his thoughts. When he spoke again, his voice held a vulnerability that left her defences waving a white flag.

'Let me be honest, Rowan. You terrify me.'

She laughed. 'You're a six-foot, uber-rich control freak and *I* terrify you?'

His thumb swept over her knuckles, tender and certain. 'Because you see everything. Every wall, every mask. And you don't look away.'

Tears pricked at her eyes.

'You make me want things I never let myself want,' he said.

Her stomach dipped. 'Like what?'

'Like hearing you sing in the shower. Like you on my desk, reminding me there's more to life than work and money. Like—' He hesitated, shook his head. 'Like waking up next to you every day, knowing I get to fall for you all over again.'

His other hand found her cheek, fingers trailing like he needed to memorise the shape of her. 'I love that you throw yourself into everything. Your work, your family, and every lost cause that crosses your path. You never hesitate. Even when it costs you.'

She made a small, broken sound.

'I love that you dug through the Drummond past and found things everyone else chose to ignore. I love that you make people laugh, even when they've forgotten how. That you walk into any room and claim space like you were born to take up more of it than anyone else.'

'Max—'

'Still not finished. I had a long drive to think.' A wry tilt of his mouth. 'I love you because you make me brave.' His voice wavered between confession and surrender. 'Brave enough to get in a car. Brave enough to sit in this hospital. Brave enough to take on the trust. Brave enough to look at you right now and tell you…' He took a breath. '…that I fell for you the second you trespassed into my life. Hard.'

A sob lodged between her ribs, trying to claw its way out.

'I love how you make me believe I can be better, even when I don't see it myself. I love you, Rowan Drummond. Not because of a contract. Not because of an arrangement. Because it's you. It can only be you. I drove through a rainstorm because the thought of losing you was worse than thirteen years of fear. You're the only wife I want. If you don't… I…' He leaned his forehead against hers. 'Just let me love you. Please.'

A ragged breath escaped her. Then another. And then she was folding into him, his arms solid and certain around her.

'Drummond, you absolute arse,' she whispered against his neck. 'Coming in here with your perfect speech and your perfect face, making me *feel* things.'

He huffed a soft laugh against her hair. 'Ditto.'

She pulled back. 'I had a plan, you know. Sulking until Tuesday, maybe some light forgiveness by Friday.'

Any trace of amusement slipped away as she felt the slight tremor in his hands from hours of gripping a steering wheel.

'You seriously *drove* here. You faced everything, just to sit in this awful chair and drink disgusting battery acid coffee with me.'

'For my wife? Worth every white-knuckled mile.'

Something inside her gave way, flooding her veins with warmth. 'I've spent my life running and hiding,' she admitted. 'From feelings, from commitment, from anything that felt too real. But… For the first time… You make me want to stand still.'

'As if you could ever—'

'No. My turn.' She pressed a finger to his lips. 'I'm shite at this, but I need to say it properly. I love you, too, Maxwell Alexander Drummond, Laird of Dunmarach.'

Colour crept into his neck and face. And he stared. Like a man who'd never expected to hear those words and didn't know what to do with them now. Like a fortress giving way to the siege.

'I love that you're a ruthless shark in the boardroom and with Blackwood, but so kind to Mrs Mac and Ollie. I love that you wear suits like chain mail, but let me see all your battle scars. Also, I love how you get really, really filthy when you're turned on.'

A brisk inhale, almost a flinch. He raked a hand through his hair – flattered, embarrassed, or both.

'I love that you see me and never once asked me to be smaller or quieter or anything less than who I am. And I love that you're scared of the same things I am, Max. Letting people in. Trusting someone with your heart. But you do it anyway. With me, you do it anyway.'

A hot blur crept into her vision, but she blinked it away. 'I've always been too much – too loud, too independent, too hungry. But you never tried to dull my edges. You…match them with your own.'

'My fierce little fighter.'

'You're worth fighting for, Max. Worth loving.'

In that moment, surrounded by institutional beige and the beeping of medical devices, everything slotted into place.

Rowan smiled against his skin. 'I love you,' she said again because now that she'd started, she couldn't stop. 'Because somehow, in this mad world, we fit. We found each other.'

His kiss silenced her. Sweet enough to soothe, wild enough to leave her dizzy. When they broke apart, his smile could have illuminated Glasgow's night sky.

'Don't let it get to your head, but you're the only husband I ever want.'

He picked up his coffee and handed Rowan hers back. 'Even when I colour code my socks?'

'Don't push it, Drummond.'

His laugh ran through her like a low current, and Rowan knew this was home. Max's arms. This was where she belonged. Where she'd always belonged.

A soft sound from the bed drew their attention. Her gran

stirred, eyelids blinking open. Her gaze flickered to the paper cup and then landed on Max. The confusion in her eyes gave way to joy.

'Joe.' Her voice was thin and brittle as a frail smile lit her face. 'Ye finally came.'

Chapter Twenty-Three

The Drummond legacy was on the chopping block, and Blackwood had sharpened his axe.

The low swell of Edinburgh's mid-morning traffic drifted up from the streets below, muffled by the floor-to-ceiling windows. The trust was gathered to pick apart their marriage, every glance and whisper weighing whether Max and Rowan were frauds. And whether Dunmarach would be ripped from their hands.

Ironic. They had been a genuine couple in every way. Waking up holding each other, her hand finding his beneath the table without thinking, his shirts migrating into her wardrobe. Her scent marking home.

And yet here they were, on trial for pretending.

Max's mind was oddly clear despite the weight pressing against his sternum.

Blackwood's voice droned on. '...clear suspicion of premeditation and fraud. A hastily arranged marriage license. No prior relationship history with Miss MacKay. The pattern suggests—'

'Mrs Drummond.' The correction left Max's lips before he

registered speaking. Every head at the long table turned toward him. 'My wife's name is Rowan Drummond.'

Blackwood's lips thinned. 'The pattern suggests a calculated arrangement designed to circumvent the trust's requirements and the will's inheritance clause. Mr Drummond's reputation in the financial sector precedes him. He views everything as a transaction.'

Blackwood had nothing tangible, that much was clear by now, but he tried anyway. Beneath the table, Rowan's hand found Max's thigh, grounding him. It always did.

'Furthermore,' Blackwood brandished another document, 'their living arrangements at Dunmarach raise questions. Separate bedrooms—'

'…which merged within days. There was…snoring,' Max noted. Several trustees shifted uncomfortably.

'After I monitored compliance.' Blackwood's tone dripped with insinuation. 'This trust was created to safeguard the Drummond estate. We might lose the chance to restore its value, potentially even finding a new owner with the vision to capitalise on its true potential.'

Max ground his teeth, a silent battle with his temper. Blackwood's idea of 'true potential' was turning Dunmarach into a museum with a gift shop and offloading the distillery to an overseas conglomerate.

Loyalty to the Drummond legacy, my arse.

Beside him, Rowan radiated quiet fury. He sensed her gathering breath for a blistering retort and touched her wrist – the barest pressure of skin on skin.

Not yet, my fierce little warrior.

'The trust must consider,' Blackwood concluded, 'whether this marriage serves the spirit of the requirements, or merely exploits their letter. Does Miss MacKay – Mrs Drummond – truly understand our heritage? Our responsibilities? Or is she simply—'

'Enough!' Max stood, the word falling like a sword stroke.

Sunlight caught his wedding ring as he planted both palms on the table. 'You want truth? Here it is.'

The room held its breath.

'You're not challenging our marriage. You're trying to take this estate away from us. To control its future, the distillery's profits. Yes, I married her because the clause demanded it. But I stayed because I *love* her.'

The trustees exchanged glances. Blackwood's face mottled.

'You question our – Rowan's – understanding of heritage?' Max gestured to the stack of research papers before him. 'She's spent *weeks* documenting Dunmarach's history. Not the glamorous parts, the hard truths. The clearances. The exploitation of labour. The involvement in the transatlantic trade.'

He met each pair of the trustees' eyes in turn. 'She taught me that true legacy isn't preserving what was but acknowledging where we went wrong.'

'And more than acknowledging it, working to right those wrongs,' Rowan interjected. 'That's why we started the history project. Because no one else will give those stories the respect they deserve. Not Blackwood, not the conglomerates he'd sell us out to. I couldn't live with that, and I don't think you could either.'

'Pretty words,' Blackwood sneered. 'If this sham of a marriage compromises the trust's ability to maintain Dunmarach, we'll ensure it's handed to someone who understands its wo—'

'I drove to Glasgow.' Max's confession silenced Blackwood. 'When her grandmother was in hospital. First time behind the wheel since...Martin died. Thirteen years of avoiding it, letting fear win.'

Rowan's inhale carried in the silence. He didn't dare look at her. He would lose his composure if he did.

'You want more proof?' he asked. 'We're not draining Dunmarach. We're building it up. And the numbers prove it.'

Rowan's eyes burned holes into Blackwood's lapel as she began to speak. 'The distillery's output has increased by twelve per cent. We're tapping into new markets through storytelling, especially by targeting niche audiences and young female consumers.'

'And look at our community engagement initiatives,' Max added. 'The history project my wife has started with local families. She doesn't just understand our heritage. She's writing its next chapter.'

He pushed away from the table, pacing the length of the windows. All eyes were on him. 'You're right about one thing, Richard. I do calculate everything. So here's the maths: My wife makes me better. She keeps me in Scotland. And she turned Dunmarach from a graveyard into something alive. That's a hundred per cent improvement. And the best ROI of my life.'

Turning back, he pinned a stare at Blackwood. 'Love isn't proved by how we met. It's proved by choice. And every day, I choose her.'

'This is hardly appropri—' Blackwood began.

'I'm not finished. You want to talk legacy? Here's mine: I chose to examine my family's mistakes instead of hiding them.'

He turned to the trust members. 'You knew my parents. To them, appearance mattered more than truth. That's why they never questioned the accident that killed Martin. Never asked why their seventeen-year-old son took all the blame.'

Susan Campbell's expression gentled. 'We always wondered what happened. But your parents made it clear it wasn't to be discussed.'

'Martin took the Porsche and got so drunk he couldn't walk. I had no experience, but I had no choice. I had to drive. Martin wasn't the perfect golden boy everyone wanted him to be. But he was my brother. And I forgive both of us for what happened. My wife taught me that.'

Max took a breath. 'If preserving the Drummond legacy means denying what Rowan and I are building – then keep the castle. Keep the distillery. I keep her.'

Rowan stood and before anyone could object, she crossed to Max and took his hand.

'Though preferably,' she added, her voice carrying notes of steel, 'we keep it all. Because that estate?' She met Blackwood's glare. 'That's our future. Not Max's inheritance or my meal ticket. You question my commitment to this estate, but you've done nothing to help it thrive. All you want to do is sell it. This trust isn't meant to line your pockets or indulge your ego. Unlike you, I care about what Dunmarach means to the people who depend on it. The trust isn't your personal chessboard, and Dunmarach isn't for sale.'

Max's chest swelled. She wasn't just standing by him, she was standing with him, fierce and unshakable. He felt the solid presence of her ring. Their ring.

She smiled up at him. The sight didn't knock him off balance. It reminded him why he would never stand steady without her. How perfectly she fit, how right this felt.

'So.' Max turned back to the trust members, Rowan's small hand in his. 'Judge our marriage by whatever metrics you choose. But know this: I love my wife. She makes me want to be worthy of the name Drummond. Not by clinging to the past, but by creating something new.'

Murmurs filled the conference room like waves against shore. Max kept his spine straight, Rowan's hand clasping his, as chairman Archie MacKenzie cleared his throat and began to speak.

'The trust acknowledges the unconventional nature of this union in its early stages.' MacKenzie's face creased. 'However, Mr Drummond has more than demonstrated his commitment to both wife and legacy. Maxwell, you're married and you live in Scotland. The clause is hereby fulfilled. Your father always placed his trust in Blackwood's pragmatism. Perhaps he believed it was necessary, but I'm not sure I agree anymore.'

Blackwood's chair screeched against marble. 'My Lord, the evidence shows—'

'...two young people who are bringing new life to a traditional estate.' MacKenzie's tone allowed no debate. 'This trust's purpose is not to preserve the past in amber or to profit, but to shepherd our heritage into the future. Strictly speaking, the marriage may not have started in the spirit of the will's requirements. But intentions evolve and so do circumstances. We have to weigh intent against outcomes. What matters is what is being achieved, and whether this union is bringing stability or risk.'

Relief cascaded through Max's limbs. Rowan's fingers tightened around his.

MacKenzie let his glance slide over the other trustees. Everyone nodded in agreement. 'The trust finds no cause to challenge the marriage's validity. Furthermore, we suggest Mr Blackwood's supervisory services are no longer required.'

Blackwood's nostrils flared. 'This is highly irregular. You'll regret this – when she's bled the estate dry. Numbers can be manipulated. What happens when those little pet projects drain resources instead of adding value? Sentiment doesn't keep the lights on!'

'And yet, those so-called pet projects have already increased engagement and revenue.' Rowan smiled. 'Sentiment might not keep the lights on, but neither does your greed. What does is vision. And that's what we have.'

'How dare you, you little—'

That's enough, Blackwood.' Max adjusted his cufflinks, voice razor-sharp. 'What's highly irregular is how long we put up with you. You never protected Dunmarach. You only wanted to sell it. We're done.'

The solicitor's angry exit left silence in its wake. MacKenzie rose, the others following suit.

'Congratulations, Mr and Mrs Drummond.' His handshake was firm. 'We look forward to seeing Dunmarach's next chapter unfold, and of course, the release of the thirty-year-old single malt.'

Minutes bled together as hands were shaken, pleasantries exchanged. Max moved through it on autopilot. Only when they reached the Maybach did reality sink in.

'We did it,' she said.

'We did. Wouldn't have happened without you. You're a star, Mrs Drummond.'

The long drive north stretched before them. Max took the driver's seat. Oliver still handled the occasional long trip, but Max enjoyed the independence and the pride of knowing he didn't have to rely on anyone else anymore. Rowan's playlist filled the cabin with Taylor Swift as Edinburgh's spires receded in the mirrors.

'What you said in there...' She toyed with her ring. 'About choosing me over the estate.'

'I meant it. I would live in a shed with you. Though I'm glad it didn't come to that.'

'Mhm. Me too. I've grown rather fond of our castle. Also, a shed for you is probably a small penthouse in Kensington.'

'Our castle.' The words tasted right. 'Speaking of which, I've been thinking about renovations.'

'You have?'

'The old library. What if we turned it into a public archive? Display space for your histories, research materials for visiting scholars, and collaboration with universities.'

Rowan's eyes lit. 'Really?'

'Really.' He changed lanes smoothly. 'You're right – Dunmarach's story isn't about the Drummonds. It's about everyone who has shaped it. It's time we acknowledged all of that.'

Eventually, the dramatic Highland hills rose around them, as familiar as breathing now. More than London ever was.

'I love you, husband.'

'I love you, too.' Max lifted her hand to his mouth and kissed her knuckles. 'We should celebrate.'

Her grin turned wicked. 'Take me home. Then I'll show you how I celebrate.'

He smiled. The road unwound before them, each mile carrying them closer to Dunmarach. To their future, written in old stones and modern dreams. Some choices shaped destinies. Some loves rewrote legacies.

This, Max knew with bone-deep certainty, would do both.

Chapter Twenty-Four

They barely made it through the front door. Victory pulsed through Rowan's chest, the rush of the trust meeting crackling in the air like static.

Max shrugged off his jacket and tossed it onto the nearest chair. Then came his tie, sliding free with a smug hiss that was louder than the breath Rowan sucked in through her teeth.

His stare burned into her, sharp as a blade and hot as embers. 'Come here, Mrs Drummond.'

Heat licked its way south like it had an appointment to keep. She stepped forward, her body answering him before her brain had a say. Until she stood toe-to-toe with him.

'You were magnificent today.' He traced his thumb along the bow of her upper lip.

Her tongue darted out, tasting him.

A muscle near his temple jumped. 'If you don't stop teasing me like that, I swear to God, I'll take you right here.'

'Then I'm *definitely* not stopping.'

Max dug his fingers into her waist, pulling her in, dragging her under. His mouth seized hers. Hot and consuming and restless. His kiss didn't ask. It took.

He tasted of triumph. Of admiration. Of love.

Rowan clutched the front of his shirt. She pushed him back against the stone wall of the foyer, beneath two medieval battle axes, and kissed him with the fury of a thousand hard-fought victories. Like a conqueror claiming her prize.

Which she kind of was.

His mouth met hers with equal fervour. His lips bruising, his smile breaking through the hunger, a taste of triumph sweetening every stroke of his tongue. She would never, ever get enough of this.

Of him.

Of them.

Max cradled her face with both hands. 'Every fight, every win… It's nothing without you, Rowan. You have no idea how much I need this. How much I need you.'

'I'd say it's obvious.' She pushed against him. 'It's, erm, a bit difficult to hide.'

He laughed and pulled her closer, hands sliding down to grip her ass, grinding her into the hard evidence of just how far gone he was. 'Ready to fulfil your marital duties?'

'If you're ready to fulfil yours.' Her voice straddled the line between tease and plea. 'I've been on active duty non-stop for weeks. I don't know how *you* do it. Not that I'm complaining.'

Max's response was a low, deliberate hum. Like he was considering something. 'Pull up that dress. Bend over.'

Rowan reached for the hem, lifting the soft fabric over her hips as she turned around. She couldn't see it, but she heard the whisper of leather sliding free. The pull of his zipper.

A slick stroke.

Is he…?

The glide of his fist working his cock came in a steady rhythm.

Rowan drew in a shuddering breath and braced her hands against the wall. She arched her back and tipped her hips, giving him a better view.

The rugged groan he let loose nearly sent her to her knees.

'Don't you dare turn around.' His voice was dark with lust like he was one breath away from losing it.

She loved this. The knowledge that Max was behind her, fisting himself at the sight of her, fuelled a surge of power through her entire system.

A sharp inhale. 'I can see the stain growing on the satin. You're getting ready for me.'

'Yes.' She was burning to feel him, and he hadn't even touched her yet.

He groaned. 'I can *see* how turned on you are.'

Her entire body fought to stay upright, to withstand the force of her need for him ripping through her.

He wrenched the thin fabric of her thong aside. Cool air licked at her sensitive flesh. The faint rustle of fabric, the clink of his belt on the tiled floor. And then—

His thick head, nudging at her entrance.

'Look at you, Rowan. You don't even need foreplay.'

'Watching you…kick Blackwood's ass…was all the foreplay I needed.'

A sharp exhale pushed through his teeth. 'Jesus. You're making me lose my mind.'

And then he drove into her.

Hard. Deep. Unrelenting.

Her body seized up, fought against the impossible stretch. She let out a broken cry.

'Max, I—' Whatever she'd meant to say splintered into raw, choked sounds, her body shaking, trying to catch up.

'You can take it.' His grip on her waist turned punishing. 'You were made for me.'

Her fingers clutched at the stones in the wall, knuckles white, body jolting as he fucked her, each stroke carving him deeper, branding him into her.

'Y-yes…I am…' The words were breathless. 'Don't…hold back. I need you rough.'

He made a sound somewhere between a growl and a groan like she'd just handed him his last shred of sanity and told him to set it on fire.

His rhythm turned ravenous.

Her body rippled with every powerful thrust, her moans escalating to panting cries. 'Yes! Yes! Oh…OH!'

And then Max—

Fucking *stilled*.

Buried deep, pulsing, holding back.

'I need you on top. I want to watch you.'

For once, she had no retort. No quip, no tease. Just a pulse between her thighs so pounding it blurred the edges of reality.

'I want to watch you fall apart for me,' he said and closed his fingers around her neck. 'And I want you to watch me fall apart for you. Admit it. You love being the woman who undoes me.'

Before she could reply, Max pulled out, leaving her aching and empty. He took her wrist, hauled her toward the broad stone staircase, and sat down on the step.

She sucked in a breath.

His cock was hard, glistening, waiting. A king demanding tribute. But it was the way he looked at her – as if she were the only thing that could save him from himself – that snatched the air from her like a rough hand at her neck.

'Come here.' The hunger in his voice could have levelled a person.

Rowan didn't hesitate. She climbed over him, knees hitting the cold stone as she straddled his thighs. Her hands clung to his shoulders, and she hovered for a second, her body screaming for him.

'Now, Rowan.'

He closed one hand around his shaft, clamping the other onto her hip as he pulled her down onto him – right where she belonged. She cried out as he seated himself deep, so deep inside her, and her head lolled forward against his.

'Jesus, *fuck*—'

The angle was so perfect, it wrung a long moan from her.

He lifted her chin. 'Look at me.'

She did.

'Ride me. Make your husband proud.'

The stone bit into her knees as she rolled her hips, but the only thing she felt was him.

'Do you have any idea what you're doing to me?' His teeth scraped her lip. 'You're… God, you're wrecking me, and I'm letting you.'

'That's…good.' Because she couldn't go down without taking him with her. They were one.

He groaned against her mouth. 'You're so beautiful. I want this etched into my memory. You. Like this.'

'I'm…doing…my best.'

'You love knowing I would burn the whole world just to feel you like this, don't you?'

She laughed on a moan. 'I'd burn down right alongside you.'

'Jesus Christ, Rowan. Goddammit.'

His hands branded her, sliding over her back, down to her ass – gripping, using his hold to slam her onto him.

'Oooh God. Max. OH!'

'I want you to remember this. Every second. Every touch.' His voice was gravelly. 'Do you know how much I love you?'

She did. God, she did.

'Yes, yes! I love you. I love you!'

With a shuddering breath, she pushed up from her knees and rolled onto her heels. She needed him deeper. Harder.

And fuck, she got it.

Max planted his strong hands on the underside of her thighs. Supporting her, holding her. Every nerve ending fizzed with pleasure, and tension coiled low in her belly.

'Max…' Her voice broke. 'Make me come. God, make me come. Please. *Please.*'

'You coming on me? My favourite thing.'

His grip tightened on her inner thighs, keeping their rhythm. She couldn't stop moving even if she tried – her own weight driving her down, thighs burning as she met every thrust.

'Max… Oh! Oh my God—' Her thighs trembled, body seizing under the sharp, perfect agony of it.

'Yes, that's it. That's my good wife. Give it to me. Let me feel it.'

'AH! Max!' Her voice shattered into a scream as the world fractured around her. Her vision flared white-hot, every nerve pulled to a breaking point, every muscle locking down in surrender. Sensation tore through her. No control, no escape –just the devastating force of him, wringing her out, dragging her over the edge so far it felt like she was dissolving.

She should've collapsed. Should've sunk into him, gone soft and pliant in his arms.

But she couldn't.

She needed him to come undone.

'I-I can…take more. Don't stop me, Max. Don't stop.'

His growl scraped her skin. 'Rowan. Fuck.'

'That's right.' She held his face in her hands. 'Now come for me. Show me. Show me…how much…you love…your wife.'

And then he lost it.

One, two, three, four devastating, body-splitting thrusts.

'I love you. I love you. Jesus Christ. Rowan. Oh FUCK!'

Heat flooded deep inside her, each pulse wringing another wrecked sound from his throat.

She melted into him, chest to chest, her fingers tangled in his hair, her world narrowing to this moment, to this man, to them.

He buried his face in her neck, arms wrapping tight, holding her like he never wanted to let go.

'You're my queen.' A kiss, soft and lingering, at her temple. 'My queen.'

'Damn right, I am. And don't you ever forget it.'

She *was* his. But not his possession. She was his wife, his partner, his equal.

'As if you'd let me. Believe me, I could never be happy with any other woman.'

'I bloody hope so.' She lowered her head, capturing his lips in an unhurried kiss. 'I really do love you, Mr Drummond.'

'I really do love you, too, Mrs Drummond. I love you so much it hurts. Where have you been all my life?'

'It's all just as it's supposed to be.' She sagged against him, a lazy smile on her lips. His heart thundered beneath her ear. Their bodies still one. The stones of Dunmarach held centuries, but this moment felt brand new.

He tightened his strong arms around her, his fingers tracing gentle, grounding patterns over her lower back. Her skin was flushed with satisfaction. A laugh bubbled up, loose and giddy.

'What's so funny?' Max nudged a kiss against her chin.

'I was thinking about Blackwood's face when you eviscerated him.' She twined her arms around his neck and threaded her fingers through his damp hair. 'So this was our victory lap, right?'

'Only the first round.' He kissed the tip of her nose, then each eyelid. This tender gesture from a man who seemed made of steel and stone sent a sharp pull through her chest.

God, how she loved him.

'Speaking of victories…' Her voice wavered. 'I've been thinking.'

'A dangerous pastime, especially for you.' He nuzzled the nape of her neck.

'Prick. I'm trying to be serious here.'

'Go on then.'

'There's this wee parish church near my gran's care home in Glasgow. Nothing fancy, stone walls and stained glass. But it's where my grandparents got married, and my gran could be there, and…' She took a wavering breath. 'What I'm trying to say is… Maybe we could get married there. Properly this time, with friends and family.'

Max went still. 'Are you proposing to me, Rowan Drummond?'

'Well, technically you're already my husband, so it's more like…proposing we make it real?' She wrinkled her nose. 'Though if you're going to be pedantic about it…'

His mouth caught hers in a kiss that tasted of wonder and hope and forever. When he pulled back, his smile lit up his entire face. 'Yes. Name the date.'

'Yes?'

'Yes to marrying you properly. To you. To us. To everything.'

His rare, beaming smile was worth every moment of uncertainty, every fear she'd conquered to get here. Every hard decision she had to make, every heartache and loss and piece of hell either of them had to endure.

Maybe, Rowan thought, the best stories weren't the ones you came looking for. Maybe the best stories were the ones that found you when you least expected them.

Epilogue

Max had never planned for this life. But two years and one impossible woman later, he understood what it meant to belong.

He adjusted his laptop screen, fighting a smile as Mrs MacPherson's voice drifted up from the forecourt, scolding Old Grant about tracking mud across her clean floors earlier. A while ago, such interruptions would have irritated him. Now they were part of Dunmarach's daily rhythm.

In two years, Dunmarach had become a living, breathing home, and the distillery was thriving, expanding into new markets while keeping its soul intact.

The study had transformed alongside its occupants. Martin's trophies no longer dominated the glass cabinet. They shared space with new milestones: the crystal tumbler from their wedding toast, the deed to the community trust, Rowan's first published history of Dunmarach. A photo of her grandmother at the care home – dressed in her Sunday best for her and Joe's anniversary. She still recognised her family, though more often than not, she searched their faces like the answer was just out of reach.

Max and Rowan's wedding photo sat on his desk. A moment captured outside the small Glasgow parish church. No society photographers or elaborate ceremonies. Just them, bathed in rare Scottish sunshine, while Rowan's grandmother beamed from her wheelchair, Mrs MacPherson swooned, and Oliver pretended not to cry.

Max outlined the frame with his fingertip. Even now, the sight of Rowan in that vintage lace dress, her hair crowned with white heather, made his heart swell. She had refused the traditional pearls his mother would have insisted upon, instead wearing her grandmother's simple silver pendant.

The study door creaked. Another sound he had grown to love. She slipped in, carrying two steaming mugs and wearing one of his old Cambridge rowing jumpers like a dress.

His favourite look on her.

'Thought you might need rescuing from those quarterly reports.' She set his tea beside him and ran her finger around the rim of her mug, eyes tracing the room like she was taking stock of her life.

'Mum says hi, by the way. She's still smug about our mother-daughter Paris trip. Apparently, I'm the workaholic now. As if she didn't march me into every bloody museum.'

He smiled. Paris had done her good. Less stress, more sleep, more laughter. He liked to think he had something to do with that, too.

'Can you believe I've gone full "local historian"?', she asked. 'People stop me in the Co-op to tell me about their great-granny's nineteen-twenty-seven sheep feud. It's sweet. Ah, I see – you already found a distraction.'

He lifted the wedding photo. 'Just remembering how beautiful you looked.'

'Smooth talker.' But her smile held tenderness as she

hopped up on his desk. 'You weren't so bad yourself. Even if you did wear a three-piece morning suit to a tiny parish wedding.'

'Some standards must be maintained.'

She snorted. 'Says the man who now wears jumpers instead of suits because his wife needs easier access to his pecs.'

'A shocking lapse in protocol.' His hand found her knee. 'I blame your corrupting influence.'

'Hmm.' She took a sip of tea. 'Speaking of corruption and influence...'

Something in her tone made him sit straighter. 'What have you done now?'

'Why must I have done something?'

'Because that's your "I reorganised the library by colour"-voice.'

'Once! That happened once! And yeah, it doesn't make sense when most of the books are somewhat brownish.' But her laugh held a hint of nervousness. 'I need to tell you something important.'

Max's thumb traced circles on her knee. 'I'm listening.'

She set her mug aside, fidgeting absently with her – his – jumper hem. 'Remember three months ago, when I had the stomach bug and vomited like a fountain?'

'Vividly.'

'And remember last month when we talked about writing new chapters and our vision for Dunmarach?'

'Equally vividly.' The community trust launch had sparked intense discussions about family, responsibility, and the future.

'Well.' She took his hand and guided it to her stomach. 'Looks like we're starting a whole new book.'

The universe split open, swallowing everything but her and those words.

'Rowan...' Her name came out jittery. 'Are you saying...?'

'That your obsessively organised sperm and all the barfing conspired to bypass my birth control? Yes.' Her attempt at humour wavered. 'Looks like I'm pregnant.'

The quarterly reports scattered as he stood, gathering her close. Her arms wound around his neck as he buried his face in her hair, breathing in the familiar scent of her shampoo and underneath it, something new. Something that made his chest hurt with joy.

'When?'

'I found out yesterday afternoon. I wasn't shopping, I've been to the GP.' Her voice muffled against his shoulder. 'Wanted to be sure before I told you. Though Mrs Mac's been giving me knowing looks for weeks. Apparently, my sudden aversion to porridge and whisky fumes was a dead giveaway. She caught me gagging at the bowl a while ago and hasn't stopped smirking since.'

'I… didn't think this was in the cards for us. God, yes, I'm happy. But I'm with you, whatever it is you want to do. I mean, should you… You know, if you're not feeling ready.'

'The wee one is staying. Aye, I'm scared shiteless,' she admitted. 'But so happy. And when is one ever truly ready for a baby? A Mini-Drummond. How cute is that?' Her hand came to rest on his cheek. 'You?'

They had not yet discussed children, both carrying too many inherited fears about parenthood. But as Max looked at his brilliant wife, those fears evaporated like mist.

'Ecstatic.' His forehead touched hers. 'Terrified. Grateful.'

'Good.' Her smile brightened. 'Because I've already started planning the nursery. That weird room off the suite? Perfect size. Though we'll need to move your surplus sock collection…'

Max laughed. 'Anything you want, my love.'

'Beware.' Her emerald eyes sparkled. 'I'll hold you to that when pregnancy cravings hit.'

'And I'm happy to comply. Even if you demand haggis ice cream at three in the morning.'

'Ugh. Don't even joke about that right now.' She tucked herself closer, fitting against him like she had always belonged there.

She had, he knew that now.

'This is happening, Max. You're having a baby with your favourite trespasser.'

'I can't wait to meet them. I hope they have their mother's fierceness.' His hand splayed across her stomach again, protective.

She laced her fingers through his. 'I love you, you know. Even when you're being annoyingly proper about everything.' She stretched up to kiss him. 'Though if you insist on silly names like Bartholomew, Percival, or Gandalf, we're going to have words.'

Max gathered her closer, memorising this moment. Autumn light painting copper in her hair, love bright in her eyes, their child growing beneath his palm. Two years ago, he thought legacy was the past. Now, he knew – it was the future they built together.

'I love you.' It came easier now, natural as breathing. 'Both of you.'

Rowan's smile carried the weight of everything they'd fought for and won. 'Gandalf and I love you too.'

Outside, leaves danced gold against the crisp blue sky. Inside, Max held his heart, his world, and his entire future in his arms. Living proof that legacies weren't inherited, but chosen and built and loved into being.

– THE END –

Fancy a little extra hot Scottish romance? Get a free spicy audio chapter when you sign up for my newsletter! Claim your audio here: **beatricebradshaw.com/free-audio**

Thank you so, so much for reading. If you enjoyed Max and Rowan's story, **please take a minute to leave an honest review on Amazon**. It doesn't need to be epic. Just two sentences can help the book a lot, and I'd be grateful. <3

Read on for a sample of *Love in the Scottish Winter Highlands*!

Love in the Scottish Winter Highlands

Pale morning light pierced through the clouds. The cold air smelled like peat fire and rain, like smoke, like frost, like everything that she loved about winter. The hills around this small town were almost as chalky as the sky. From a distance, they looked like folds of a wool blanket. It was still early. Marla flipped up the collar of her peacoat and walked along the cobblestoned street. Despite the November chill, her face was glowing.

This place, half-snuggled in a valley, was a far cry from the busy, tiring city of London she had called home for fourteen years and left behind yesterday morning.

Yet here she was. In Scotland.

Marla swallowed, unsure of what lay ahead. The past few weeks had been a whirlwind. A swirl of conflicting emotions surged in her chest. There was a rush of anticipation, yes, but also a warning that nagged at her mind, reminding her of the risks. It was the glimmer of possibility, too hard to ignore, that made her cheeks flush.

I'm really doing this, aren't I?

As she sauntered to her appointment with the solicitor, she took in the sights and sounds of Kilcranach's old core. Side roads led up the hill and wound their way through the village like a gemstone necklace that someone had carelessly dropped. In contrast, the high street was built in a straight line and flanked by quaint shops with whitewashed facades. With their slate roofs and pointed gables, the houses looked like they had been there since the time of Mary, Queen of Scots. Or at least since some enlightened, eighteenth-century landowner had stuffed his crofters into efficient lodgings so they could collect kelp while sheep grazed on what used to be their land. The sea, as the screeching chorus of gulls in the background announced, wasn't very far away.

Behind a bend, Marla noticed the small castle looming in the distance. A structure with blonde sandstone walls, over-grown with ivy. Even from afar, it appeared as sad as in the photos. And calling it a castle was a stretch. It looked more defeated than defensive. Although it must once have been an inviting eighteenth-century country house. Marla imagined glamorous balls and hunting parties with people wearing tweed.

In truth, she had no concept of what the Scottish nobility used to do in their extensive spare time two hundred years ago. Even two years ago, for that matter.

Today, the former grand house was a neglected three-storey building with dull panes in its many large mullion windows. It seemed tired, forgotten, and lonely. This house had the weight of well over two hundred years pressing down on it – and it appeared as if it was done pushing back.

Her house now. Her weight.

Marla snorted in disbelief, and a frosty cloud of breath formed in front of her nose. What the hell had happened? Four weeks ago, she had been living her life in London, working as an oncology nurse for the National Health Service NHS. Mostly reading books while curled up on her couch. Completely unspectacular and utterly intentional. After everything, Marla had designed her life to be as stable and safe as possible. A solid wooden drawer with cosy velvet lining.

Until one phone call changed it all.

She had just returned from running errands when her mobile rang. At first, she thought it was a prank. Who wouldn't?

'Good afternoon! Marla Wilson? You will not have heard of me, but I have something important to tell you,' said the male voice on the other end.

'Not at all a bizarre thing to say. Bye.'

'Wait! There is something you must know,' the unknown caller cut in.

'Oh, really? Must I?' Marla's day off had been unpleasant so far. She was in a *mood*. 'Let me guess: you're calling in the name of Prince Harry and need cash for a charity? Or better still, you're a Nigerian prince and need my help with wiring four million dollars to my account? Guess what, I don't believe in princes and—'

'Miss Wilson, there seems to be a misunderstanding. My name is William Collins. I work with Arniston Solicitors, and the reason I'm calling you today is to inform you of an inheritance.'

'Ha! I knew it. No thanks,' she scoffed.

'Does the name Gordon Wilson ring a bell?'

Marla gasped. That was her grandda's name.

How does he… What…?

Anger welled up inside her. 'What do you know of my grandfather? Is this a cruel joke? My grandda died two years ago. Don't you feel ashamed using dead people's names in a scam?'

'No, no! Of course not, Miss Wilson. It is just… How do I put this delicately? It seems that in his youth, Gordon Wilson had made an acquaintance of some…emotional significance. Let us leave it at that.'

'Pardon me?' She noticed a trace of shrillness in her voice.

'I would much prefer to discuss the details with you in person. But as far as we know, he knew the young Lady Hamilton, and it appears that Gordon Wilson…made a lasting impression on her.'

'Lady who?'

'Lady Helena Cecilia Hamilton,' he said.

'Never heard of her.'

'I see. Well, that is not at all surprising. She lived a secluded life. Lady Hamilton passed away six months ago.'

'I don't know what to say. Eh…I'm sorry for your loss?'

'Thank you for your sympathy,' Mr Collins said.

Something in his voice resonated with Marla. She recognised the incorruptible truth of grief. He must have held that lady in great esteem. Marla paced up and down her hallway, the shopping bags still by the door.

'She was our client for many decades,' he continued. 'A good person, an amiable woman. One of a kind. She died without an heir, but her will – here the entire affair becomes more than a little unorthodox – unmistakably states that in these circumstances, the castle and estate should pass to the living descendants of Gordon Wilson.'

'What? Okay. That's…mental. My grandfather mentioned no lady. Ever. And I'm sure my gran wouldn't have approved of other women in his life. If you know what I mean.'

'Certainly, Miss Wilson. I did not intend to insinuate—'

'Right. So, wait. You're telling me that a complete stranger left a castle – an entire castle – to my grandda and his offspring? You can't be serious.'

'I assure you, this is not a joke to me, Miss Wilson.'

'Oh, I don't think this is funny either. And I have a lot of questions. Like why didn't he tell anyone about any of this? Ever? What on earth is going on?' Her voice rose. 'How am I supposed to even know who my grandda was dating in his youth? That's wrong,' she huffed. 'And who in their right mind doesn't give their godforsaken castle to the National

Trust instead of leaving it to a stranger? Doesn't that sound suspiciously wrong to you?'

'To you.'

'Who?'

'To you. She left Hazelbrae House to you. We have done some digging, you see. Since he passed two years ago and your mother in 1992, you are the only living blood relative of Gordon Wilson. Unless you have children, of course, but we could not find any records,' he explained. 'Hence, it follows – according to Lady Hamilton's will – that it is you who inherits her estate.'

Marla flopped onto a chair, ungracefully landing on the cupcake she had bought herself as a treat and placed there when her phone rang. She didn't notice it. All she noticed was a tingling numbness ascending from her legs, along with an uncomfortable ringing in her ears. After a pause, she said, 'No siblings. No children. Neither existent nor planned.'

'I apologise if this sounds intrusive. But you certainly see that we—'

'Estate,' Marla mumbled. 'What does that even mean?'

'I would much rather discuss everything in person. But for now, I can tell you that the inheritance encompasses a large, listed house with a few acres here in Scotland. Although the building is in a state, most unfortunately, and the land is a fraction of what it once used to be.'

'Sorry, I have to ask, for the record – are you for real? Do you have any proof of whatever you're saying, like…right now?' Not that any serious, self-respecting scammer would answer that question with anything close to the truth. Nonetheless, she had to ask.

'I guarantee that this is a most serious and lawful matter.'

She let out a breath. 'You understand that I can't simply believe everything a random stranger tells me on the phone? That's one thing my grandda taught me,' Marla said, mostly to herself, feeling the comforting weight of Gordon's small knife in the side pocket of her jeans. Along with the all-too-familiar twinge of loss.

'Yes, Miss Wilson. That is sensible. I would expect nothing less. I can send you all the relevant information and preliminary legal documents, the title, photographs, et cetera. And then, if you're interested, Arniston Solicitors would love to welcome you to Kilcranach.'

That had been one month ago. The town hall clock towered above Marla. Its long, thin hands showed a quarter past nine. Almost time for her meeting with William Collins to finalise the particulars of this odd inheritance. She was a few minutes early. But her mind was racing, and she couldn't sit in the car for one more second.

I can't believe it. What if it's too much for me?

Initially, she'd been less than thrilled at the thought of inheriting a castle from a stranger – everybody knew those houses were bottomless money pits – let alone the mystery surrounding her grandda's dubious ex-lady-friend or whatever position Helena *Whatshername* Hamilton had once held in his life.

It was Marla's pal Trish who had encouraged her to take the leap of faith, stuff her car with her favourite clothes and books, and move to Kilcranach to take on her inheritance – a property she hadn't even set foot in.

'Marl, what are you talking about? A flipping castle in Scotland, for fuck's sake. That's an amazing opportunity. Think what you could do with that!' Trish had squealed from beneath her cloud of brown curls. 'That's how all those Mills & Boon novels start! And if it's shit, you can sell it for a few million pounds to a Danish billionaire and bam! No more worrying about pensions or any of that. That's you, sorted for life!'

Marla couldn't help but smile at the memory of Trish's innate enthusiasm and unwavering faith in the world. Most of the time, it was unfounded. But it somehow still made things better. Inexplicably. Or maybe even magically.

She moved past the bookshop. A narrow, three-storey, timber-framed building with a small café on the ground floor. A few people were grabbing a coffee to go. There was a pair of American tourists in trainers, hunched over their phones.

Probably a lot fewer of them in the Highlands in November than during summer.

The faint aroma of roasted beans and the scent of yellowed books wafted into the cold air. A young woman wearing a pointy hat and a black coat was peering into a shop window. Her long, emerald-green hair was fashioned into a braid and flowing down her shoulders on top of a woollen tartan shawl. She looked like a witch. Maybe this tiny town had more edge than Marla had imagined.

Whatever her doubts, and there were plenty, she was here now. After having drained a reassuring bottle of Bordeaux with Trish, Marla had made a promise to herself. Come rain or shine – and considering that this was Scotland, rain was the much more likely scenario – she would find a way to make it work.

This wasn't just an unexpected inheritance. It was a once-in-a-lifetime opportunity to give back to her colleagues in the NHS, who worked so hard to save their patients' lives. Create a retreat for tired doctors and nurses. Like herself. Like the ones that tried to save her mum twenty-five years ago or the ones who took care of her grandparents at the end. Renovating Hazelbrae was also a way to be connected to her grandda. To honour his memory, to find out who he had really been and where he was from.

And to start over after all the loss and sorrow.

The solicitor's office was in one of the historic buildings just off the town square. The heavy door creaked as Marla opened it, revealing a claustrophobically small lobby. It wasn't even large enough to contain a gathering of five people. Two timeworn oak chairs and an equally ancient wooden reception desk testified to the age of the office. The darkly panelled walls were adorned with antique paintings of ships conquering raging waves. It smelled of dust and varnish, with a slight salty tang. The entire room seemed like the wooden sea chest of a nineteenth-century naval officer.

Behind the panelled desk sat a woman with white streaks in her red bob, knitting what looked like a Fair Isle jumper. She didn't so much as lift her head when the door creaked.

'Hi. Good morning.' Marla plastered on a polite smile.

Now the woman looked up. She gave a nod and put down her needles. 'Morning. Welcome to Arniston Solicitors. How can I help you?'

Marla explained who she was and why she was there. The receptionist nodded again. This time, with squinted eyes. As if she couldn't believe it. Neither could Marla.

'Of course. Mr Collins is expecting you, Miss Wilson.' She rose from her chair. 'Please follow me. And watch your step. It's a wee bit uneven.'

Marla walked behind her up a narrow spiral staircase with ornate cast iron steps and rails that were cold and coarse under her fingers.

'Ah, Miss Wilson,' Mr Collins called from the back room. 'Welcome to Arniston Solicitors! Glad you made it. How was the journey? Not entirely unpleasant, I hope?' Mr Collins emerged from his office wearing a tweed suit with a waistcoat and a pocket watch, round glasses perched at the end of his pointed nose. He looked like an obscure side character in an unpublished Sherlock Holmes story, scholarly and anachronistic to the point of eccentricity. Much more interesting in person than on the phone. Marla liked him right away.

Mr Collins ushered her into his tiny office, where several stacks of documents were scattered around the room. The slope of the roof was low and crooked, Marla could hardly stand upright. A square window let in a few resilient rays of winter morning sunlight, illuminating several shelves of books lined up like soldiers at attention.

Over a cup of tea, Mr Collins explained the legal details of the inheritance. There was no family dispute, since this was a minor branch of the Hamiltons without relatives. The property had been surveyed and valued, the inventory and other forms completed, taxes and debts paid. So was the basic upkeep for a year, excluding insurance. Now was the time for the title transfer.

Marla understood all of it, or so she hoped. Dealing with small print had never been her core strength. She would inherit Hazelbrae House with about ten acres of surrounding land. Apparently, Helena Hamilton had declared that the house was not to be turned into a museum. 'Hazelbrae is neither a shrine nor a zoo, it is a home,' were her words, as related by Mr Collins. Miraculously, there was no remaining debt on the estate, but there had been no renovations since the 1980s. Good bones, neglected state. The estimated renovation and conservation costs were... Astronomical didn't even begin to describe it.

And yet... Marla had felt drawn to Hazelbrae since she had first seen the pictures in Mr Collins' e-mail.

It was still baffling, though. 'What about their relationship? Were they...' Marla trailed off.

'Lady Hamilton and your grandfather?'

'Yes, those two. Who else would I be talking about?' She narrowed her eyes.

'Sadly, there is not much more that I can tell you.' Mr Collins adjusted his glasses. 'She changed her will shortly before her serious health problems started, and I never had the opportunity to ask her personally. It is all a mystery. Or simply private.'

He dug out a document and followed the lines with his index finger. 'According to Lady Hamilton's will, in which she bequeathed her estate to his family, Gordon Wilson was, and I quote, "the truest, dearest friend I ever had. I owe him my life and more than I could ever repay." End of quote.'

'What's that supposed to mean? Did he give her a kidney or something?'

'I could not tell you. Lady Hamilton was a private and fascinating woman.' Shifting his glasses again, he continued. 'My guess? Since your grandfather was from this area and moved away when he was twenty, if our research is correct, they most likely knew each other in their youth. Mr Wilson must have been a friend or confidant to Lady Hamilton. Class difference aside.'

Mr Collins leaned back in his squeaking swivel chair and folded his hands in his lap. 'We could try to investigate further. Although I have not the slightest idea how. We looked at her correspondence, but it didn't include any significant private letters or documents, unfortunately.'

Marla shrugged. 'I'm just so curious. I mean, who wouldn't be? There must be more to this story, but it seems we're not getting anywhere right now. So be it.' She straightened her shoulders. 'All right then, Mr Solicitor. Let's do this.'

With the legal details outlined, explained, and mostly understood, Marla picked up Mr Collins' pen in her right hand, her left hand on the document. She felt the tight weave of the paper fibres under her fingertips. The pen had an old-fashioned shape and a black, lacquered finish that had been worn smooth by generations of signers. Marla took a deep breath.

A few circles and scratches later, Mr Collins announced, 'Congratulations, Miss Wilson. You are now the proud owner of Hazelbrae House. Good luck.'

Marla left the solicitor's office exhilarated, bordering on terrified. To calm her jittery limbs, she decided to walk from the village to the castle and explore the area. It was eleven. Plenty of time in the day.

Time to make plans.

Marla would restore Hazelbrae House, find a new purpose and her roots here. It dawned on her how much she had been longing for a new beginning.

There was no way back. She had rented out her tiny flat in London and quit her job. A half-ruined castle in this remote Scottish village was her home now, which left only one possible conclusion: she must be insane.

Chapter 2

Niall trudged along the churned-up dirt path through the forest on his inspection rounds, his boots squelching in patches of moss and mud. Winter had stripped the trees of their foliage, leaving behind brittle branches outlined against the hazy sky, like a charcoal sketch.

A heaviness crept into the air. He knew the Highland weather and these woods like the back of his hand. This was his land, after all. It had been his father's and his grandfather's before that. But Niall didn't feel a sense of connection. Not anymore. Only obligation, to an extent.

Besides his own forestry, he had been an estate manager on the Hamilton land for thirteen years now. Close to a third of his life. It was a job that needed to be done, and he happened to be the one doing it. There was nothing more to it.

'Barclay? Barclay!' Niall called out for his dog. He paused and listened. Nothing but the long, rolling sigh of the breeze as it rustled through the branches. Niall turned around to survey the territory, to reassure himself that everything here was fine, that nothing was out of place. There were only familiar sights, like the old, gnarled ash tree with its branches twisted into shapes resembling faces. He called again, and this time he heard a bark in the distance.

That silly bugger can't help himself, he thought affectionately.

Thirty seconds later, the black and white border collie came shooting out of the thicket towards him. Niall smiled and scratched Barclay behind his ears. 'You sure love to run off on your own, don't you, boy?' At this time of year, there was nothing to be wary of on this part of the estate, and he allowed his faithful companion these independent excursions.

At least Barclay always returned to him, no matter how far he had run off. It was some comfort that there was one thing he could always rely on – the unconditional love of his dog. 'Let's get going, eh?' And the two of them plodded along the same trail they always followed, Barclay alongside his owner and friend. It was in fleeting moments like these when Niall was almost at peace.

Almost.

As they walked, Niall noticed the ambassadors of winter, like a stray snowflake settling on his shoulder, the chill in the air, the flurries of fallen leaves being tousled by the breeze. Out here, in the middle of the forest behind Hazelbrae House, there was always an air of peace, a serene atmosphere that he had come to cherish.

Hazelbrae.

It had been over half a year since old Lady Hamilton had died in the care home where she had spent the last months of her life. A heart attack, they said. Niall still didn't know what was going to happen to that place. That unsettled him. He didn't like loose ends.

But, more importantly, it had brought his plans to an indefinite halt.

He had mulled over it for much longer than anybody in Kilcranach would ever have suspected, but when the developer had approached him with an offer to buy his land about a year and a half ago, Niall had been ripe and ready to make a deal. He wanted to move on. There was no spark of excitement or new beginning about it. This wasn't about opening a new chapter.

No. It was about finally closing an old one.

Because, more often than not, Niall felt trapped – like a solitary wanderer in the frame of a gloomy landscape painting. Forever doomed to roam the moors.

Or forest, in his case.

With the money from selling his acreage, he would likely never have to work again. At least if he lived sensibly. He could buy a boat and live on it. Go sailing. It used to be his favourite hobby when he was a student, his soul unbent, his heart unbroken, his light undimmed.

Before…everything.

He hadn't done it in ages. But he rather wanted to be at the mercy of the elements than at the mercy of the memories that surrounded him here at every turn.

Niall stopped and zipped up his lined wax jacket. He emitted a cloud of white breath and resumed the walk while his thoughts wandered in their own direction. He couldn't say that he had been pleased with the plans the developer had for the area – a huge luxury hunting, shooting, and fishing billionaire playground with a spa for clients with helicopters and such – but it could bring a few jobs to Kilcranach. To people who needed it. Frankly, he cared little about the details. Times were changing. That was a fact. Better to change with them and make the most of it. He had been looking forward to it.

But just when he had started to feel something akin to hope, Niall had learned that Hazelbrae, sitting in the middle of it all, was a crucial part of the deal. They wanted the entire bloody thing. Not just his land. No, the crumbling mansion on the hill was the cherry on top of their billionaire-property cake.

Niall had tried to convince them otherwise. In vain. He had also made several attempts to persuade old Lady Hamilton to sell. To no avail.

A part of him knew she would never be willing to cut ties

to her home of over seventy years, the place where she had been born.

Still, he had to try.

Not that he didn't understand her. Hazelbrae was her home, the place where her family's memories lived. Their presence was tangible in every nook of the house, starting with the faded pictures and paintings that spoke volumes about family roots that ran generations deep within this forgotten corner of the world.

No matter how eloquently Niall argued when they discussed estate matters, neither facts nor feelings made any difference. Lady Hamilton's friendly but firm response was always the same.

'My dear, dear boy,' she would say in her commanding voice, only a little frail. 'Don't you know that all of Hazelbrae is part of me? And I wouldn't sell my own arm now, would I? And what would your father think of that?' she had asked, patting his hand and shaking her head.

How am I supposed to know? It's not like you can phone people in the afterlife.

The last time they had spoken about it was a month before she suffered a second stroke and had to move away into care. A good six months before her death.

She had finally left this place for good. He was still stuck here.

Niall had even tried to sell his land discreetly to other candidates. Unsuccessfully. Unless it was an absurdly large acreage with a romantic castle, a potential nature reserve, or one of those tiny symbolic bits of land with a fantasy title, no one seemed prepared to buy land in the Scottish Highlands.

The canopy of wiry branches parted to reveal the decaying grandeur of Hazelbrae in the distance, a splendid house in a state of forgotten glory. Grass, moss, and birch saplings sprouting from the black rain gutters. All giving silent testament to its neglect.

Only a few harsh winters away from falling into utter disrepair, Niall reckoned.

Astonishingly, the roof still held up, withstanding the years, the wind, and the intense rain here in the West. He hadn't set foot inside of Hazelbrae since… not in a long time. There was a quick sting of pain and loss. A feeling as familiar to him as these ancient woodlands. Relentless murmurs of his unforgivable mistake. Niall shook his head in an attempt to shake off his memories.

He didn't know how Lady Hamilton had spent her last time there or what the inside of Hazelbrae might look like. All he knew was this half-ruined grand house stood between him and his ticket out of Kilcranach. Between him and his hope of lifting the crushing weight that had been suffocating him for six years. Whether he liked it or not, Hazelbrae was the key to his freedom and peace.

Barclay dashed towards a babbling brook beneath a small slope. Following the path to the left would lead them past the gates of the grand old house.

Och, why the heck not? Let's see how deep those cracks really are.

He whistled. Barclay obeyed and came back as fast as an arrow. Niall and his dog walked side by side through the woods.

Suddenly, he heard a voice from somewhere in the nearer distance.

'You treacherous damn shitty shit tree!'

Barclay pricked up his ears. Niall frowned.

What the…

'I hate you! I hate you from the bottom of my heart! Stupid fucking tree!'

Yes, that sounded like a woman. An *angry* woman. The only problem was that her voice seemed to come from…above?

Barclay jolted towards a mature oak tree and barked.

'Well, hello there! Awww, look at you. Such a good boy,' the voice said to Barclay, all anger vanished. Niall took a few steps closer to the tree. He squinted in disbelief as he peered up at the top.

A woman in a dark blue pea coat was clinging to one of the oak's branches. Her jeans were splattered with mud, and her complexion was bright red. She stared at him with a mix of surprise and suspicion. Niall blinked in bewilderment. He had no inkling who this woman was or what she was doing here.

In a tree, no less.

One of his trees, by the way.

'Hi,' she called out. 'Hello! Oh, thank God. Do you think you could help me down? I can't seem to do it on my own. Not that I would normally admit that to anyone.' She laughed nervously.

The warm sound of her voice tingled in his ears. Niall furrowed his eyebrows in puzzlement. Why would a normal grown-up person climb a tree? He scoured his brain for explanations, but there were none that made any sense to him.

'What are you doing up there, if you don't mind me asking?'

'Major Tom to ground control: might I suggest I tell the tale once I've returned to Planet Earth?'

'I'm afraid I sold any spaceships or flying tin cans to the charity shop ages ago anyway,' Niall replied.

'Ah, so you're a funny one. But I'm about ten seconds away from a proper panic attack, so if you don't mind.'

'*You* started with Major Tom.' Niall noticed he was smiling. Barclay wagged his tail in excitement. That there on the tree was not the usual squirrel.

'Get me down. Now!' she insisted. 'I mean…please?'

'All right, all right. Let's see.' Niall examined the situation. It seemed that the crucial branch about halfway down had broken, preventing her from descending the same way she must have got up. He would have been irked by the sight of damage done to the trees under his care and supervision. But he knew the inhabitants of his forest well. This particular tree was a bit of a troublemaker that had been worrying him for a while. 'Can you turn around?' he asked.

'Are you joking?' She sounded slightly angry again.

'You know, I could continue my walk and pretend this never happened.' He was oddly enjoying this bizarre encounter.

'You would not.'

'Try me.'

'Okay, I guess I could make a quarter turn.'

'Brave girl,' Niall said. 'If you turn and slowly try to sit down on the branch that you're standing on right now, you could jump.'

'And break my ankle? Not a fat chance,' she said resolutely.

'I could catch you, you know.'

'You? But you're a stranger! How do I know you won't take a step to the side and let me land face-first in the mud?'

'Guess you won't know for sure until you try.'

'Honestly.' She looked dispirited. 'This is not a good way to encourage someone with trust issues.'

He folded his arms. 'Sometimes you have to take a leap of faith.'

'Really? Okay, as soon as I'm on firm ground again, we'll go into town and get matching "Live, Laugh, Love" tattoos.'

And Niall laughed. A sound so rare that Barclay barked twice in confusion.

The woman in the tree shifted her feet awkwardly, still clinging to the higher branch. Gradually, and with wobbly knees, she lowered herself into a sitting position, while holding onto the bark of the thick tree trunk.

'Okay, I'm sitting.' She looked relieved.

'I can see that.'

'And now I jump?'

Niall positioned himself underneath her. It was less than six feet, not too terrible. He spread his arms out. 'And now you jump.'

She landed on him like a hundred sacks of flour. The momentum pushed Niall backwards, staggering. She wasn't a fairy, this was a woman of substance. He lost his balance, and with a thud, they both landed on the mossy, leafy forest ground.

Barclay ran circles around them, while Niall lay flat on his back. Judging by the pain, his coccyx must have hit a thick pinecone or something.

'Ouch.'

'Sorry,' she replied, sitting astride him.

Niall stared into a pair of grey eyes with a silver glint under long, dark lashes. Tiny beads of sweat had formed a tiara at her hairline. There was a dab of dirt on the tip of her nose.

She bit her lower lip. 'I'm Marla, by the way. Thank you for being my mattress, Major Tom.'

Barclay licked her cheek and she let out a low, contented giggle.

Deep inside, Niall had always suspected that there must be some magical creatures living in these woods.

He just never thought they would be so…gorgeous.

Get *Love in the Scottish Winter Highlands* today!

Glossary

Aff yer trolley = completely nuts
Awright = alright
Bampot = a fool, a mad person
Baws = balls aka testicles
Bevvy = drink
Cannae = can't
Ceilidh = Scottish country dance in groups and pairs
Da = dad
Daft = silly, foolish, stupid
Dinnae = don't
Doesnae = doesn't
Eejit = idiot
Fae = from
Faffin' aboot = wasting time, messing about
Gie's a break = give us a break, stop bothering me
Haud yer wheesht = hold your tongue/ shut up and listen
Hogmanay = New Year's Eve
Isnae = isn't
Ken = know
Maw = mum
Nae/naw = no

Numpty = idiot
Ootside = outside
Pish = piss
Sgian Dubh = ritual dagger
Steamin' = very drunk
Weegie = Glaswegian
Yous = Scottish plural of you

Resource: Dictionary of the Scottish Language https://dsl.ac.uk/

Author's note

Dearest Reader,

If you're reading this, you've made it to the end of *Hired by My Rich Highland Husband* – and for that, I owe you a dram of whisky, a warm scone, or at the very least, a heartfelt thank you.

I had so much fun writing this book! It's got some of my favourite things: a broody hero in desperate need of being taken down a peg, a smart, sharp, delightful heroine who does *not* suffer posh men gladly, a marriage of convenience with plenty of inconvenient feelings, smutty smut, and, of course, Scotland in all its beautiful, historically complex glory.

Speaking of Scotland's complexity, that's something I couldn't ignore while writing this book. I'm a historian, which means I have a particular fondness for pointing out that behind every picturesque Highland castle, there's usually a money trail that leads somewhere deeply questionable. Scotland isn't just misty glens, peaty whisky, and men in kilts. It's also a country shaped by centuries of land grabs, forced removals, absentee landlordism, and staggering wealth inequality.

In the course of the 1800s, landlords cleared entire communities from their homes, sometimes to make way for sheep or deer, sometimes because they were more profitable harvesting kelp on the coast. While Gaelic people were being forced from their land, Scotland's mercantile elite was growing rich. And that included profits tied to the enslavement of human beings. Glasgow's Jamaica Street? Not a coincidence. The city became one of Britain's wealthiest trading hubs through its deep entanglement in the transatlantic economy. Scottish merchants dominated the tobacco trade, controlled sugar plantations in the Caribbean, and later profited from cotton grown by enslaved people in the American South. When slavery was finally abolished, those investors were handsomely compensated for their 'losses,' while the people they had enslaved received nothing. And many of those fortunes, built on human suffering, still linger in Scotland's old country estates, its merchant-built townhouses, and the names of its streets.

When I decided to write about a man who grew up in such a castle and has a lot of money, I decided he would *not* be a billionaire. Nothing against wealth, money can be lovely, but millionaires are quite enough. When a handful of people hoard more resources than entire countries, while others can't afford heating or healthcare, that's grotesque and dangerous.

That being said, Max *is* a rich man, but he's also a deeply unhappy one. Because money doesn't protect you from grief, guilt, loneliness, or feeling like you'll never be enough. The real joy of writing this book was giving him a heroine who sees straight through his money and tailored suits to the boy beneath. A fierce woman who challenges his worldview at every turn, loves him for who he is, and who does everything for her family. Especially her gran, who is struggling with cognitive decline.

This brings me to something close to my heart. Dementia is a cruel, slow thief. I watched my grandfather struggle with it in his final years – not in a way that entirely changed who he was, but in more and more moments of disorientation and confusion that were heartbreaking to witness. One moment, he'd be completely himself. The next, he'd be trying to eat a flashlight because he thought it was a bundle of parsley. He had to live in a care home at the end and it was tough. But even in those painful moments, there was humour and love. That's how we got through it. With love. So much love.

I suppose that's what I try to do in all my books – hold all those things at once. The pain and the joy. The fury at the way things are and the hope that maybe they can get better. The sharp edges of grief and the ridiculous, wonderful moments that remind us why we keep loving anyway.

So, thank you. For reading. For laughing along. For making space in your heart for Max and Rowan, for reluctant lairds and wild-hearted women, for Scotland in all its messy, magical glory. I hope this book made you smile. I hope it made you *feel*. And if you ever find yourself in a castle with a ridiculously broody man and a bottle of whisky… well. Don't steal his coffee. But do challenge him to a debate on wealth inequality and maybe ask where that money came from.

With love, gratitude, and a toast to inconvenient feelings,

About the Author

Beatrice Bradshaw crafts spicy contemporary romances set across Scotland – whisking readers away to glens and windswept coastlines without the need for a plane ticket!

By day, she's a German journalist, translator, and Scottish historian; by night, she transforms into a purveyor of page-turning passion and fun.

Beatrice Bradshaw is the pen name/ pseudonym of Jessica Beatrice Wagener – chosen so as not to have German narrative non-fiction confused with her (English) romance books.

And after trading Berlin for Scotland in 2018, Beatrice has been smitten with her adopted homeland and not once looked back.

With her knowledge of Scottish history and literature acquired at the University of Glasgow, she sprinkles authentic Scottish experiences through stories that venture well beyond predictable clichés. Her heroines are fierce, funny, and delightfully flawed. The kind of women who trip over their own witty comebacks but land on their feet with style. Her books deliver wit, heat, and men who are actually worth the emotional investment: charming, filthy, and capable of both finding the G-spot and the grocery store without assistance.

When not hunched over her laptop in her Glasgow flat (fuelled by industrial amounts of coffee and pastries), you'll find her hunting for inspiration in crumbling castles, exploring Scottish landscapes, or striking up conversations with the residents of ancient cemeteries. Her future grave-stone will immortalise the time she convinced David Hassel-hoff to sing, a tale best shared over whisky. And while she throws herself into ceilidhs with the same enthusiasm as karaoke nights, her dancing has been described as 'enthusias-tically hazardous'.

Connect with Beatrice here:
instagram.com/beatricebradshawauthor
facebook.com/beatricebradshawauthor
www.beatricebradshaw.com